GRIFFIN: RED AND THE BIG BAD REAPER

50 LOVING STATES, NEVADA

THEODORA TAYLOR

Griffin: Red and the Big Bad Reaper

by Theodora Taylor

Copyright © 2021 by Theodora Taylor

First E-book Publication: March 2021

Cover Design: Qambar Design & Media

Editing: Authors Designs

Free Book Alert!!!

Want a FREE Theodora Taylor Book?

Join Theodora's mailing list to get a free welcome book along with newsletter-only exclusive stories, author giveaways, and special sales.

Go to theodorataylor.com to get your free book

CHAPTER 1
GRIFF

"ALRIGHT, I'M BORED," I TELL THE GROUP OF REAPERS sitting around the roadhouse's banquet table. I'm not the president of our biker gang, but I do expect plenty of answers when I demand to know, "How're we going to fix this shitty vibe?"

Waylon, who actually is one of the Reaper's presidents, rolls his eyes and ignores me. Like I'm some mouthy brat—not the guy paying him six figures a year to run security at all my shows.

With the mood I'm in, that'd normally be enough for me to put a fist through his mouth. Nothing cures a bad case of the Bored as Hells like knocking out teeth. But I let it slide.

Waylon and Hades, the other Reaper prez, are two of the only guys I could call true friends prior to my music fame. Waylon's the one who pinned me with my road name, Rockstar, years before I signed my record deal. And, trust, it's a whole lot better to have him as a best friend you tolerate than an enemy you punched because he pissed you off.

I don't want to use the word psycho, but Waylon has a reputation for ending anybody who crosses him. There's a reason **DON'T**

PISS OFF WAYLON is written in huge block letters on the list of rules hanging above the roadhouse owner's office door.

It's probably a sign of our enduring friendship that he just ignores me instead of pulling a gun and shooting me in the face. That could 100% happen with our co-prez. We call him Viking sometimes because he's been known to go totally berserk when crossed.

Besides, I am acting kind of bratty. Borderline '80s-era Mötley Crüe. That happens when I get bored—which Waylon's probably thinking I shouldn't be, considering we're at the Reaper's favorite Tennessee roadhouse with friends who know how to party, top-shelf blow, quality weed, and biker groupies willing to do just about anything to get invited to our table.

One of my hit tracks is playing overhead, and two topless blondes with big smiles and even bigger breasts appear to replace all our empty bottles and whiskey glasses with fresh pours of bourbon and Yazoo beers.

Yeah, this scene is as close to biker Valhalla as you're gonna get.

"You want a mug for your Yazoo, Griff?" one of the waitresses asks. She presses her fake breasts into my shoulder as she sets a bottle of local craft beer down in front of me. It's so cold, it's got a wisp of smoke wafting up from its mouth.

Hmm . . . there's a good chance I've fucked this girl on a previous occasion. But I can't remember.

A few of the Reapers eye me expectantly—probably because the last time a waitress batted her eyes at me this hard, I convinced her to crawl under the table and give us all blow jobs. Now that was real '80s-era Mötley Crüe.

But tonight, my dick does nothing in response to her rubbing up against me like a cat in heat.

All I feel is dead inside as I answer, "Nah, I'm good."

I take a swig of my fresh Yazoo to end any further conversation, then announce to rest of the Reapers, "Still bored."

"I got Molly," Rowdy yells over my song. He's one of the Reapers who've been on tour with me all year. I've been letting him stay at my place in Nashville during the holiday lead-up to my record label's big New Year's Eve show, along with Crash, another Reaper on my security team.

Unlike Waylon, these guys know how to entourage. They start making suggestions as soon as they see the under-the-table blow job thing isn't going to happen.

"We could throw down with The Bandits," Crash says. "They've been looking over here funny all night. And Waylon hasn't shot nobody in a while."

Waylon tilts his head with a thoughtful frown, like the opportunity to dead somebody might just get him out of his seat.

But Hyena, who came up as a prospect with me over a decade ago, points out, "The last time we tried to beat down another gang for staring, we got over there, and all they wanted was Rockstar's autograph. It was stupid as shit."

I turn to glare over my shoulder at The Bandits anyway. A weird, ugly energy's been brewing inside of me since I turned thirty a few weeks ago. I could use a good fight to blow off some steam.

But I guess The Bandits want to prove Hyena's point. As soon as I make eye contact, most of the heavily bearded MCs sitting at the table behind us start pointing up at the song playing overhead.

The few guys not pointing tear off pieces from one of the shitty brown napkin rolls placed at each banquet table and pantomime the international symbol for *Can I have your autograph?*

Meanwhile, The Bandits's prez shouts across the distance, "I requested them to play this one soon as I saw you in here. You're my favorite rapper of all time."

My record label prefers the term "country trap artist" since I sing too. But whatever.

Hyena laughs with the signature sound that inspired his road name as I heave myself out of my chair and go over to sign all their shit and thank them for being fans. Instead of getting my fight, I get promises that I'll see a few of them standing front row at the New Year's concert I'm headlining in two weeks.

"Well, that was a bust, and I'm still bored as fuck," I inform Crash when I return to the Reaper's table. At least he has the decency to drop his eyes. Yeah, he should feel guilty.

"What else?" I ask the rest of the table.

"I got Molly," Rowdy offers again.

"There's a whole bunch of extra holiday help this year," Hyena points out now that he's over his laughing fit.

"You should see the hot redhead Vengeance's got lined up for later tonight," Crazytown, one of our old-timers, brags, nodding over at Hyena, Vampire, and Des-E. "She's got a set of cans on her you wouldn't believe."

Vengeance is what we call the three guys in charge of doing the Reaper's grislier enforcement duties. One laughs and smiles like a Hyena. We already covered that. One carries not one, but three Desert Eagles on him at all times, hence the shortened road name.

And one's a pale and broody as . . . well, a vampire. Anyway, they don't just work together, they fuck together. One girl always gets all their attention after one of them—almost always Hyena—picks them up.

Not my thing. But, hey, I'm not judging. I grew up in Los Angeles. Hell knows, I've seen stranger arrangements.

"That's what's up. Good for you, guys," I say, throwing Vengeance a chin nod.

Crash comes out of his guilty head hang to suggest, "Bet you could do the same thing. But, you know, in reverse," he quickly adds. "Three girls all to yourself."

Yeah, the prospect of that would be intriguing to 99.9% of straight guys. Me, not so much.

"Been there, done that," I let Crash know. "Not as fun as you'd think. Three girls is a fuck ton of condom work. And my number one goal in life is to make sure I don't become some chick's eighteen-year child support check."

"Yeah, but I got Molly, man," Rowdy says again like there's a chance I didn't hear him the first two times. "And I heard there's at least three new waitresses from Rydell, that all-girls school, working tonight."

"All women's college," Des-E corrects.

We all turn to stare at him. Three words are two more than Des-E's nightly average. Hell, I've seen whole weeks go by without him saying three words, especially all in a row like that.

"Doc went to Rydell, and she gets pissed when you call it an all-girls school," Hyena explains off all our confused looks.

Crazytown and the rest of the Reapers who haven't been touring with me all year nod like this makes 100% sense.

But since this is the first chance I've gotten to hang out with my old crew for a while, I have to ask, "Who's Doc?"

Before anyone can answer, my song is abruptly cut off and replaced by an AC/DC anthem I've been thinking about sampling for my next album.

"Okay, Mama Red Bird is in the house!" an amplified voice calls out over Brian Johnson scream-wailing about the girl who shook him all night long. "I've got shots, and I'm looking for my biker birdies! Chirp-chirp, baby! Bring your twenties to the bar, and line up if you want somethin' good!"

I look up, and *holy fuck*.

A girl . . .

A girl like no other is standing on top of the bar that runs the length of the roadhouse's back wall—a girl with silky brown skin stretched over curves that call my name like a siren song.

She's a waitress. I know that because her supple breasts are bared for the world to see, and she's dressed in high-rise cutoff shorts and cowboy boots—the official uniform for all servers at the Reaper's favorite roadhouse. But unlike the rest of the roadhouse girls, she's wearing a pair of huge wings. I'd call them angel wings, but she sounds pretty damn committed to that bird imagery. Plus, they're cherry-red—the same color as the hair spilling in long waves over her breasts down to her waist.

Her eyes are huge in a way that makes me think of innocence. But her smile is 100% wicked as she waggles a spouted bottle of some clear alcohol above her head.

Our gazes lock across the distance, and she stutters, the come-hither look slipping off her face as she stares at me staring at her.

Suddenly . . .

Suddenly I'm not so bored.

My cock stirs, and that dead inside feeling fades away along with everything else as the entire world becomes a single question:

Who are you?

CHAPTER 2
RED

WHO AM I?

That question was so easy to answer . . . four weeks ago.

Four weeks ago, I was Boring Bernice. I lived in the same town I grew up in and attended services at the same Methodist church every Sunday, rain or shine.

I reported in promptly at nine a.m. to the same nursing job for an obstetrician who stuck to a rigid 8 a.m. to 6 p.m. schedule—no middle of the night calls for us. Those moms who went into labor at inconvenient hours just had to deal with whoever was on-call at the hospital.

Four weeks ago, I was known by my coworkers as Bernice Daniels. I spoke quietly and kept my thoughts to myself, just like my grandma taught me growing up. I had a nice boyfriend, a practical diagnostic medical sonographer who let me know last Christmas that he'd be proposing to me by this one if everything went to plan. The only thing surprising that ever happened in our relationship was me dumping him just six weeks before his promised proposal.

It wasn't him. It was me. Seriously. A few hours after letting him go, I put in two weeks' notice at my steady job.

I'm somebody different now. Somebody who bartends topless at a nameless biker roadhouse. Somebody who everyone here calls Red—even Allie, the friendly med student who hooked me up with this job. Somebody who knows how to use her feminine powers and get paid for being a wicked vixen.

I smile and flirt and entertain, and the bikers give me huge tips for being the most interesting topless bartender they've ever met.

Here, I'm the opposite of boring. The other servers glare with jealousy whenever I come out on the floor to bartend because they know I'm about to overshadow them. And the bikers cheer because they know I'm about to make their night a whole lot more interesting.

At least that's what they usually do.

When I arrive for my shift that night, nobody acknowledges me. They're all too focused on something happening near the Reaper's usual table—a blond guy walking into the roadhouse with both arms held up like he's the Second Coming of Biker Jesus.

Maybe he is. I wouldn't say the music stops when he arrives, but he definitely gets a lot of attention. Waylon and the rest of the Reapers rise from the table to greet him with bro hugs and slaps on the arms.

Crash and Rowdy, those two bikers who are always offering the waitresses cocaine and other drugs to come upstairs with them, they clear a space for the blond biker on the bench right next to where Waylon's sitting, as if royalty has arrived.

I thought the Reapers only had two presidents. One for each of their chapters. Waylon and Hades, who left with the other

Louisiana members to go back down to New Orleans a couple of days ago. But maybe this guy heads up some chapter I don't know about? The other Reapers are acting like he's a huge deal.

And The Bandits wave him over to their table to say hi. A few of them even take selfies with him.

Too bad Allie was catching up on her med school lab hours all week. Her step-uncle owns this place, and she always has the inside dirt on all of the biker gang guys who come through here. Maybe she could explain why these 1% criminals were acting such a fool over this random Reaper's arrival.

Right after I take up my position at the beer tap next to the servers' station, a squabble breaks out between Tawny and Kitten, two of the blonde year-rounders. That's what Allie calls all the non-seasonal servers who work at her step-uncle's roadhouse.

I thought Tawny and Kitten were best friends. But each is insisting that *she* should be the one who brings the Reapers their next round of beers and whiskey.

Candy, the bar manager, has to rule on the case like King Solomon. She tells them they can either stop arguing and do the job together, or she'll let one of the holiday-help girls have the table.

They grudgingly agree to both taking the assignment, which means a split tip. And I make up two crates of Yazoos, thinking that would be the end of it.

But Tawny snatches her crate and makes a beeline for the new arrival before her supposed best friend can grab hers.

And I'm no expert at body language, but I don't have to be to tell Tawny's flirting hard with the popular Reaper—and that he turns her down with a hard, dismissive glance before he picks up his beer bottle.

Her rejection doesn't stop Kitten from acting pissed off, though.

"Oh my God, Tawny! I can't believe you did that!" she says as soon as they return to the bar to put in non-beer-and-whisky drink orders for the Reapers' table. "He already let you take him upstairs last year, and everybody knows he doesn't allow girls to hook up with him twice. It was my turn!"

Doesn't *allow*? Who does this guy think he is? Also . . .

"Don't you have a boyfriend?" I ask Kitten, thinking of the guy I'd seen dutifully drop her off and pick her up in a Suzuki mini-truck a few times since I started working here right before Thanksgiving.

Kitten shrugs. "Mike's about to go back on the road, and Rockstar's my hall pass."

Wow. Rockstar. Is that really the Reaper's road name? I roll my eyes. It's obvious from that tag and the way he turned Tawny down like she wasn't worth more than a few words that this guy thinks he's all that and a bag of chips. He might be even worse than Hades in the arrogance department.

"Is this guy really worth fighting over?" I ask Kitten. "I mean, you saw the way he treated Tawny. And just because Mike's going on the road, that doesn't mean—"

"He's my *hall pass*," Kitten repeats, as if that somehow negates any argument I could possibly make. She glares at her best friend. "Or at least he would've been if *Tawny* hadn't swooped in, even though she knows he doesn't do seconds!"

"There's always an exception to the rule," Tawny answers in as haughty a tone as one can pull off with her breasts hanging out. "And there was a chance he didn't remember me. He was pretty wasted the first time, so he only let me suck his dick."

Okay, so many problematic statements in their argument.

But as Allie had warned me before my first shift at the roadhouse: "Abandon ye here all sense of ethics, sis. Especially the kind that begins with 'fem' and ends with 'ism.'"

Tawny and Kitten get to arguing so bad I decide to do the Bird Call a couple of hours early just to distract them from their fight.

It works. Tawny and Kitten go from arguing with each other to glaring at me.

Ever since I came up with the highly lucrative Bird Call game and Allie used her niece-of-the-boss privilege to tell the other bartenders they couldn't replicate it, the year-rounders have banded together in hating me behind the scenes. So, Mission Stop the Catfight is easily accomplished within a few bars of the devil music I had to love in secret while growing up with my grandma, who only allowed me to listen to, sing, and buy gospel. Thanks, AC/DC!

I waggle the bottle above my head, and all the biker criminals come running like panting dogs. Rockstar, who?

Not going to lie. Diverting their attention makes me feel some kind of powerful as I watch them converge on the bar.

I paste on what Allie calls my "welcoming sex goddess look." It's not for real, though.

They can look all they want. But Red never lets them touch. She calls them "baby" and acts like she's known them forever. But they're not allowed to know her, even for a little while. She smiles and flirts and takes their money. But she'll never let any of them—

I feel his gaze before I see it. Powerful and burning, even before I notice him watching me across the bar.

The biker Kitten called Rockstar. He's standing now, but instead of approaching the bar like the others, he's looking at me. Just looking at me. And it feels like he's staring into my soul.

Red doesn't care about the bikers. They're only a temporary means to an end until we save up enough money to finally make our new dream come true.

But my Red mask slips when my eyes lock with the biker's. I falter and forget that I'm no longer Boring Bernice. Why is he staring at me like that—like a wolf who's found his dinner?

My heart flips over, and my stomach flutters. I'm no longer Red. I can't be. I'm too nervous and afraid.

For a moment, the whole world disappears and becomes one question:

Who is he?

"Hey, Red, you going to pour my shot or what?"

The real world comes back into focus. Gritty and wild, with an AC/DC song playing overhead. I tear my eyes away from the unknown Reaper and find one of The Bandits who took a selfie with him earlier. He's now standing belly up to the bar and waving a twenty.

"Sorry, baby." I exhale and pull the Red mask back on to focus all of my transactional attention on the biker with the money.

"Mama Red Bird's got what you need right here," I promise him with a wicked smile.

Then I proceed with the Bird Call—doing my level best to pretend like I don't feel the other biker's eyes on me.

But I'm beginning to understand why they call him Rockstar.

CHAPTER 3
GRIFF

I'M ROOTED TO THE SPOT. BUT ALL AROUND ME, BIKERS scramble out of their chairs and rush toward her. Crash, Rowdy, Hyena, and the entire table of Bandits belly up to the bar and tip back their heads while waving their twenties in the air.

The girl with red wings just laughs like this is a typical day in her life. Then she squats down—butt out and knees spread like a music video vixen—and starts pouring measured shots of alcohol into each of their waiting mouths.

I can't hear anything over the AC/DC song. But she leans down to murmur something into the ear of each guy after she "feeds" them and tips the bottle back up. Then she smiles and plucks the twenty-dollar bill out of his hand before moving on to the next dude.

As she moves down the line of open-mouthed bikers, they look exactly like the image she painted when she called them to the bar: leather-clad baby birds, eager and waiting to be fed by their mama.

For some reason I can't figure out, an ugly jealousy boils in the pit of my stomach. I'm tempted to go over there and start slamming heads into the bar. Just because she's touching them, and not me.

But the thing is, I've actually dated video vixens. Dated them and passed them on to members of my entourage when I was done. I don't get jealous. Especially of some chick I just laid eyes on a few seconds ago.

Still, when I try to look away, my eyes stay glued right where they are—on her as she makes her way down the length of the bar. Once, then back again for a second line of guys, then back again when a third line replaces those guys. And yet again, when a few of the guys from the first couple of lines come back for second shots. By the time she picks up the mic again, her waistband is stuffed with twenties.

"Thank you!" she calls out. "Mama Red Bird's all out of shots. But I'll be on the stage in a little bit for tonight's Deep Cut."

The bikers she baby-bird-fed shots hoot and holler as she descends from the bar and disappears from my sight, which abruptly releases me from the trance I fell into while watching her.

"Who is she?" I demand as soon as Crash, Rowdy, and Hyena return to the table. "You know what, actually, her name doesn't matter."

I grab Rowdy by the shoulder and turn him back toward the bar. "Tell her to come over here. I want an upstairs meeting."

"Upstairs meeting" is always code for "sex" when it comes to roadhouse girls. But for once, Rowdy doesn't immediately jump to do my fetching.

"Aw, Rockstar, don't even bother, man," he advises, even though he's usually my biggest cheerleader.

"She's a dick tease," Crash adds with another apologetic look. "You cain't get close to her unless you're waving a twenty."

Even Waylon decides to weigh in. "She's been here since Thanksgiving, and just about every biker in here's tried with her. But she's turned all of them down."

"Even Hades," Hyena adds as he plops back into his seat and takes a swig of beer.

Gotta admit, the Hades thing surprises me.

The girls that work behind the bar at the nameless roadhouse are strictly off-limits. Everybody knows that. But sometimes, they can be coaxed upstairs. For the right price or for the right guy. And Hades, with his smooth New Orleans accent and next-level flirting game, are what most girls working at the roadhouse would consider the right guy.

I've seen him drop a few honeyed words into the ear of a waitress he likes and her set a whole tray of drinks down to follow him upstairs to one of the fucking rooms.

But the girl with the wings turned him down.

The crowd erupts into cheers before I can finish processing all this new information. And the chick who called herself Mama Red Bird appears above us again, this time on the roadhouse's stage where I've been known to perform Garth Brook's "I've Got Friends in Low Places" when I've had a few too many.

The girl's wings have disappeared, but that doesn't make her any less mesmerizing, especially now that she's carrying a guitar under those fantastic tits.

"Hey, everybody, I'm Red! Y'all ready for tonight's Deep Cut?" Her slow drawl lets me know she's a local Tennessee girl, not a Nashville transplant like me, or from one of the twangier lower southern states like Hyena.

"What's a Deep Cut?" I ask Crash and Rowdy.

"It's this game she plays," Crash answers.

And Rowdy adds, "She sings a song, and if you can guess it—"

"Ssshhh!" Waylon hisses, cutting him off. "I wanna hear. I almost won last night."

When Waylon gives an order, none of the Reapers dare to disobey it. Crash and Rowdy immediately clamp their mouths.

But up on stage, the girl with long cherry-red hair explains everything, as if she heard my question.

"I play a song, and if you know the name of it, shout it out. Whoever guesses first gets a free beer on me. But fair warning, this is Waylon's favorite game, and boy, does he hate when folks cheat. He *will* pull a gun if he catches you Shazaming or looking up the lyrics any other way. So keep your phones in your pockets and just remember rule number four."

She points to the sign hanging above Nestor's door, and just about everybody in the bar shouts back, "Don't piss off Waylon!"

She laughs, like Waylon's well-earned reputation for sudden violence is a funny story.

But then she starts strumming her guitar with a meditative look on her face, and the whole bar quiets to play her game.

I recognize the song immediately, even before she starts singing about a lamp that won't light in her poetry room. But I don't call it out. No, I don't say a goddamn thing.

Her singing isn't professional. Hell, she wouldn't even be able to get through the door at Big Hill, my family's record company. But her voice has something a lot of better singers can't replicate. Personality, mood.

The song she's chosen is melancholy and bittersweet. And that's exactly how I feel as I listen to her sing—like the stone wall I've constructed around my heart is cracking in a few places with old memories from before I joined the Reapers.

No, I don't call out the song's title. I don't disturb her mini-concert, even for a moment.

I've performed on stage with R&B legends. But for the few minutes of her amateur rendition of this particular song, all I want to do is listen.

There's a moment of rapt silence when she finishes. Then every biker in the bar burst into applause, including me.

"Thank you!" she calls out with a laugh. "Oh, my goodness, thank you so much! But did any of you know it?"

Nobody but me answers.

"Boat on the Sea," I call out.

She smiles down from the stage, and an engine revs in my chest when she looks straight at me with those big brown eyes and says, "Yes, sir. You got it exactly right. Good job!"

"Hey, no fair!" The Bandits prez, who was so eager to get my auto-graph earlier, calls out. "'Boat on the sea' was the main hook on the chorus. Anybody could have guessed that!"

I keep my gaze locked on her, but I let that Bandit and everyone else know, "It's the song that ends that movie, *Grace of My Heart.*"

"Right again, sir," she says with an impressed nod. "What's your name?"

All the Reapers look at her, then at me. Probably because they're way more used to waitresses coming up to me and squealing, "Oh, my God, you're G-Latham!"

I'm startled by her question myself.

But the PR bros at Stone River did warn me just a few days ago at our branding meeting that my fan numbers are glaringly white and majority male.

So, a lot of people love my particular brand of outlaw country trap, but they're usually not women of color.

I reset my ego and answer, "Name's Griff."

Then I give her a slow up-and-down look and ask, "What's yours?"

The question's meant to throw her off the same way she did me when she pretty much announced to the whole bar that she has no idea who I am.

But she just grins and answers, "Come on, Griff, you know who I am. I came out in a pair of bird wings earlier? Remember that? And now I'm playing guitar half-naked on stage."

She shakes her head at me like an exasperated teacher. "But if you really can't remember it. Boys, let's remind him."

She cups one hand around her mouth and calls out, "What's my name?"

"Red!" the whole bar shouts back.

Like she's the music star, not me.

"What's my name?" she shouts again.

"Red!" they cry even louder.

A wicked grin spreads across her lush mouth. And this time, she gives *me* the up-and-down look as she calls out, "One mo' gain—just in case Griff has as hard a time hearing important details as he does remembering them."

Even Waylon and the rest of the Reapers join in to yell back, "Red!"

Red laughs big and loud, filling the gritty roadhouse with the sound of her delight. "Okay, Griff, meet me at the bar to get your free beer on *Red*."

She walks off the stage to cheers and laughter—mostly at my expense. But I'm not too bothered.

"I don't care what any of you say," I declare as soon as she disappears from my sight again. "I'm fucking her."

Waylon snorts. "Yeah, good luck with that."

Crash and Rowdy, my two biggest fanboys, refuse to meet my eyes.

And Hyena repeats, "Even *Hades*," like maybe I didn't hear him the first time.

"Hades ain't me," I remind him—remind all of them.

I could lie and say I'm not cocky. But why bother? I know what I look like. Even hotter than Hades, with more money and fame on top. I've never been turned down, especially here in the roadhouse where I'm big shit. And I'm sure that record won't be broken tonight.

Plus, I want this girl. Bad. Them telling me I can't have her only makes me want her more—at least until I nut between her legs and then instantly lose interest.

"I'm going to have her," I tell my fellow Reapers. "Watch me go over there and close this deal."

I'm met with a whole bunch of skeptical looks, but Rowdy rises to the occasion.

"Yeah, Rockstar'll be balls deep in no time," he tells the rest of the Reapers, finally falling back into hype-man mode. "All he has to do is let her know who he is. When she finds out he's G-Latham and his family owns a record label, them legs will fall right on open for Rockstar. You'll see!"

I squint at Rowdy. "You don't think I can get this girl without her knowing who I am?"

"Uh . . ." Suddenly Rowdy's real interested in what's happening on the roadhouse's concrete floor.

But Hyena isn't afraid to make his feelings on the subject known.

"Yeah, playing the fame card is probably the only thing that will get you in that particular girl's pants."

That ugly, weird vibe that's been plaguing me since my birthday boils and bubbles at his words.

I'm back in the gym at the boarding school my dad tried to ship me off to after my mom went home. And the rich boys with famous last names are calling me "Surfer Dude" because I'm from California and wondering out loud during a lacrosse game if I even would have gotten into the place if my last name weren't Latham.

Back then, I proved that I wasn't one to cross with my fists. Breaking all those teeth was worth getting expelled from my first of many schools before I dropped out and joined the Reapers.

But this time, I decide to prove myself a different way.

When they tell me the girl I want is untouchable—that there's no way I can have her without using my fame or name to get it in—I ask them, "Wanna bet?"

CHAPTER 4
RED

KIKI: *Have you decided yet on Christmas? Need to give the caterer a head count.*

I IMMEDIATELY REGRET PULLING MY PHONE OUT WHILE waiting for that good-looking Reaper who guessed the Deep Cut to come get his beer. And my fingers hover above the touch-screen's keyboard as I try to decide how to answer the latest text from Kiki.

She's my cousin, but also my best friend—which is why we call each other "best cousins" even now that she's a highly in-demand songwriter who the rest of the world knows by her married government name, Kyra Fairgood.

We're so close. How can I look her in the face at Christmas and not tell her what I've been up to since Thanksgiving? That I quit my job and my boyfriend. That I'm moving to New York at the beginning of the year to begin a completely new career outside of my field.

That I decided to work here in a topless roadhouse to earn the money I need to make my secret dreams come true instead of just asking her—my now super-rich cousin—to give me the money.

If I told her, there'd be yelling. So much yelling. Then would come the questions, followed by worry. I'm sure she'd assume I was having a nervous breakdown.

Maybe I am.

I've felt so lost and restless since I held my grandma's hand as she took her last breath.

"How does my hair look?" Candy suddenly demands, grabbing hold of my arm. She smooths her hands over her striped brown and black extensions. Then she cups her breasts and asks, "Is there anything on my tits?"

You'd have to serve hot wings and alcohol topless to realize how much of your breasts you can't see by just looking down. How often have I found random smudges of buffalo wing sauce after my shift while walking past the big mirror in the back room where all the serving staff changes? So, I totally get why she's asking me this question.

"You look great," I answer, grateful for the excuse to return my phone to the back pocket of my cut-off shorts without answering Kiki.

Then I get to feel like the total opposite of Boring Bernice when I assure her, "Your tits are all clean"—five words I would never have imagined myself saying before Thanksgiving.

"Oh, good." Candy lets out an audible breath of relief. Then she squeals, "Here comes Rockstar!"

Sure enough, the Reaper who cockily introduced himself as Griff after my song was done is coming straight this way. Bikers and groupies part like the Red Sea as he strides up to the server station where I'm waiting to pull his beer behind the tap.

And wow . . . he is even hotter up close. Chiseled good looks and a straight patrician nose. He's also tall and well-built. And unlike some of the bikers wearing bandanas to hide their receding edges, he's got a full head of platinum blond hair. It's so perfectly tousled, I'd bet all my Bird Call tips that there's a whole bunch of gel and care involved to make it seem like he just rolled out of bed.

I'd almost call him pretty, but he's covered all his conventional handsomeness with tattoos. They cover his entire neck and extend down from underneath his jacket sleeves to cover the back of his hands. He even has a few on his face: a black rose sitting directly above his left razor-sharp cheekbone and some lettering underneath his right eye.

Other than his beauty and tats, I can't see anything that screams, "Okay, everyone, treat me special!" though. He doesn't even have a president patch on his jacket, like Waylon and Hades.

I bend sideways to ask Candy, "Is there some reason people are acting like this guy's such a big deal?"

She laughs like I've told a joke.

"You're so funny," she tells me—right before she breaks off to say, "Hey, Rockstar!"

"Call me Griff."

He answers her, but his dark-blue eyes laser in on me.

My stomach swoops—in the way it does when I'm nervous and don't quite know what to do with myself—which is crazy.

No matter how wild and confident I act inside the roadhouse as Red, I'm still Boring Bernice outside of it. And the person I am in real life would never dream of being attracted to somebody who looks like this guy.

Things Boring Bernice would never approve of:

1.The kind of biker criminals who frequent roadhouses.

2.Biker criminals with face tattoos.

So, I have no idea why my heart stops and my stomach starts doing acrobatics when his eyes find mine.

"What can I get for you, *Griff*," Candy asks, interrupting my stare-fest.

Somehow Candy manages to make the common bar question sound like a request to take her upstairs, especially when she places both her hands on the serving station's bar top and strikes a sultry pose.

I've never been to the second floor of the roadhouse myself. Allie warned me against making the trip up there unless I was looking to confuse guys about my willingness to sleep with them. Which I wasn't.

Red is just a mask, a character to scratch an itch I've never indulged and get me the kind of money I need to go to New York City. And yes, it's fun playing her. And yes, she makes me feel free for the first time in my entire adult life. But actually sleeping with one of these guys would be taking it a step too far. I couldn't do that.

I peek over at the biker from the beer tap. Could I?

My heart skitters and skips a few beats.

"This one owes me a beer," Griff answers Candy. He has one of those accents that Kiki calls country adjacent. It lopes like a Southerner's but doesn't twang and hum like somebody born and raised in the south.

"On her," he adds. Then he shifts his eyes back to me.

I squirm under his burn of a gaze, uncomfortable and embarrassed for reasons I can't quite explain.

"I'll get that beer for you," Candy offers, even though I'm already in position at the taps. "I don't mind. What are you drinking?"

"Gran Patron," he answers, even though that's a tequila, not a beer. And I'm pretty sure we don't have it in stock.

"Nestor keeps a couple of bottles special for me in his office," he explains to Candy. "Can you go get it and take it straight to the Reapers' table? Just tell Waylon I sent you, and he'll take care of your tip."

"Sure thing," Candy answers. Her voice is eager and bright, even though she's the manager, not one of the servers. And she rushes off to fulfill the order before I can offer to do it myself.

Not the nicest move since that means I won't get the tip from the premium bottle of tequila. I can feel myself slipping back into the role of Boring Bernice. The background character in everyone else's story.

But, okay, whatever. There are plenty of other bikers here to serve.

Since Griff doesn't want his free beer, I turn back to the main side of the bar, push back my shoulders, and paste a welcoming smile on my face. As Allie advised on my first day, "Big smiles and big tits get big tips."

"Hold up. Where you going?" Griff grabs my arm before I can leave.

And when he touches me, my heart doesn't just skitter. It stops. But I play it cool.

I take back my arm and tell him, "Hey, I've got other customers needing drinks before I go home, run myself a nice bath, and put on the latest Roxxy Roxx album."

He wrinkles his nose, like he's smelled something weird. "You still listen to whole albums?"

"Yes, and I still buy CDs too," I admit. "Though I prefer vinyl, especially when it comes to Roxxy Roxx."

I laugh at his mystified look. And I really should get back to my customers, but I have to ask, "Speaking of CDs, how did you know that song from *Grace of my Heart*?"

A shadow falls over his eyes. "It was my mom's favorite movie."

I nod in immediate understanding. Kiki made me watch that movie with her so many times. I guess, "So your mother was a singer/songwriter?"

He shrugs. "She was trying to be. She never got anywhere with it except bitter."

Again, I nod. "Yeah, there's a lot of that, especially in Nashville."

"You know what, I don't want to talk about my mother." He leans forward on the server station. "What if I told you I was the only customer you needed to worry about tonight?"

Okay, we're back to flirting. I reset to Red and answer, "I'd say that's simply not true. Candy's going to be real upset with me if I leave these bikers thirsty."

"Candy . . ." He sneers a little, like he doesn't quite like the taste of her name in his mouth. "Is that the girl I sent away so I could talk to you in peace?"

Aaannnd cue another stomach swoop. But I calmly tell him, "I really do need to see to the rest of my customers."

He gives me an assessing look. "I'll take a bottle of Glendaver from the top shelf."

Top-shelf bourbon. I should be beyond thrilled. We charge premium prices for the bottle of thirty-year Glendaver I have to stand on a stool to retrieve from the bar's literal top shelf. I've never even had to get it down for a pour, much less to sell the whole bottle.

But a funny feeling grumbles in my gut as I check the price list taped to the side of the liquor shelf. What was supposed to be a free beer for him and a nice tip for me is turning into something way more complicated.

And as Red as I'm trying to be, I have to work to keep my voice from shaking when I let him know the high three-figures price tag.

He reaches into his jacket pocket and places enough twenty-dollar bills on top of the server station to pay that amount with another five hundred dollars on top.

I just made more in three minutes than I've made in the first three hours of my shift.

"Thank you, baby," I say, putting extra Red oomph in my voice like I always do when bikers overtip me. "That's very generous."

"Don't thank me." He ignores the bottle he overpaid so much for and leans back in. "Just tell me how much more it will take on top of that to get you upstairs."

This isn't the first time a biker has propositioned me. Usually, it leaves me feeling dead inside my cut-off shorts.

But when the biker they call Rockstar asks me to go upstairs, my entire body goes haywire. What would it be like to sleep with the cocky biker? Would he take me in missionary, like my last boyfriend, Paul? Caress my breasts fondly? Ask if I was ready before he carefully entered me like he was having sex with a precious G-rated princess?

Or would he flip me over and grab on roughly to my breasts before he—

Wait, what the heck am I thinking? I blink away those R-rated visions. Too far. Definitely too far.

"I don't do that," I answer, putting a few icicles in my voice. "I don't go upstairs."

He considers my words with a thoughtful look. "I've got some-where else I can take you, if that's what you need to seal the deal. But you feel this, right?"

He wags a finger between the two of us, and a dangerous hunger stirs below my waist, curious and electric.

"I'm not looking to seal any deals," I answer, nonetheless. Then I tell him and remind myself, "I've got goals and dreams. And this job is just a means to achieve them. So, you can keep your tip and just pay me for the bottle. I'm not for sale."

He jerks his head back like I'm speaking a foreign language he can't quite understand. "So, you're saying you're the only one in this place who can't be bought for the right price?"

"Not everybody is for sale," I let him know since he's apparently never heard of that concept.

"That's not my experience, here or outside this roadhouse." His voice is flat, like I'm pissing him off. "You have a price. I just haven't figured it out yet."

Okay, enough of this. I pull the plug on the conversation by taking just enough from the pile of twenties to pay for the bourbon.

"You can keep the rest," I inform him.

There. Transaction done.

But he grabs my wrist again before I can move away and pushes the remaining bills into my hand. "Take this. I insist."

He's touching me again, and my mind spins with terrible, bad, bad, wanton thoughts. Working at the roadhouse is fun and liberating—easy too, since it plays surprisingly well into my outside-nursing skillset. Whatever this thing is sparking between the biker and me is the opposite of that. It's dark and dangerous territory that fills my belly with fear . . . and an anticipation that I cannot reconcile.

"If I take this money, will you leave me alone?" I ask, desperately trying to get ahold of myself. "Let me go back to serving the rest of my customers?"

He stares down at me, his eyes gleaming and intense.

But then he says, "Sure."

With that, he lets go of my hand and simply disappears back into the crowd of bikers, waitresses, and all the other women who like to hang out in this underworld.

It's like tugging on a rope and suddenly having it go slack. He's gone. I can breathe again. But I'm still shaking on the inside. For the first time in my mostly boring adult life, I understand the meaning of the term "totally shook."

"What's his deal anyway?" I try to ask Candy when she finally returns to the bar after delivering Griff's Patron. "Why does he think he's God's gift to women?"

Candy averts her eyes and answers, "I don't know. I guess because he's really hot?"

She *guesses*?

I squint. The one time Hades, the Reaper's other co-president, came onto me, Candy and every waitress who heard I turned him down spent an entire shift telling me how crazy I was.

They extolled his virtues—not just his good looks, but how rich and powerful he was. One waitress who'd actually slept with him before told me it was my loss because he was hung like a horse and then went on to describe the magnificent cock in detail.

But now Candy doesn't seem to be able to string more than a few words together to talk about the outrageously good-looking guy who tried to pay me to go upstairs with him?

And it's not just her. Every waitress I ask about Griff catches a severe case of the vagues. Somehow, they don't seem to know anything about the good-looking biker beyond his road name of Rockstar.

And as for Griff himself, I throw him quite a few wary glances, but he just laughs and jokes with his fellow bikers all night. As much as I find my eyes wandering to him, he pretty much ignores me for the next few hours of my shift.

Good, I tell myself. I no longer have his attention, and that's what I wanted.

Right?

Griff flags down a waitress about an hour before my shift is due to end, and she comes up to the server station to put in an order for a Coke.

That probably means he's fixing to leave. 1% bikers aren't always the best when it comes to drinking and driving laws. But the more responsible ones switch to nonalcoholic beverages about an hour or two before they're due to get back on the road. Good for him.

Still, I carry an uneasy feeling in the pit of my stomach as I put some ice in the clear plastic cups we use instead of real glasses and pour him some Coke from the soda gun.

Then a different kind of feeling twists my gut when a blonde appears at his table—one who's definitely not a waitress.

Nestor requires all of us to wear extensions so that our hair scrapes our bottoms, but her hair is styled in a sharp bob. And she looks way too classy to be one of the biker bunnies. She's dressed in a sensible beige wool coat buttoned up all the way to the top. And I can't tell from here, but I think she might be wearing panty-hose—like actual *pantyhose* underneath her wedge boots.

Griff greets her with a smile and a hug. They have a short conversation, and she hands something to him in a large brown bag. What could it be?

"Red? Red? Earth to Red!"

I don't realize I'm full-on staring until I look up to see Stormy, the graveyard shift bartender. She must be here to relieve me. I don't even want to know how long she called my name before I snapped back to attention.

She follows the direction I was looking and throws me a knowing grin. "Oh, hey, Rockstar's back! No wonder you were staring. I can't believe he's actually one of the—"

Before she can finish, Candy shows up out of nowhere and takes her by the arm. "Hi, Stormy. Let me go get you set up on the register, babe."

My chest swirls with suspicion and confusion as I watch Candy pull her away. Since when did our manager start overseeing us logging into the bar's system?

It only takes a few taps on the register for Candy to set her up. Then they start talking about something with their heads together. At one point, Stormy glances back at me. What the . . . ?

I'm feeling so paranoid that I almost give in and text my friend Allie. But she's taking her med school finals right now, and I don't want to disturb her.

"I'm back," a voice announces.

I turn to see Griff standing in front of the server station, this time with the brown bag in his hands.

"Like Jesus?" I tease, lifting an eyebrow. But curiosity makes me walk over to the server station to ask, "What's that?"

He smirks, like he knew I'd have to ask. "Your price. But we can call it a gift to help you change your mind about coming out from behind that bar."

My mouth drops open at his audacity. "What kind of gift do you think would possibly make me agree to . . . ?"

The rest of my words fall away when he pulls the item out of the large brown bag.

CHAPTER 5
GRIFF

I HAVE HER. I KNOW I'VE WON AS SOON AS RED TRAILS OFF, and her expression goes from "No way" to "Holy shit!"

I'll admit, I had my doubts before. Returning to the Reapers' table with nothing but a bottle of Glendaver to show for my trip was an ego blow, for shit sure. Everybody but Waylon laughed as soon as I arrived. And Waylon doesn't count. He never laughs or smiles.

"*Even Hades*," Hyena repeated. This time with a smug singsong. Like I was Icarus or something, and he was the dad that warned me not to fly too close to the sun.

I ignored them all and pulled out my phone.

"Whatcha doing?" Crazytown, one of the old-timers in the club, asked. "Calling that little secretary of yours to drop off all the money you owe us?"

Yeah, the bet had gotten out of hand.

Red did a hell of a branding job on herself before I came along. The other Reapers were so sure I'd get shut down, they'd all anted up, and everybody but Waylon had wagered big against me—to the point that the pool grew to five figures in size.

I didn't care about the money. I was probably going to piss that out in blow and booze by the time the two-week holiday in Latham County with the Reapers was done and I returned to Nashville for the Stone River Records New Year's Eve show.

But my pride refused to go down without a fight. I only got in five minutes of game with her before she officially shut me down. But I *felt* that five minutes, and I knew she did too. Something was crackling between us—something that made me want to fuck her even more for reasons that went beyond the bet.

"Assistant. Nobody calls them secretaries anymore except for old fucks like you," I answered Crazytown. "And yeah, I'm texting her. But not for the reason you think. I got a plan."

"What kind of plan?" Hyena asked. "You know what, man, never mind. Ain't no plan in Tennessee going to open up those legs without you telling her who you are. How about we double down on the bet?"

Damn Hyena. He acts like a fun-times guy with nothing on his mind except the next laugh. But ask any of the people we send Vengeance to collect on—all fun and games disappear when there's money on the line.

His sly eyes shone like a Wall Street banker when he asked, "You game to go or too scared to raise the stakes?"

I went back and forth with myself—the ego my mom gave me warring with the good Latham sense that my dad and half-brother were always telling me I had to start using. There were no guarantees my idea would work, after all.

But in the end, my ego won out. Not to mention the raging hard-on I had gotten from just talking to her.

"How about we triple it?" I asked, glaring back at Hyena like Clint Eastwood in the eighties.

But unfortunately for me, that fucker, Hyena, agreed without even a millisecond of hesitation.

And all he had to do was say, "Even Hades" a few times to get the rest of the gang on board.

Even Waylon joined in this time.

He just shrugged when I gave him my "What the fuck, et tu, Brute?" look. "She ain't happening for you tonight. Might as well learn you that the hard way."

So yeah, I'd been real close to doubting myself when I walked up to the bar.

But now I have her.

Her entire face lights up with shock when she lays her pretty brown eyes on the item I took out of the bag—a first edition vinyl copy of Roxxy Roxx's first album.

This wasn't one of those items her fans could get easily.

When Roxxy Roxx signed the deal for her first few albums, it had been under one of those horrible hit-job contracts that her original label, Majesty Records, used to be known for—the kind of deal that made artists like Prince write the word SLAVE across his face. And fortunately for me, it had been around that time in the early 2000s when vinyl had fallen out of favor. So there'd only been one pressing of her original albums before she parted ways with Majesty Records. And for various reasons, Majesty hadn't bothered to do a second pressing after they went down in a dumpster fire flame of embezzlement and lawsuits.

The album in my hand is worth over five thousand dollars on the open market. I knew that because that's what Jenni, my assistant, told me she paid for it before driving it up here herself from Nashville to hand-deliver it to me in the freezing cold.

She was even more passive-aggressive than usual when I thanked her for her assistance. "Sure, Shelli and I were planning on going to the closing night of *Chrysanthemum* tonight. But anything for my boss."

Well, I'd been scratching my head to figure out what to get her for Christmas. A weekend off while we're on the European leg of the G-Latham tour and tickets to go see that opera everybody's been talking about, *Chrysanthemum*, in some East Coast city with her girlfriend would do the trick. If they were still together by then, that is.

I stayed touring, and girlfriends got clingy and whiny when they couldn't see you—one of the many reasons I never bothered with them. So far, none of the women who came before Shelli had stuck around waiting for Jenni to get back. That's probably why she chose to complete my errand over a night out at the opera. Girlfriends come and go, but there'll always be asshole bosses willing to pay for assistants to be at their beck and call.

Anyway, pissing Jenni off and the money I paid for the album was worth it.

When Red breathlessly asks, "How did you find this?" I know I'll be able to pay for Jenni's Christmas present and the Roxxy Roxx vinyl with all the bet money I'm about to win.

"That's something I'd love to discuss with you, " I answer smoothly before adding, "on this side of the bar."

I confidently wait for her answer. The internet says this vinyl's worth a few thousand dollars, but to a Roxxy Roxx megafan, it's priceless. A true stan would find it almost physically impossible to turn this gift down, even if it comes with strings attached.

She wets her lip, and her expression weakens.

"What do I have to do to get that album?" she asks, confirming my guess about her true-fan status. "Have sex with you?"

Sex . . .

My pulse sprints at just the thought of it. I can already see all the stuff I want to do to her—all the positions I'll put her in for making me work so hard.

But something inside of me won't let me say yes to her question.

Damn ego again. It's telling me that it won't be much fun conquering her if she's only hooking up with me because of a round piece of plastic. I have to prove to Red that she wants this too. Just as bad as I do.

"Another five minutes," I decide. "Another five minutes with you on *this* side of the bar. And then the album is yours."

She squints at me in a way I'd describe as adorable if she wasn't making my cock so stiff and achy.

"Five minutes doing what?" Her voice is laced with suspicion. "I've got a feeling you're not interested in just talking with me for five minutes to see if we truly connect."

She's got me there. Yeah, we had that weird moment when I told her about my mom for some reason. But like the "F**kin' Problems" A$AP Rocky track I keep at the top of my workout playlist, I'm not one for the long talkin'.

I run my tongue around my teeth and admit, "I wish I could do the small-talk dance with you. But this thing between us is burning too hot for that."

I dip my head down and promise, "There's gonna be kissing involved. Touching too."

I heroically manage to keep my eyes on her face as I tell her this, but I can already feel the weight of those glorious breasts in my palms. And maybe she can tell what I'm thinking.

She crosses her arms over her breasts, hiding them from me. Then she looks up as if she's seeking some kind of consultation from above.

I can tell her brain's working overtime to reconcile my terms. It shouldn't be that hard of a decision. I mean, look at me. I've had girls beg to suck me off on their knees. And I know deep in my gut this desire isn't one-sided.

"That's all I have to do?" she asks eventually. "Let you kiss me on that side of the bar? With a little touching?"

I nod.

"Okay, five minutes."

She says the words on a rush of air, like she's sighing and giving in at the same time.

"You can kiss me. But you can't take any of my clothes off. And no touching below the waist. I'm not looking to star in a porn video for your friends."

She glances to the side, and I follow her gaze to the Reapers' table. Those damn lookie-loos are watching us like a TV show. A few of them are even standing to get a better view.

Luckily, I'm a music star and used to doing all sorts of stuff in public that most guys can't even manage in the shower by themselves.

"Deal," I answer. Because I'm Griffin fucking Latham. And even if she doesn't know who I am, she's going to submit to me.

One kiss . . . five minutes . . . That's all I have to work with.

And I'm going to make 'em count.

CHAPTER 6
RED

ONE KISS. JUST ONE KISS.

That's all I have to do to get a priceless Roxxy Roxx album.

I'm a grown woman. I can handle one kiss.

I take a deep breath and lift the server station, and then . . .

I'm standing in front of the weirdly magnetic biker. Be cool, be cool, be cool. You can do this. You can do this. You can do this.

"Hey," he greets, his voice low, like were two past people who just happened to find themselves standing face-to-face in front of the same bar.

"Hey," I say back, swallowing hard.

Allie warned me so often about not being caught without a tray on this side of the bar. I glance all around. It feels like I've wandered into a foreign country.

Looking beyond Griff is a bad idea, though. Everybody's staring at me. Bikers are as rowdy as rowdy can be, but the room's gone quiet, save for some country song playing overhead that I don't recognize.

But then again, I hate country music. Unless it's something my best cousin wrote. Even then, my enthusiasm for her songs might be more encouraging than truthful. Okay, stop thinking about Kiki. You're Red right now. Be Red. Just be Red and don't let your mind chew on anything else.

"This is a one-time thing, y'all!" I call out to our audience. "One rare kiss in exchange for one very rare record. A fair and square deal. That's all."

Griff raises his eyebrows, his expression skeptical and amused— like he's caught me lying even though I'm speaking nothing but the truth.

I raise my Apple Watch and inform the gorgeous biker with my most businesslike tone, "I'm setting a timer for your five minutes."

He grins down at me and steps closer with the same look Olympic athletes wear when they're getting set up to run a sprint. "You're kinda adorable. You know that?"

Before I can answer, he gently shoves me backward to plop onto the serving station's single barstool. Whoops and hollers go up all around us as he wraps my legs around his waist and presses into me.

He's wearing black jeans, but I can feel his erection. It presses into the space between my legs, declaring itself as loud and obnoxious as the bikers egging him on.

"Yeah, Rockstar, that's it. Fuck that dick tease! Show her!" a few of them shout. Like he's some kind of biker bro hero for putting on this display.

I squirm, instinctively wanting to extract myself from this situation. But Griff wedges himself even tighter between my legs, keeping me pinned to the stool.

"Ignore them." His blue eyes bore into mine. "Focus on me. Focus on this."

Yes . . . focus. I rip my eyes away and press the five-minute clock icon on the Apple Watch's timer display.

"Your five minutes starts n—"

He slants his mouth over mine before I have a chance to finish my declaration, and the strangest thing happens.

All the noise—all the bikers jeering and calling out rude things— they all disappear in an instant. The moment his lips touch mine.

One rough hand curves around my neck, and the other finds my breast. My nipples tighten, and goose bumps break out across my skin. Not because I'm cold. No.

My eyes flutter closed. And did I say I didn't like any country songs?

"This Kiss" by Faith Hill suddenly blasts into my head as the world becomes an eddy of sensations I've never felt before.

Heat sparks across my skin, lighting me up, consuming me in flame. And my legs fall open like a marionette.

He instantly takes advantage of the additional access I've given him. He groans against my lips, his heavy hips pressing into mine, demanding and insistent.

He doesn't reach down to remove the barrier of my shorts, though. He's keeping his promise. I should be grateful. But I whine inside, a sick and needy ache coming over me like a fever as I grind against the thick erection encased in his jeans, begging him with my body to take the kiss even further.

He catches one of my earlobes between his teeth. Then he drops his mouth to my neck to kiss all the spots I didn't know could make me whimper and moan—make my entire body shiver with arousal.

He makes it worse. The need . . . the ache . . . He only makes it worse.

I forget myself. Forget the deal. All I can do is kiss him back, on his face, his neck—anywhere my lips can find skin. This feels so good. Better than anything I've ever experienced in my G-rated life.

And then he captures my mouth again, this time pushing his tongue into mine. Oh, sweet invasion.

Somewhere in the distance, a beeping sound goes off. I ignore it.

Kissing Griff . . . Touching Griff . . . That's the only thing I care about.

But then some little voice reminds me, *That beeping is from an alarm. The watch alarm you set to prevent things from going too far.*

It's like waking from a trance. My eyes flutter open.

The sound of the bar comes back. Bikers are calling out all sorts of coarse things, and I'm pretty sure I hear Candy somewhere in the background calling me a lucky bitch.

The five minutes are up, but Griff hasn't stopped. His tongue twists in my mouth as he pistons between my legs. It's like we're having sex with our clothes still on, and for a moment, I join him, undulating into the heavy shove of his hips. I almost get dragged back down underneath his spell.

But no . . . no . . . *We have to stop!*

I pull back, tearing my lips away from his.

He immediately tries to follow me, but I grab onto my last piece of sanity to gasp out, "Griff, no. You have to stop. You promised you would stop after five minutes."

He blinks his eyes open, and he looks like he's coming out of a trance too.

"What the hell was that?" he demands, as if I'm the one who cast a spell over him and not the other way around.

"I don't know," I whisper back.

Because it sure as heck wasn't just a kiss.

The crowd gathered around us is losing their mind, like we put on a show just for them.

Embarrassment creeps in, and I stiffen, trying to figure out how I should handle this so that I can keep working here without getting harassed too badly on a daily basis.

He takes off his jacket and puts it on me, pushing my arms through it.

"I'm sorry," he says, zipping me up in leather and covering my breasts. "I didn't mean for it to go that far."

Me either. But I squint at him and have to ask, "What were you trying to do when you kissed me like that?"

He dips his head and presses his forehead into mine. "Convince you. I don't want you to leave with me because of some record. I want you to leave with me because you want me as bad as I want you."

His explanation is so simple. Yet it sets off a volcano of emotions inside my chest, and I realize something at that moment.

I do. I do want him too—as bad as he says he wants me.

Not because he's a nice guy and we've been dating an appropriate number of months to introduce sex. But because for the first time in my life someone has kissed me in a way that makes me feel something other than mild curiosity and duty below the waist.

"I know I gave you my word to stop, and I didn't stick to it," he continues. His eyes are boring into mine again, hot and tortured. "But that was because I didn't want to stop. I want you, Red."

His voice is thick with lust and frustration as he tells me, "I want you. In my bed. Now. And I'm pretty damn sure that kiss proves you want me too."

More than proved it. Even zipped up in his jacket, my whole body continues to tingle like I'm still naked and exposed.

"I . . ." I swallow, carefully lower my legs from around his waist, and tell him, "I don't want to go upstairs with you."

His whole expression crumples, like I kicked him in the stomach.

So I imagine he's almost as surprised as me when I add, "You mentioned having somewhere else you could take me to earlier. Take me to it. Take me to it right now."

CHAPTER 7
GRIFF

WHAT THE HELL WAS THAT?

I ask myself this question again as I watch Red's car pull up at my dad's cabin—the cabin I've never invited my fellow Reapers to, much less some girl I just met.

But that kiss, man . . .

Don't blame it all on the kiss. You were all set to invite her here before you even got those five minutes, my brother snidely points out inside my head. *You're breaking all your rules for this woman.*

This isn't the first time the imaginary version of my brother has called me out. Most guys have a voice of reason that sounds like either themselves, whatever god they're into, or an imaginary cricket. But ever since my older brother, Geoff, decided I wasn't "ready" for a deal with our family's record label, I've had his voice inside my head. Correcting me. Telling me I'm not good enough.

But now isn't the time to be thinking about my asshole brother.

It doesn't matter why I got Red here. I'm winning the bet. Also, I get to bang her. That's the only thing I decided to care about as she shuffles up the pathway in my leather jacket.

Another first. I've never invited a girl to my dad's cabin, and I damn sure have never let one wear my Reaper's jacket. I don't know why I put it on her after that kiss—or why I didn't ask for it back after she agreed to follow me in her car to my dad's cabin.

I told myself it was because I didn't want to risk breaking the spell. Candy, that one waitress who made sure none of the other servers told Red who I really am, had just brought all her stuff out to her in one of those zip-up totes that some girls carry as a purse. Everything was set. Why risk asking for it back?

But my chest pangs with a weird feeling as I watch her jog up the cabin's front steps huddled in my jacket. Like I'm proud or something because it's my leather keeping her warm and protected on this cold Tennessee night.

She stops on the top step when she sees me waiting at the door for her.

"Hi again," she says, her voice soft.

"Hi again," I answer.

I'm tempted to close the distance between us. Pull her in the rest of the way. Then I remember I'm Griffin Latham—even if she doesn't know that.

I make myself stay right where I am. Wait for her to come to me, like she should've from the start.

But as cold as she looked coming up the cabin steps, she doesn't appear to be in any hurry to get inside. She also stays right where she is. And she tilts her head quizzically at me. "Why are you looking at me like that?"

"Like what?"

She shifts from boot to boot, her expression wary. "Like me shivering on your front step is something you want to eat for dinner."

"I already had dinner tonight, but I could do with some dessert," I answer, leaning hard into the innuendo, same as I do when I'm rapping about weed and pussy. "That will warm you up, I bet."

"Smooth." She squints at me in that adorable way of hers. "Are you always this slick? Is that why all the other servers were practically lining up to go upstairs with you?"

"All the other servers except you," I point out instead of answering her loaded question. Then before she can throw something else at me that I don't want to answer, I ask, "You want to come in and stop being cold or what?"

"Yes," she says.

But she doesn't step forward, and my stomach hardens with a new possibility. "You chickening out?"

"No," she answers quickly. "Once I make a decision, it's made. No turning back. That's my personal motto. I'm just remembering this time my cousin texted me out of the blue that she was meeting some random guy at his cabin in Latham County."

"What happened?" I ask, hoping to hell this isn't a story about her cousin getting axe murdered.

She glances nervously at the woods surrounding the cabin. "They ended up getting married. She just gave birth to their first kid, and they're already talking about having another one."

Red looks from the woods back to me.

"But that's not gonna happen here, right?" she asks, squinting at me. "This is just a one-night stand? All challenge, no substance?"

I think she's teasing me. But, just in case, I answer, "I'm not a fan of marriage or kids, if that's what you're trying to ask."

She grins at me, letting me off the hook. "Okay then, yes, I'll come in just for one night."

She finally walks forward, and I step back to let her enter.

But there's a weird, awkward churning in my gut where the anticipation should be as I close the door behind her. I've finally got Red where I wanted her, but it feels like I've just told her another lie to get her in here. Even though it's true. I've never wanted marriage and kids. I consider that a fate worse than death. So why did it feel wrong to say that out loud to her? What the hell is wrong with me tonight?

"Whose home is this?"

I come out of my weird thoughts to find her looking around the cabin's front room with a suspicious frown.

"This place is too nice to be a vacation rental—especially in Latham County. I don't think most people around here could even tell you what an Airbnb is. But I know it doesn't belong to you."

"How do you know it's not mine?" I ask. I'm more curious than insulted about her assumption.

She glances around. "Dark, elegant furniture, rustic stone fireplace, raised beam ceiling, built-in wet bar, ski chalet window overlooking the lake. So many antlers, I can practically hear Gaston from *Beauty and the Beast* singing about how he uses them in all of his decorating. Yeah, I don't think so. Unless there's a gentleman hunter who smokes cigars under all that Reaper."

I close the distance between us. "I'm trying to figure out whether to be impressed or amused by all these detective skills you're showing me right now."

"How about just answering the question?" She takes a step back and gives me another of those adorable squints. "I'm not going to be able to enjoy our hot one-night stand if I'm worried about the cops busting in here to arrest us for breaking and entering. This is Latham County, and I'm Black."

I don't pretend not to know what she's talking about.

At the ceremony where they renamed the county after him, my dad told a story about how Blacks and Whites lived on separate sides of the lake when he was growing up here. And the county-wide rename was partly to patch over the whole scandal that came after the feds raided the compound of the white supremacist motorcycle club that used to sit on a large patch of land on the "white side" of the lake.

But . . . "The cops here know better than to cross the Reapers," I assure her. "Doesn't matter what color you are. You're here with me."

"Okay, fine." She holds up her hands. "I'm not worried about the cops anymore."

Hyena said she was new, but she must have heard about our reputation. The Reapers transport illegal shit all over the South, and Waylon and Hades are looking to expand up to the Midwest and the East Coast. The police here either agree to work with us behind the scenes or mysteriously disappear.

"But I'm still nosy," she says, glancing around. "I want to know who actually owns this place."

"Relax, the cabin belongs to my dad."

"Your *dad*," she repeats, her eyes going wide. "But you're a Reaper. Reapers crawl out of holes, not cabins that look like they could be featured in the Tennessee edition of *Town & Country*."

I'm not supposed to let her know who I am, or that I share a last name with the whole damn county. So I just shrug and say, "I'm the black sheep in my family," and leave it at that.

"Hey, me too!" she answers to my surprise, clapping me on the arm like Geoff does whenever he meets somebody else who also went to Vanderbilt.

But then she winces and admits, "At least I'm trying to be. I guess you could say I'm going through a rebellious phase right now. Hence me working in the roadhouse and you know . . . being here with you. But why did you decide to become a black sheep?"

I shake my head, a little confused. Every word out of this girl's mouth seems designed to throw me off my game.

"It wasn't really a decision," I answer. "My parents got divorced when I was pretty young. My mom was kind of shitty, but she was, you know, there. But then she went home when I was still in high school, so I ended up having to spend more than holidays and a couple of weeks in the summer with my dad and brother here in Nashville. Turns out I couldn't cut it at any of the private boarding schools he sent me to, so he tried to ship me off to military school. But fuck that. I dropped out and joined up with the Reapers instead."

I don't know why I told her all of that. That's not the part of my backstory I share in the media or even in private.

But she nods like she completely understands where I'm coming from. "That's a lot of good reasons to rebel. And I'm sorry about your mom. It's horrible to lose a parent before you're ready."

This is way more deep talk than I wanted in a one-night stand. Part of me is telling myself that I've already said too much. But the other part of me can't help being curious about her backstory too.

I find myself asking, "How about you? Why did you become a rebel?"

"Mainly for the opposite reasons," she answers with a wry note in her voice. "My parents were really great. But then they died in a car accident when I was still a kid."

She lets out a sharp breath, and I can tell the memory still pains her. "For a long time after that, I thought I had to be exactly what they would have wanted me to be. Get everything exactly right to preserve their legacy. But then, the grandma who raised me after they died passed away too . . . just a few months ago. And I guess that's when I kind of lost my mind. I realized that no matter how good I try to be, that's how everyone I love will end up eventually —dead in the ground. Including me."

She chuffs, and the sound comes out bitter and a little sad. "I guess I just got sick of trying to be my parent's legacy. I decided to live my own life. That's why I took the job at the roadhouse. I'm saving up money to move to New York."

I nod, understanding her reasoning. "New York kicks ass. That city's the opposite of dead."

She gives me another "we both went to Vanderbilt" slap on the arm. "Right?! I've lived in small-town Tennessee my whole life. All people do there is work jobs until they die. And most of them don't ever leave. I didn't even dare to get a passport until a few months ago. But now, I can't wait to live somewhere else."

Her face goes from sad to excited, and her eyes take on a new light as she tells me, "I was looking online, and it's a whole lot cheaper to fly to places like Paris and Rome from New York than from Tennessee. And I'm real good at saving. Maybe in a year or two, I could actually start traveling the world during my time off—not just going into Nashville to visit my cousin."

I open my mouth to tell her I'm about to go to Europe myself, but then I stop when I realize that would violate the terms of the bet —the bet I still haven't fully won.

"Oh, wow, look at me yammering on," she says, mistaking the reason I'm not responding. "This isn't how a one-night stand is supposed to go, right?"

"Yeah, usually there's not so much talking." Totally true. But for some reason, I feel like an asshole for pointing it out.

She raises both hands to her face and hides behind them with a self-deprecating laugh. "Okay, this is the part where you offer me a glass of something from your dad's elegant, enclosed wood wet bar so that I stop talking and we can start hooking up."

I could use a whiskey myself. But I have to tell her, "I don't let girls drink too much when they're with me."

"Why not?"

Instead of telling her the truth, which involves a whole bunch of unsexy legal ramifications and the kind of bad press PR companies can't fix, I ask, "Why do you need alcohol, Red? You scared?"

I expect her to deny it, but she answers, "Of course I'm scared. I mean, look at you. Who wouldn't be nervous? You're really hot underneath all those tattoos. And I really wasn't expecting to break the one rule I have at the roadhouse and have sex with a biker criminal tonight—hence, all the talking. Too much talking. I can hear that, but I can't quite figure out how to make myself stop."

Talking too much has never been a big problem for me, but I instantly know how to solve it for her.

"Red?"

"I know! I know!" She looks up at me with an apologetic wince. "I've got to stop. Are you sure I can't have any of your dad's alcohol? That would—"

I raise my hand to the zipper of her—really my—jacket and pull it down. And all her words disappear when her breasts fall out, luscious and real.

Leaving me free to say, "Shut up and let me kiss you."

CHAPTER 8
GRIFF

I GRAB THE OPEN FLAPS OF MY JACKET AND PULL HER forward to claim another kiss.

But she leans back before I can reach her lips. "Hold on. Do you mind if I take the steering wheel this time?"

Is she yanking my chain? I've got hours of blue-ball buildup from imagining all the take-charge shit I would do to her when I finally got her alone.

But the "hell no" doesn't immediately roll off my tongue.

I've got to admit, I'm kinda intrigued by her request. Maybe because no girl has ever asked me to let her drive before. Take a selfie while I'm fucking her from behind? Sure. More than once. Let her take charge? Not ever.

Until now.

Curious about where this is going, I let go of my jacket and give her some room. "Okay, you lead."

"Yes!" She pumps her fist, her whole face lighting up like I gave her exactly what she wanted for Christmas. "I promise I won't lose control like I did at the bar. This is going to be so R-rated."

I'm already regretting my decision. I liked the way she lost control at the bar. Also . . .

"R-rated?" I ask her.

"Never mind. Forget I said that." She waves both her hands side to side, like she's erasing the memory of what she just said for me. Then she gets to work.

She's the one who's topless underneath my open jacket. But there's something weirdly sexy about the way she enthusiastically pushes my flannel off my shoulders, then reaches for the hem of my tee and pulls it over my head.

Her mouth drops open when she sees all the muscle I'm packing underneath the shirt. "Whoa, look at you!"

I preen more than I should at her admiring tone—and make a note to myself to Apple Pay my personal trainer an extra Christmas bonus to thank him for getting me to this moment.

I like that Red's so obviously not regretting coming home with me. Just the opposite. She runs her hands over my chest and says, "I've never been with anyone with more than one or two tattoos— and none had what I would call artwork. You've definitely changed my mind about tattoos being sexy."

A strange mix of pride and something way too close to jealousy surges through me at the thought of her dating other guys—especially ones with shitty tattoos.

"How long did it take to get all of these?" she asks.

I tamp down the jealousy I don't want to be feeling. "I got the first couple of them when I dropped out of school, just because I could. But I learned the hard way that good artwork takes planning and vision. Now I've got an artist in L.A. who I hit up . . ."

I almost say "between gigs" but substitute "Uh . . . when I can" at the last moment.

"May I kiss them?" she asks, her voice polite, like she's requesting something at a restaurant.

Another new request.

"Sure." It's no big deal what she's asking, but my voice comes out a choked growl.

She kisses me once on the bird covering my right pec, then again on the roses covering my left clavicle. My dick pulses with each touch of her lips against my ink-covered skin, sending tremors of lust up my belly.

"And these?" She hovers one hand over the small tattoo underneath my right eye and the other over the black rose on the side of my face. But she doesn't touch me or kiss me there.

A strange disappointment makes my revving engine sputter. I liked her touching me like that, putting her lush mouth on my ink. I want more.

"Griff?" she asks again, reminding me that I still haven't answered her question about my face tattoos.

"When I started getting a bunch of tattoos, my dad said, 'Fine, just don't mess with your face.' He can't stand when m—" I catch myself again just before I slip and say "musicians."

"He can't stand when *men* get face tats," I tell her.

She lowers her hands and grins up at me like I'm an old friend she already knows. "So, let me guess, you immediately messed with your face?"

"Not *immediately*," I answer, chuckling low. "You gotta play the long game when it comes to pissing off my dad. I let him think he won the argument for, like, a whole year. Then I showed up to Thanksgiving dinner with my face art. That's how real rebels do it."

She laughs, and the sound makes something warm pop off in my chest. "Did it work? Was he pissed off?"

"I think so." I shrug and admit, "He's not the kind of guy who lets others see when he's upset. And he just changed the subject when my brother pointed out my face ink."

"So, that's where you get it from." She nods to herself, as if I've explained something clearly. "Your dad."

I screw my face up. "I'm nothing like my dad."

She clamps her lips, like she's trying not to laugh at me. "Just so you know, the only guys who say that are people who are in serious denial about being just like their fathers."

"Seriously, how are we back to talking about my dad again?" I ask, shaking my head at her. "Plus, you said it yourself. I mean, look at this place. This isn't me at all."

"Yet," she says, holding up one finger like a professor. "This place isn't you, *yet.*"

"You think I'm going to become a gentleman hunter?" I ask her, not bothering to hide how crazy I think she sounds.

She bounces her head to each side with a thoughtful look. "I think there's more than one way to hunt. I mean, you didn't just give up when I asked you to go away. You tracked down a Roxxy Roxx album, and this is where you brought me when I said I didn't want to go upstairs at the roadhouse. So no, you're not a gentleman hunter, but you're comfortable enough here. And who knows how you'll be when you turn your dad's age? Maybe you'll start smoking cigars and using antlers in all your decorating too."

She's fucking with me. Teasing me. And that makes me grit my jaw. "I didn't bring you here to talk about my dad. I think we have better things to do than that. Unless you're stalling."

"And *now* you're changing the subject, just like he did at Thanksgiving," she crows, pointing at me.

I just stare at her. Hard.

And she gives in with an apologetic wince. "Okay, you got me. I'm totally stalling. I'll stop that now."

She looks at me for a long, strange time. Then she takes my head in both hands and pulls my face down to her lips, pressing her mouth to the under-eye tattoo on the left.

My dick pulses again, like a bomb about to go off.

What the hell is wrong with me? It's just a peck. Not even on my lips.

Why am I acting like some weak virgin when I get pussy thrown at me every time I leave my Nashville penthouse?

I don't like this. I need to take back the reins.

But when I reach for her, she says, "Un-un-uh, you said I could be in control. Keep your promise. Let's not have a repeat of what happened at the bar, Griff."

The memory of not being able to stop when her timer went off pulses just like my cock.

"You are driving me crazy, and I wish I never agreed to let you take the wheel," I growl into her hair. "How's that for admitting when I'm upset?"

She laughs. "Thanks for letting me know. That gives me all the confidence I need to do this."

She reaches down and starts unbuckling my jeans.

Yes . . . finally. But I have to hold myself back from taking over the job myself. I don't think I've ever wanted to be inside somebody as bad as I want inside Red, and it feels like she's moving in slow motion. It takes her way too long to get to the part where she undoes my zipper then pushes my pants and underwear down my hips to free my dick.

But I get to peacock again when her eyes widen at the size of me.

"I guess all that big-dick energy you were throwing off at the bar was the real deal."

I don't bother to try to tamp down my cocky grin. But I also tell her the truth. "I've been waiting for this. Since the minute I saw you."

"Maybe I have too," she admits with a shy peep up toward me. "Do you have a condom?"

Yes! Game time! I play it way cooler than her, but inside, I'm pumping my fist just like she did earlier.

I purposefully caress her breast on the way to pull a condom out of my inside jacket pocket.

But before I can rip it open, she asks, "Can I do the honors?"

Is she kidding? I would never let some random I picked up at the roadside bar put a condom on me. That's a one-way ticket to becoming a child support check.

But for some reason . . . some reason I don't want to think too hard about, I trust her.

I'm barely holding myself back from ending this game and just putting her beneath me. But I hand her the condom package and say, "Go for it."

Big mistake.

I've never been a patient guy. My low frustration tolerance was the subject of many a lecture before my dad booted me off to military school.

But I find out just how too impatient I am the hard way when she touches me. One stroke of her hand sends an unexpected shudder up my back. And the second brings disaster.

I come.

I come before I'm ready, splashing the both of us with an unexpected jet of semen.

Fuck! Fuck, fuck, fuck! What just happened?

"Shit. I'm sorry." I don't know how to explain this. To her or myself.

"It's okay," she answers quickly. But her eyes are wide with shock, even as she assures me, "It happens."

"Not to me," I answer between clenched teeth. "Never to me."

She wipes away the shock with a reassuring smile. "There's a first time for everything. Seriously, don't feel bad."

She's trying to be sympathetic, but I feel worse than bad. I am fucking dying inside. This is not me. What kind of shitty *Twilight Zone* episode is happening to me right now?

"Give me a few minutes," I tell her. "I don't have a long refractory period when I want to go again."

"That's really impressive," she says, but her face is a careful blank. I can't tell if she believes me or if she's just humoring me.

Either way, this shit is fucking humiliating.

"Um, is there a bathroom I can use?" She glances down at the forearm I covered in my way-too-early spunk. "I should clean this up. And um, wash off the condom."

The condom she didn't even get to take out of its package before I came like some incel nutjob in her hand. Dude, I could not be more embarrassed.

But making her stand there with my jizz growing cold all over her hand and wrist won't make it any better. I point toward the hallway. "First door on the right."

She rushes into the bathroom and closes the door behind her. Then comes the sound of water running.

Then . . . nothing.

She stays in there for way longer than I'm expecting. But eventually, the toilet flushes, followed by the woosh of more sink water.

Then she comes back into the main room with a sheepish look on her face. "Turns out, we wouldn't have been able to do anything anyway. My Aunt Flo is in town."

I stare at her. Is she for real? Or is this some story she's giving me to end the evening early after I came like what the English drummer for my touring band would call a "Johnny No Mates."

"I know that sounds like a tall one, given what just happened," she says, as if reading my mind. "But I'm telling the truth. It's just really unfortunate timing. I guess the universe, as my best cousin calls it, didn't want us to hook up tonight."

First thought: Okay, I believe her.

Second thought: Fuck the universe.

Then a bunch of crazy thoughts pop off in my head.

I want you. I want you right fucking now. I want you even if you're bleeding. My body roars with the need to be inside her.

"So, um . . . I guess this awkward walk on the wild side is over for me." She grabs the tote she set down on the couch and jabs a thumb toward the door. "I should go. Thanks for trying this with me. Bye, and if I don't see you at the roadhouse again before I leave for New York . . . you know . . . have a nice life."

Have a nice life?

She gives me a little wave and ducks out the door before I can come up with a response. Then she's gone.

Have a nice life?

The words rip through me. Mock me. Even though I have plenty of money to cover that bet. And she's left me with enough time to go back to the roadhouse and score a less complicated chick—one who's not on her period and willing to follow me upstairs to the fucking rooms.

Have a nice life . . . Have a nice life . . . Have a nice life.

Why won't those words stop echoing in my head?

CHAPTER 9
RED

SO, THAT WAS A BUST.

My Toyota Camry's not even cold yet—that's how little time I managed to pull off Sexy One-Night-Stand Red. I toss my bag on the passenger seat and start the engine. Real talk, I'm not sure whether to be ashamed of myself or totally relieved things turned out the way they did.

On the one hand, I just got period-blocked out of my one chance to have wild and anonymous sex with a hot-as-sin bad boy.

On the other hand, do I really have what it takes to pull off wild and anonymous sex with a hot-as-sin bad boy?

I mean, I'm not a bad girl—not really. Underneath all this weave and makeup, I'm still Boring Bernice.

So sure, I'll never be able to find out what might have happened on the other side of those scorching kisses. But there'd also be no embarrassment when he found out my secret—that I'm not nearly as wild or experienced as I pretend to be with the "Red" mask on.

The phone inside my bag dings, interrupting my thoughts. I pull it out and find a text message from Kiki.

KIKI: *Seriously?! Still no answer? What's going on with you, best cousin? You're starting to worry me.*

See? More proof that I had no business going home with that bad-boy biker. No business at all.

I type back, *Sorry! I was busy at work. Yes, I'll be there for—*

A knock on my window makes me jump before I can finish the text.

It's Griff. Despite the low temperature, he hasn't put his shirt back on—just pulled up his jeans. So, he's crouched over shirtless, his dark-blue eyes blazing as he regards me on the other side of the glass. He makes a motion for me to roll down the window.

And that's when I realize I'm still wearing his Reaper's MC jacket.

Dangit, dangit, dangit! Can I do nothing right? Not even make a final exit?

I reluctantly roll down the window. "I know I still have your jacket. Just give me a moment to put on my shirt."

The shirt I should've put on *before* walking into his house.

Go in wearing his jacket with nothing underneath, Red said. *It's sexy*, she insisted. *He'll think you're such a bad mamma jamma.*

Why did I listen? All sorts of regrets pop off in my head as I haul the tote bag into my lap so I can change into my shirt and return his gear.

"Come back into the house," he says, his voice severe and commanding.

I'm pissing him off again.

I rummage even harder through the bag, trying to find my shirt in the dark car and having no luck. Geez Louise, did Candy bury it at the very bottom?

Still, I flash Griff a reassuring smile—the kind I used to give the kids when I volunteered for Sunday school.

"You don't have to invite me back inside to change. That's very nice of you, and I know you must be freezing. But I just need a few more seconds to find my shirt. Then I'll have your jacket back to you in a jif—"

"Red!" He splays his hand against the car window, and his expression is the same kind of tortured it was when he didn't want to stop kissing me at the roadhouse.

"Come back inside," he says again. And he looks nothing at all like a Sunday school kid when he adds, "Spend Christmas with me."

CHAPTER 10
RED

SO THAT'S HOW I END UP AGREEING TO SPEND CHRISTMAS
week with a biker.

Griff says I don't have to have sex with him on my period. He also
offers to triple pay my lost wages from the roadhouse! And, after
some inner hand-wringing, I agree to his terms.

I'm aware he's a criminal—that I'm getting paid in crime money.
But Allie let me know before I took the job that her step-uncle
was just as shady as any of the 1% bikers who frequent his
roadhouse.

"It's good money. Like better money than anybody could ever
make without an advanced degree," she told me before agreeing to
set up a job interview that consisted of Nestor telling me to take
my top off and turn in each direction. "But you've got to check
every moral you have at the door."

So that's what I did after I got the job. And that's what I do when
Griff hires me to "keep me company, and maybe cook and shit
until you're done bleeding and we can finish what we started."

My stomach flips at his words. And Boring Bernice has some thoughts. A lot of them.

But at this point, my curiosity wins out over my fear. Why would someone who looks like Griff triple-pay me, of all people, to keep him company when he could go to the roadhouse any time before Christmas and find a girl who's not on her period to one-night stand?

After making our agreement, he turns and shows me to a room opposite the bathroom, where I discovered my time of the month had come early. It's small but cozy, with a quilt laid out on a sled bed. There's a small drawer set that looks like it's made of the same honey-blond wood as the floors and walls. And there's even a single French door leading outside.

He leans against the wall. "This is where you'll sleep."

I don't realize how nervous I was about the nighttime arrangements until I find myself exhaling a small sigh of relief. "Thanks for giving me my own room."

He shrugs. "No way I'll be able to respect your no-period fucking boundary if you're sleeping in the same bed as me."

I swallow. I'm really not used to, or comfortable with, being addressed so directly when it comes to things like sex—or my period. But a small thrill goes through me. A biker who wouldn't have looked at me twice when I was Boring Bernice is basically saying he couldn't be trusted to keep his hands off me if we were to sleep in the same bed.

Griff steps forward and tilts his head. "Is that a hard no, by the way? I don't know what you're into yet, and we still need to have a conversation about your boundaries."

My boundaries? He's standing so close now. Still shirtless. Still tall and powerful with a body chiseled to perfection. My mind fills up with static.

But I manage to squeeze out, "Um, *yes*, that's a firm boundary. A really, really firm boundary."

"That's too bad." His voice is gruff with humor, but he has a frustrated look in his eyes. Like a wolf who's been chained up.

And I have to ask, "Do you have a lot of period sex. I mean, with other girls?"

"No. Never," he answers. "But you're not other girls."

His eyes blaze again as he says that, and he stares down at me in that wolfish way. Like he'd eat me alive. If I let him.

"Okay, I'm out," he says, turning to leave.

I watch him go with his mention of boundaries ringing in my head. Why did he think we needed to have a whole conversation about it?

I don't know whether to anticipate that answer or fear it.

THE WAY GRIFF'S BODY IS CUT, I FIGURED HE'D BE ONE OF those guys who got up at the crack of dawn to run around the lake like Rocky or something. But I don't hear him come out of his room the next day until after one p.m.

I immediately switch off the *Law and Order* marathon I'm watching and rush to the kitchen. He might not have been serious about me cooking for him, but it's the least I can do, considering how much he's paying me to stay here with him this week. And maybe it will make me feel less awkward?

Here's hoping.

Griff appears in the front room as I'm pouring more of the pancake batter I made earlier onto the griddle plate I found in one of the pull-out cabinet drawers.

He somehow looks both insanely sexy and adorably tousled as he comes into the kitchen, wearing nothing but a pair of black sweatpants and sniffing at the air.

"Good morning!" I greet. "I figured flapjacks would be a perfect cabin breakfast."

He eyes the griddle with a mournful look. "I don't do that."

"Pancakes?" I ask, confused.

"Carbs."

I eye his flawless physique. "Okay, well, that tracks. Bacon and eggs, it is."

"Thanks," he mutters, heading over to the coffee pot. But then he stops short to ask, "Where did you get all this breakfast stuff?"

He eyes me up and down with a disapproving frown. "And Christmas pajamas?"

"I hit Cal-Mart first thing this morning for groceries, period stuff, and warm clothes." I glance down at the Santa- and holly-covered fleece PJs I was happy to swap out for my less than daytime-appropriate outfit from last night. "I think I bought enough food to last us until Christmas. But if you want anything else, you can just give me a list and maybe an advance on the money you promised to pay me."

He tilts his head. "If I give you the money up front, how do I know you'll come back from the next Cal-Mart run?"

"How do I know you're going to pay me what you promised?" I shrug and crack the first of four eggs into a bowl. "If we're going to live together until Christmas, we'll both have to learn to trust each other."

"Trust," he repeats with a bitter tone as he grabs a mug from the cabinet above the coffee pot. "That's not something I fuck with."

"Then you probably shouldn't have invited some random road-house girl to spend Christmas week with you," I answer dryly. "There's still time to back out if you want. When I texted Candy to tell her I was staying the week with you, she just said to let her know if I wanted to pick up any last-minute shifts if you changed your mind."

Actually, Candy said *when* he changed his mind—as if it were inevitable. She also sent several Bitmojis, including one of her avatar stewing in a jar of jam labeled, "SO JELLY."

Long silence. Then Griff just takes a seat at the cabin's slab wood table.

I figure he's done with the subject. But when I set his breakfast down in front of him, he says, "Next time you want to go to Cal-Mart or anywhere else, just give me a list. I can get you anything you need. Anything. All you have to do is ask, Red."

My heart stops. It doesn't feel like we're talking about food and period staples anymore.

"Sit down. Keep me company," he says before I can come up with an answer.

So that's what I do. As nervous as I thought I'd be spending time with a criminal biker, Griff is surprisingly easy to keep company. We chat about the colder-than-usual weather and his thoughts on here versus Los Angeles, where he grew up after his parent's divorce. He's been living in Nashville for over a decade, and he still isn't a fan of seasons, he tells me.

"Especially last night, when I had to ride here in the freezing cold after giving some rando my jacket."

"It was only five minutes, and I'm sure your tough Reaper blood kept you warm," I tease back.

"Kind of hard to act tough with icicles hanging off your nose."

We laugh and talk at the table, then move over to opposite sides of the couch to watch TV.

That's when I find out about Griff's weird entertainment values.

"I decided about ten years ago to stop watching stuff I haven't already seen at least once unless it's for a job," he tells me, snatching up the remote from the side table where I abandoned it when he came out.

I squint. "So you haven't watched anything new in ten years?"

"Not much," he answers. "I . . . uh . . . work security for this one country music act, along with Waylon and a few of the other Reapers. He's been on tour all year, but sometimes I have to go with him to premieres or watch TV shows his agent sends to him. His team's trying to get him to do more acting stuff."

"So, is that why I didn't see you at the roadhouse until yesterday?" I ask. "Because you were catering to this country star?"

"Yep," he answers, his voice terse.

"Well, that's an interesting side hustle."

But Griff doesn't seem to feel like talking about it. He pushes off the couch. "Anyway, my Dad's got a pretty big DVD collection. Let's just watch one of those. And hey, you want to get us something to drink?"

We spend the next few days sipping on wine and whisky, smoking a seemingly never-ending stash of joints Griff kept producing out of nowhere, and watching DVDs.

Strangely, I can tell a lot about both Griff and his father by the movies he picks out for us to watch. Mostly crime films and stupid comedies from the early 2000s—the kind of movies my grandma didn't allow me to watch growing up. I get the feeling Griff was raised to value ruthlessness, winning, and the kind of women you don't have to work too hard to get.

But I appreciate the chance to finally catch up on so many movies I'd heard about but never seen. It's somehow easily both the wildest and most relaxing vacation I've ever taken.

Our unexpectedly cozy time together hits a speed bump on Christmas Eve after dinner, though.

"Uh-oh, we've run out of both whiskey and bourbon," I tell him when I go to the wet bar to make the drinks for our usual after-dinner session. Tonight's scheduled film is a Will Ferrell movie I've actually seen before, *Elf*.

Griff's just settled on the couch after lighting a joint, but he hops right back up. "On it. Dad's got a couple of bottles of Glendaver stashed away in his office."

"Oh, Glendaver . . ." I've grown so relaxed with Griff that I actually open my mouth to tell him about my Auntie Minerva—the one who's worked for the Glendaver family for decades and practically raised their two daughters. But then I remember that's a Boring Bernice detail. One that could lead to questions about who I really am.

Luckily, Griff disappears down the hallway before I can let my Auntie Minerva detail slip. He's a man on a total mission.

I pull out my phone to pass the time while I wait for his return.

Big mistake. Several messages from Kiki blanket the screen.

She's having a lot of trouble accepting that I'm truly not coming to Nashville for Christmas. She's only ever known Boring Bernice. Always dependable. Always where she wants me to be when she expects me to be there. Half the time, she doesn't even bother to invite me to stuff. She just tells me the time and place, knowing I'll show up early to help her set up because that's what I've always done.

I can tell she's truly alarmed by my supposed decision to "take on some extra shifts at work" this week instead of spending the holidays with her, Colin, and their baby. Alarmed and probably a little hurt.

My stomach tightens with guilt. And that guilt only becomes worse when I see all the additional messages from Allie, asking if it's true what Candy told her about me going off with some Reaper and wanting assurances that I'm all right.

> **ALLIE:** *If this is really you, where did we first meet, and what did we bond over?*
>
> **ME:** *At the vending machine in our medical complex's lobby. There was only one package of Twizzlers left, so we split it. Lol! I'm totally fine. But thanks for double-checking.*

I smile at the fond memory after hitting send on that reply. But there's still the million messages from Kiki to deal with—the messages I'm not ready to answer yet.

Am I losing my mind?

I think that possibility is what's made me hesitant to tell Griff my news all day.

Where was Griff, anyway? It shouldn't take this long to fetch a couple of bottles of bourbon.

The tendency toward snoopiness that I inherited from my pastor's wife grandma makes me put the phone down. Instead of texting Kiki back, I peek down the hallway. The door between the guest room Griff gave me and the primary bedroom has been locked since day one of my stay here. I know because I checked a few times.

But it's open now.

I don't intentionally try to creep up to the newly opened door. But I guess that snoop gene really does run too deep because that's exactly what I end up doing.

Griff doesn't hear me coming—not until I let out a loud gasp when I discover the secret he's been keeping from me.

CHAPTER 11
GRIFF

"WHAT THE . . . ?" RED SAYS BEHIND ME. "I CAN'T BELIEVE you've been keeping this from me the entire time I've been here!"

I freeze with the stack of G-Latham CDs I pulled from my dad's collection clutched to my chest.

I should have closed the door behind me. Should have locked it too. I'd just been so surprised to find my two albums and three mixtapes in compact disc form in my dad's collection. He claimed to hate the kind of music I put out.

"A bastardization, if you ask me. Both country and rap deserve better."

That's what he told me the last time we were in the same room at Thanksgiving. And years later, he was still pissed off that I'd signed with Big Hill's rival, Stone River, after Geoff refused to give me a contract. So pissed that a few months ago he invited me to join his latest venture, AudioNation, as the head of A&R, just to get me to stop making music.

At least that's what I'd thought.

I stared at the CDs for way too long, trying to figure out what their presence in my father's highly curated album collection meant. Then I realized I would have to hide this unexpected evidence of my real identity if I wanted to keep my situation with Red going.

The last five days have been the most easy and laid-back time I've ever spent with a girl. I didn't want it to end. But I didn't move fast enough—or pay enough attention to my six.

Before I could dispose of the evidence, Red walked in on me and caught me . . . well, red-handed. Shit! Shit! Shit!

I try to put together a plausible explanation for why I didn't tell her who I really was.

But then she says, "Your father has a huge CD collection?"

She appears on my left side, her wide eyes taking in Dad's wall-to-wall compact disc library like she's just discovered a lost treasure trove. "I've never seen one this big!"

It takes me a few seconds, but I manage to choke out, "Yeah, the old man refuses to get rid of it. He keeps insisting CDs will come back one day, just like vinyl did."

"They totally could," she insists. "That's why I still love them. And hey, look, his collection isn't just country . . . Oh wow, *Permission to Land* by The Darkness. I love that band!"

When she reaches forward to pull out The Darkness's first album, I take the opportunity to hide all the G-Latham CDs behind the long row of Garth Brooks jewel boxes.

"I never understood why they didn't become as big as Death Buddha," she says, giving the CD a fond glance. She scans the D section again and confirms. "He has all of their albums here too. That lead singer's growl, right?"

"Right?" I agree. "West Nygard was a huge influence on my—"

I stop myself right before saying "flow." Yeah, a few critics have commented that I sound like a young West Nygard decided to quit metal and make a country trap album. But now's definitely not the time to tell her that.

I clear my throat and substitute, "My listening habits. Metallica, Death Buddha, Andrew W.K., Nine Inch Nails, The Darkness—I stanned all those bands growing up."

"Me too!" She beams up at me like she's found a kindred spirit. "I had to sneak their CDs home from the library, though. According to my grandma, I was only supposed to be letting gospel past my innocent ears."

I open my mouth to tell her about how my older brother used to make fun of me for listening to so much metal and rap, even though our father owned Big Hill, one of the most prominent country labels in Nashville. But I close it just as fast with a bad feeling in my gut. Suddenly, I understand the definition of wanting to have your cake and eat it too.

I've liked not having to play the part of the famous music star with Red over the past few days—of getting to hang out with her like I'm a regular guy. But I'm also growing sick of not being able to tell her stuff.

Standing there with The Darkness CD between us, I suddenly want her to know me—the real me.

For the first time since I made that bet, I consider telling her the truth.

But then I decide against it. And not just because that would mean losing the bet.

The other Reapers assumed she'd melt into my arms if she discovered who I really was. But now that I've been talking to her over the last few days, I can't say I agree with them.

She's cooked all of my meals and fetched everything from snacks to drinks for four days straight. She's fallen asleep on the couch the last three nights in a row, then mumbled about her duty to keep me company when I sent her off to bed.

And yeah, I'm paying her, but I think Red might have something most girls I vibe with don't. I wouldn't go as far as using the T word. I still don't trust anybody except myself and my brother Reapers. But I'm pretty sure there's a bone-deep integrity underneath all those sexy curves and teasing smiles.

And if that's true, I don't know how she'll react when she finds out I've been lying to her about who I really am from the start.

Her entire face lights up, distracting me from my worried thoughts. "Hey, I've got an idea. Let's lay down on the floor and listen to this entire CD?"

She goes over to the TASCAM combination CD/Blu-ray player to push in *Permission to Land*. The old-school machine's embedded in a media center that controls the custom-built surround-sound system on the office's window-facing wall.

"I mean, sure. Why not?" I answer. "But why do we have to lie down on the floor?"

"Dunno," she answers with a shrug. "That's how my best cousin likes to listen to records. She swears it's the only way to truly take in an entire album. C'mon."

The sound of the album's first track, "Black Shuck," fills up the room as she dims the lights and lies down on the Southwestern-patterned area rug in front of the couch.

Okay, well, I was really looking forward to rewatching *Elf*. But I get down on the floor and listen to the first few tracks with her.

Not going to lie, "Growing on Me" hits a little too close to home. But as the song gives way to "I Believe in a Thing Called Love," I relight the joint I'd let go out earlier and have to admit, "Your cousin was right. This is weirdly nice."

"Kiki says it's the next best thing to being at the concert," she shouts over the loud music with a laugh.

"Kiki?" I take a lazy drag of the joint before handing it to her. "That's your cousin's name, right? You talk about her a lot."

She stiffens beside me and takes a careful drag on the joint before answering. "She's my cousin, but she's more like my sister. Actually, she's better than a sister. She's my best friend. That's why we call each other best cousins."

It's a sweet detail, but her voice sounds sad, and for some reason, I find myself wanting to pry.

"But you're not spending Christmas with her?" I ask instead of letting the subject drop.

Another long silence. Then she says, "Yeah, things between us have been a little weird lately. Growing up, she was always the out-loud one—the one with dreams she wasn't afraid to tell people about. And I guess I was kind of the quiet one who stood in her background. I accompanied her on guitar whenever she sang at church. I was the dependable person she texted when she went to meet her future husband in that cabin. She had these big dreams, and she was always doing outrageous things. And I was . . . I don't know, just staying here in Tennessee where we grew up and being boring like everybody wanted me to be."

Her voice trails off along with the song's guitar solo but then picks up again before the big finish. "She's my best friend. But I think she wants me to stay the same person. She wouldn't understand who I am now—who I'm trying to be. Someone who takes risks because I want to, even if it is just to feel that thrill going through my chest. She'd be scared and worried, and I guess I just didn't want to deal with that this Christmas."

I don't exactly understand everything she's saying, but I get it.

"I'm not spending Christmas with my dad and brother," I tell her. "And they both live in Nashville. I get not wanting to play the role your family put you in sometimes."

"How about the Reapers?" Her voice takes on a teasing note as she hands me back the joint and asks, "Do you think you'll regret staying here with me for six days of nonstop movies instead of hanging out with them?"

I take another puff. "Maybe. I kind of hope so. To be honest, my decision to keep you here feels crazy. All this week, I wouldn't have minded getting sick of you and kicking you out and going about my normal hard-partying business."

I brace myself for her to be offended, but she just laughs and takes back the joint.

"Yeah, you probably should have been kicked me out," she agrees, her Black Tennessee accent coming on a little stronger. "This waiting out my period stuff is some kind of crazy, if you ask me."

She takes another pull on the joint, so her voice sounds a little choked when she adds, "And I bet that country star you've been on tour with throws some sick parties. Let me guess. He probably lives in one of those crazy-expensive bachelor pads in the Fairgood building."

The weed must really be doing its job. Instead of panicking, I chuckle and admit, "Actually, that's exactly where he lives. Matter of fact, after Colin Fairgood decided to get married and buy a house, the guy I work for upgraded to renting his top floor penthouse unit."

"Why are you lying?" she demands, giggling as she hands back the joint.

"I'm dead serious," I answer with a wry shake of my head. "He's that big of a cliché."

We collapse into laughter as the drum intro to "Love Is Only a Feeling" sounds. And I can't tell if it's because we really find my supposed boss's situation that funny because we're on weed, or because of something else.

Something else that makes us look over at each other in the low light and stop laughing with smiles trembling on our lips.

We've been so friendly over the last few days. That's because I've managed to keep my dick down, like a good dog, with a combination of weed, whisky, and stupid after-dinner comedies.

But I never did fish out those bottles of bourbon from my dad's office stash. And tonight's stupid comedy is paused on the DVD player, still waiting to be watched.

Something ticks in the air between us, like a bomb about to go off.

Then suddenly we're kissing.

CHAPTER 12
GRIFF

IT'S JUST A KISS, I TELL MYSELF GOING IN. LIKE A BUMP OF coke to take off the edge before a performance.

I'm even mindful enough to pinch out the joint to keep from burning her before I wrap my hand around her neck and pull her in. Real gentleman. Zero Mötley Crüe.

But then our lips touch, and even coke doesn't rush through me like this.

A firebomb explodes between us, and we go up in flames. We claw at each other, our lips wet and messy as we burn alive.

The dick I thought I'd tamed fills with lead. I press it into her soft body to relieve the ache, but that only makes it worst.

No, not just a kiss.

I thought I had this under control. I thought I had myself under control, but I instantly turn into an animal. I do not give one fuck about her boundaries. Just one kiss, but I'm starving. And it feels like I'm going to die if I don't get inside of her.

All I know is the want. All I know is the hunger. Nothing else matters until she pulls back and gasps out, "Hold on, hold on . . . Let me try something."

Her voice carries both apology and a promise—a promise I don't understand until she starts pressing feather-light kisses down my chest toward my . . .

"What are you doing?" I ask, even though my cock is pulsing —*pulsing* in anticipation of what it already knows she's doing.

"What does it look like?" She glances up at me, and that wicked smile is back on her face. "You don't strike me as the kind of guy who's never been offered a blow job before."

She's right. I'm not that guy. It's no longer the eighties as far as the music scene goes, but it's still rock 'n' roll. Girls offering BJs are a dime a dozen. But . . .

I tell her the truth. "You're not other girls."

She smiles in a kind of goofy way. I can't tell if I've embarrassed or pleased her.

Either way, she ducks her head and focuses on pulling my cock out. Her eyes widen when she sees it for a second time, as if she thought maybe she'd only imagined how big it was before. And damn, if that look doesn't fill my chest with stupid pride.

"Can I put my mouth on you?" she asks, her voice a little breathless.

Can she . . . ? I nearly laugh, and a strange, tender sensation pops off in my chest. Does this girl have any idea? Any idea at all what she does to me?

"You don't have to ask permission," I grit out.

"Consent is important." That teasing note creeps back into her voice.

And the tender feeling vanishes. Dark ideas warp through my head. Ways I could punish her. Ways I could make her beg.

Wait until I—

All thoughts of my imminent revenge cut out when she takes me in her mouth.

Fuck. I'm not going to come early again. I refuse.

But the feel of her, warm and wet around my aching cock. And the sight of her . . . She can't take all of me, but she wraps a hand around the part of my shaft below her hot mouth, dragging it up and down as she suctions the rest.

Then, for some reason, she looks up at me in a tentative way. Like she's afraid she's not doing it right.

She's doing it right. Fucking hell. Too right.

My spine's rippling again. She's got me revved up and ready to shoot in a matter of seconds. Not minutes. Seconds.

But maybe that would be a good thing.

Maybe I should have thought of this that first night instead of asking her to stay. A blow job satisfies the bet I made with the other Reapers. And after this, that done feeling I always get after nutting with some new girl will swoop in, and there won't be any reason to keep her here. I could go back to the roadhouse for Christmas or maybe even throw a last-minute rager at my place in Nashville—one of those sick parties she mentioned earlier.

But for some reason, the thought of ending this with a blow job, of sending her away because I'm done with her, hits me like a bucket of ice water.

"Stop." My voice comes out as something between a growled whisper and a plea.

She keeps on going, and I don't think it's because she didn't hear me. She's testing me, poking at my boundaries like she did when she asked to take control that first night.

"Stop," I say again, and this time there's no plea in my voice, only steely command.

I grab her by the hair and pull her off my cock. She comes off with a wet suck that sends another dangerous ripple down my back. I immediately miss her mouth wrapped around my dick, but I don't need her to suck me off.

Not as much as I need to sit up and move my hand from her hair to her throat.

"When I tell you to stop, you stop." I squeeze the hand around her neck. Not enough to choke her, just enough to let her know who's boss. "No more going against my orders."

Her entire body quivers like a small animal caught underneath the paw of a wolf. But then she asks, "And what if I don't stop when you tell me to? What happens then?"

Her eyes flash with the question, defiant and . . . something else— something else I think I might recognize.

I tighten my hand around her throat, testing to see if I'm right.

Squeezing off her air.

She squirms, but just as I suspected, it's not fear that flashes across her eyes. More like excitement. Anticipation. And my cock, still semi-erect from having her mouth on me, pulses with new life.

"You like that, don't you?" I say, squeezing even tighter. "You like me dominating you like this. You're squirming at the thought of me doing the same thing to you in bed."

She hits me with a wry, helpless look, reminding me that she couldn't answer, even if she wanted to.

I loosen my grip, just enough to let her breathe and talk, but not enough to let her think she can get away from my question.

"Answer me."

She gives me another helpless look, but this time it carries a hint of her usual dry humor. "Actually, I was today years old when I discovered I don't hate being choked."

She rubs at my hand as she tells me this. And she's not pushing me away. It's more like a caress.

"Do you . . ." She peeps up at me in that weirdly innocent way of hers. "Do you do this domination stuff often . . . with other girls?"

She doesn't sound jealous or accusatory. But for some reason, guilt turns my stomach into a hard knot. I tell her a semi-version of the truth.

"When the girl's into it. I used to like it . . . back before I started, um . . . working security. But there are rules on tour. Risks you shouldn't take without paperwork. And I don't fuck girls twice, so it was always more trouble than it was worth."

"But you're not on tour now."

Her expression has gone carefully neutral. I can't tell what she's thinking, but the dark, warped part of me has to ask, "Are you into it? Do you want me to do that to you when we finally have sex? Hurt you, make it rough? Punish you?"

Her pulse quickens underneath my palm, beating a rapid little drumbeat against my thumb. "Just as a thought exercise, tell me what all that would involve."

My dick pulses dangerously at her request for more information. This conversation is just as bad as the blow job. Maybe worse. That BJ's not going to happen tonight, but I can already feel her body pinned underneath me as I punish her for making me wait.

"We'll have to establish some ground rules," I answer, working hard to keep my voice level. "You'll tell me your boundaries, so I know how far I can go. And, of course, we'll need to do the whole safeword thing. You know about that, right?"

She gives me a little nod. "I've heard of safewords, even if I've never used one. But how about if I don't know what my boundaries are?"

She says that. Then she looks up at me with those big brown eyes. Jesus. She's the living personification of a bad girl. But sometimes, she says things that make me feel like I'm talking to an innocent. Someone way too inexperienced to line up a bunch of bikers at the bar for a Bird Call or even work at a roadhouse.

I can't tell if she's really asking or teasing me again.

Either way, I have to swallow down a lump of lust to answer, "I'd test you out. Establish the boundaries for both you and me."

"How would you do that?" she asks. "What tools would you use?"

She's got to be fucking with me. She knows exactly what she's doing to me when she says stuff like that, I assure myself.

I don't like getting played. Plus, there are about a thousand legal reasons I shouldn't even be having this conversation with her.

Nonetheless, I answer. "My words . . . at first. I'd give you a bunch of orders and threats. See how well you heel."

She looks to the side, giving me a moment of reprieve from what surely must be a faux innocent gaze. But then those big brown eyes swing back right up with a new question. "And what if I don't do what you say?"

Fuck me. The images that pop off in my head. I bear down so as not to spray again.

"Then I use my body to make you do it," I answer between clenched teeth. "And I punish you for making me take it to the next level. I make you heel. If we do things my way, you don't get away with defying me."

I watch her carefully. Not every woman's okay with even minor degradation language or the idea of having sex the way animals do it. With the male dominating and the female being held down.

But Red . . .

Red just stares at me. And trembles.

A mirroring shiver runs down my own back. We're not even kissing. I've only got my hand around her throat. But I'm fighting myself not to blast past the only boundary she's established with me.

"Griff, I have something I need to say."

I know she's about to ask another question, but I can't do this with her. Not anymore. Not without . . .

I release my hand from around her neck and pull my sweatpants up over my throbbing cock. I'm going to have to beat off to get to sleep. And sure, I've had to do that every evening since I invited her to stay, but tonight it pisses me off.

She's in my head. How did she get in my head?

"No movie tonight," I bite out. I spring up from the floor and head toward the door with a weird feeling gonging inside my chest. "I'm not in the mood for Will Ferrell."

"That's a first," she says with a chuff, rising to her feet as well. "But we don't have to—"

"I'm not feeling a movie tonight," I say before she can suggest something else. I go to stand by the open door. "You can watch *Elf* by yourself or do whatever. But I can't have you in my dad's office without supervision. I don't know you like that."

She blinks, then squints a little, like she's trying to figure me out.

But in the end, she doesn't protest, just averts her eyes and says, "Sorry if I went too far and made you uncomfortable."

She thinks this is about *my* boundaries? A new kind of outrage thrums through me.

But I can't answer her. She's already inside my head. No way I'm letting her in any further by admitting that I'm too turned the fuck on to keep talking with her—to even do something as innocent as hanging out on the opposite side of a couch to watch *Elf.*

I don't hear the rest of whatever she has to say.

So I let her walk out past me. Let her have the last word.

I watch her sashay down the hallway in one set of those Christmas pajamas she's been swapping out every other day since her first morning here. Then I go to my room.

And did I think I'd make it all the way to the bed?

Wrong again, Griff. I barely get the door closed behind me before I'm fisting my cock. Images of her flood my mind as I jerk it with rough strokes for what can't even be a minute before I shoot my load onto the wood floor.

Then I stare at the pool of jizz I'm going to have to clean up, breathing hard.

And even though I know her name, I wonder once again who this girl is . . . and what the hell is wrong with me?

She doesn't know who I am. And suddenly, I don't either.

CHAPTER 13
RED

DID I GO TOO FAR?

I spend the rest of the night outwardly watching *Elf.* But inside I'm churning and turning in my head over everything Griff said— including the part about no longer wanting to watch the movie with me.

A spark I hadn't realized I possessed lit up inside of me when Griff wrapped his hand around my throat.

And I'll admit, I wasn't just trying to act like a sexual badass who was up for anything—you know, the opposite of Boring Bernice. I was honestly curious.

But maybe I said too much. He acted like I couldn't be trusted even to hang out in his father's office alone. And I'm pretty sure it was me, not Will Ferrell, he suddenly went cold on.

What had I been thinking, trying to give him that blow job? I don't have much experience with them, but I thought I was doing a good job—until he made me stop.

And while I was getting super turned-on by our conversation about boundaries, maybe he wasn't. Maybe he wanted one of those experienced roadhouse women—the kind who knew exactly how to handle the bikers they followed upstairs. Not someone who admitted to barely knowing what a safeword was.

The constant replays looping inside my head make me feel cringier and cringier until I have to go to bed early myself to get away from them.

The next day, I wake up at my usual hour and do the same things I've been doing pretty much every morning since I decided to take Griff up on his offer. I read some more of the latest Clara Quinn book. Not just because she's a distant cousin, who I, like all Black southern girls with huge extended families refer to as Auntie, but also because she's my favorite Sci-Fi/Fantasy writer of all time.

Griff still hasn't come out by the time I'm done, so I do some more research on Harlem, the neighborhood I plan to live in when I move to New York.

Sometime around two p.m., I just decide to make his Christmas gift in the hopes of luring him out.

It works. Griff comes stumbling into the front room about five minutes after my gift starts frying.

And why does he look even sexier than usual with a grumpy scowl on his face?

I have the weirdest, strongest urge to make it go away. To rain kisses on the criminal biker until he smiles at me like he usually does in the morning. But kissing is what led to all that awkwardness last night.

So instead, I focus on setting his Christmas gift on a plate covered with a paper towel.

"About last night . . ." he starts to say behind me. But then he stops and comes closer to the stove to ask, "Wait, is that fried chicken?"

"Sure is," I answer. "I've got an all proteins and vegetables keto version of Christmas dinner planned for tonight. But I thought maybe you'd appreciate some dirty carbs as your Christmas present, since you said earlier in the week that you never eat them. I also made biscuits and apple crisp. They're in the oven, keeping warm . . ."

I peter out, realizing once again that I might have read him wrong. Just because he mentioned not eating carbs didn't mean he actually wanted them as a Christmas gift.

"Are you fucking with me, Red?" he asks, dipping his head down low to spear me with his suspicious eyes. "Tell me right now, are you trying to mindfuck me?"

"Um, no, I was just trying to give you something for Christmas." It's hard to talk. I'm choking so hard on embarrassment. "But this was a bad idea. I get it. I'll just throw the food away."

His eyes take on a dangerous gleam.

"Red . . ." He bares his teeth at me and shoves his finger right in my face. "Do not play with me. *Do not*. If this is a game of mind-fuck. You will not win. Other women have tried before you. Tried and failed."

"I'm not trying to play with you," I answer, sputtering. "I have no idea what you're talking about. I was just making you some fried chicken."

He glares at me, his eyes scanning my face like some kind of lie detector. "Good. Then, let's eat. I haven't had carbs in fucking years."

I'm pretty sure he's exaggerating about how long it's been since the last time he had carbs, but I can't help but thrill when he houses five pieces of chicken and three biscuits slathered in butter and honey.

And I downright beam when he throws down his cloth napkin and declares my Christmas gift, "The best damn meal I've ever eaten."

"Where did you learn to cook dirty like that?" he asks, as if me cooking non-healthy meals was a secret I've been keeping from him on purpose.

"My cousin Kiki taught me. This is her grandma's secret recipe. She made these Sunday dinners that brought in our relatives from all over. So many of them came through for Aunt Bernice's famous fried chicken, we had to set up tables in the backyard to fit everybody. Luckily, she taught Kiki how to make it before she went home to the Lord. And my cousin taught me on account of me being—"

I break off, realizing I was just about to admit being named after my great aunt in real life.

"On account of you being what?" Griff asks with a curious look.

I reset with a shrug. "Real sad about her moving to Nashville. Once Kiki got married and started a family of her own, she didn't have much time for her extended family."

This is only a partial lie on my part, and Griff must sense that.

"You miss her," he says, and it's a statement, not a question.

I shake my head. "It's stupid. She's right in Nashville. But it feels like she's hundreds of miles away. Even when I'm in the same house with her. We're just so different now. It's like I don't have a place in her life anymore—not really."

Griff gives me a thoughtful look over his plate of chicken bones and biscuit crumbs. "My brother and me . . . well, we've never been best friends like you and your cousin. But we were for shit sure closer before I . . ."

He pauses, swallows, then finishes with, "Joined the Reapers. But he wasn't there for me when I really needed him. And now he's married with a kid on the way. I've probably got at least one hundred people in my phone who I talk to more than him. Some people start families and forget about everybody else."

I nod, understanding him like he understood me. "I guess that's the real reason I didn't go to Kiki's place for Christmas this year. We used to talk every day, but now she never texts me unless she wants me to be somewhere at a specific time. It feels like I'm just somebody she trots out for special occasions."

I've never dared to talk about or even inwardly explore the feelings of jealousy and resentment I carry toward Kiki. Much less had someone else take my side over it.

It's weirdly thrilling—but also guilt-inducing.

"It's not like she meant to forget me," I rush to explain. "She's doing her best. She's just . . . really busy. I'm not exactly being fair."

"Yeah, I guess that's my brother's situation too. Plus, I'm the one who said no to my dad when he asked me to join this business venture he wants to work on with the both of us. Maybe I'm not exactly being fair either."

Griff lets out a thoughtful huff. But then he shakes his head and adds, "Still feels shitty, though. Did you say something earlier about apple crisp?"

He's right. It does feel shitty, and I did say something about apple crisp. But as shitty as it feels to finally admit out loud some of the feelings I've been secretly having about Kiki, for some reason, I feel a little better as we eat the dessert I made.

And even though it's Christmas, Griff doesn't bring up what happened in his father's office—just suggests *Die Hard* to kick off today's pre-dinner movie session.

This is nice, I decide as I clean off the table. It's nice to talk with someone who won't judge you—someone who doesn't know enough about you to judge you anyway.

As I wash the dishes, I think about the tentative friendship we've managed to build over the last few days of hanging out. One that allows us to say stuff to each other. Stuff we wouldn't necessarily say to the other people in our lives. And the confession I never got around to making last night rises up in the back of my mind.

Taking a deep break, I turn off the water. Okay, courage-wise, it's now or probably never.

"Hey, Griff?" I come farther out of the kitchen and lean my hip against the island.

"Yeah?" He's already settled on the couch and pulling out a joint.

I try to look at him like a big girl . . . and utterly fail.

"This was actually supposed to be the second part of your Christmas present," I mumble.

"Oh yeah?" he says, fishing a lighter out of today's pair of sweatpants. "Now I'm feeling guilty because I didn't even get you a part one of any Christmas present."

"Oh, this unexpected vacation was present enough," I assure him. "Seriously, I've had a really great time hanging out with you."

"Okay . . ." Griff eyes me suspiciously. "But if you're having such a great time, why can't you even look at me all of a sudden?"

I try to answer, but I can't.

Griff lowers the joint he was about to light.

"What was the first part of the gift?" His voice is a suspicious metal detector, creeping closer and closer to the truth.

I open my mouth, and nothing. I can't say it now, just like I couldn't say it last night.

"Red?" Griff stands up, the unlit joint hanging from his fingers. "What was the first part?"

"Fried chicken," I answer in a rush of expelled air.

He squints. "You've already given me fried chicken. It was freaking delicious. We both agreed on that."

"No, I mean *fried chicken*," I say. "That's my . . . um . . . that's my safeword. Fried chicken."

He stares at me. And it occurs to me to add, "I'm off my period. That's what I was trying to tell you last night before you told me you didn't want to watch *Elf* with me."

CHAPTER 14
GRIFFIN

I WAS SO PROUD OF MYSELF WHEN I SAT DOWN TO LIGHT my first joint of the day.

I'd woken up hungover and weak, and I'd had a lie about having to get back to Nashville on the tip of my tongue when I came out to the front room. Yeah, I'm a Reaper, and every article I'm featured in talks about how I'm some kind of badass.

But early that afternoon, I couldn't see how I was going to possibly get through another day of just chilling with her on the couch.

Her Christmas present had saved me, though. I'd sorted myself out and gotten my mind right while inhaling all those dirty, sexy carbs.

In fact, I'd felt so satisfied after the meal she served me, I'd wondered if maybe that wasn't the real reason for all this messed-up energy I'd been carrying around since turning thirty. Maybe I didn't need to get laid. Maybe I just needed more carbs to get my head right.

Yeah, I'd thought I had it all figured out.

Then she came out into the living room and dropped that bomb on me right after I pressed play on *Die Hard*.

"I'm off my period. That's what I was trying to tell you last night before you told me you didn't want to watch Elf *with me."*

On-screen, John McClane is avoiding questions about his estranged marriage. But in an instant, the extraneous sound disappears.

All my attention, all of my senses, every single nerve focuses in on her and her exclusively. There is no movie. There is no TV.

I watch nothing but her.

"So to clarify, that means we can have sex now," she says, mistaking my silence for confusion. "You know, cross me off your bucket list. Then I can get out of your hair. Merry Christmas?"

I think she meant to say those last two words with sassy bravado, but it comes out as a question. Like she's unsure of herself. Unsure of me.

It's time to set a few things straight.

"Come here. Now," I tell her.

She regards me with wide eyes. I think I might be scaring her. But I can't bring myself to care. I think of how weak I felt last night... how many times I had to fuck my own hand just to calm down. The half a bottle of bourbon I downed just to get the job done and knock myself out.

I could have had her. She sat down across from me at that table and fed me chicken, when the only thing I wanted—the only thing I'd truly hungered for all week was her.

All that anger seeps into my voice as I repeat, "Come here."

She just stands there, glancing from side to side.

This girl is turning out to be someone who has to be told more than once. I need to show her why that isn't a good idea when it comes to me.

"Come here." My voice is a warning made of steel. "You're not going to like what happens if I have to tell you again."

She takes a tentative step toward me.

But then she glances to the side again. And this time, instead of looking back at me, she takes off running toward the hallway.

"If you want me, you're going to have to find me!" she calls over her shoulder before disappearing around the hallway corner.

I'm so shocked by her sudden flight, it takes me a few moments to put together what just happened. To connect it to what we talked about last night.

She didn't run away because she's scared, I realize. She ran away because she wants me to chase and catch her.

She wants to be hunted and claimed.

Challenge accepted.

Maybe she was right about there being different ways to enjoy hunting.

I flare my nostrils like the animal she's turned me into and go stalking after her. I'm tracking down my prey.

The entire hallway is dark, and every door except for the one leading into my dad's office stands open.

"Smart move, Red," I call out to her, a lion congratulating a mouse. "I can only imagine how good you were at hide-and-seek when you were a kid."

I walk down the hallway, peeking into each room. She also turned all the lights off. Another smart move.

But I let her know, "Neither of us are kids anymore, though. You're playing games for fun. I'm playing to win...to conquer...to overpower you in every way. When I catch you—which I will— you're going to find that out the hard way."

I wait to see if that baits her enough to make a sound that will give me some idea of which room she's hiding in, but nothing.

The hallway remains silent, save for the sound of my bare feet padding down the hall. If I wasn't half out of my mind with lust, I'd be proud of her.

I go to my bedroom first and flip the light on. "Red, you in here?"

No answer.

"I came in here first for two reasons," I tell the silent room. "Want to know why?"

Still no reply, but I tell her anyway. "One: this is where I stashed all my condoms."

I make my way over to the nightstand and pull out a gold square from the drawer as I explain to her. "I need to make sure I'm ready because when I catch you, Red, I'm going to fuck you. Doesn't matter where you are—that's where I'm going to take you. Unless you show yourself right now and get on top of this bed."

I wait, both hoping and not hoping that she takes the bait.

She doesn't. But I notice the bed's high enough to hide somebody underneath it. I drop down to my knees, but no Red.

"Guess that brings us to reason number two," I say, standing back up. "This is the last place any sane person would hide. But I'm beginning to suspect you're not sane, Red. Same as me."

I pause and listen. But the room remains still. And when I check the en suite bathroom, she's not in there either.

My blood boils with hunting lust. "I would have been nice if you told me last night. I would have been sweet as that apple crisp you served me, even though you knew your pussy was ready to go. I would have held back. Made myself take this slow. But now you're going to get it, Red. Do you know? Do you have any idea how hard I'm going to fuck you?"

I rip open the closet door. It's a walk-in, even though my dad was two times divorced when he had his old cabin razed and replaced with this. There's nothing except for an emergency suit and some hunting clothes hanging in here, along with the gun safe, sitting toward the back. And again, no Red.

I frown. Maybe I was wrong about how crazy she is. Maybe she's not in here after all—

Something rustles behind me.

I whip around. Nothing. But then I notice the floor-length blackout curtains swaying a little. Could she be hiding behind them?

I yank each side of them back. Nothing there either. And there's nowhere left for her to hide.

I'm just about to leave, but for some reason, I can't let my original notion go. I was so sure I was right when I came in here.

Instead of moving on to another room, something makes me flip off the light, walk all the way out—then tiptoe back in and close the door behind me.

At first, nothing happens. But then I hear that rustling sound again, and a shadow crawls out from underneath the bed and rises.

So that was the sound I heard. Her moving from one hiding space I hadn't checked yet to one I already had.

Clever girl. But the game is lost for her now.

My hunt is over.

She's framed by the moonlight, so I see her, but she doesn't see me. Not until I lunge at her and tackle her to the bed.

"Heya, Red," I say, grinning down at her. "Looks like you're going to get fucked in a bed after all."

CHAPTER 15
RED

DID I GO TOO FAR?

Whatever is going on with me, whatever kind of mental breakdown I'm experiencing, it's reached its peak.

This is all Red's fault.

She thought it would be fun to do it this way. She was the one who ran and threw out words of challenge over her shoulder. Red —not me—invited a criminal biker to hunt her like big game. She's a very, very bad girl.

But now Griff has *me* flat on my back with my arms pinned above my head. He's a shadow animal crouched on top of me—a feral smile glittering in the moonlight.

"I want to be on top," I tell him breathlessly, grasping at my last chance to take control of this situation. "Let me drive again."

"No," he answers with a short laugh. Like I must be making a joke.

His answer enflames me. I struggle underneath him and tug at my arms, trying to get them free. "Then let me go!"

"Sure, I'll let you up," he answers. His voice is a wolf in the dark. "Just say the safeword."

I stare up at the animal bathed in moonlight.

And he stares down at me.

Do you know how hard I'm going to fuck you?

His words from before echo in my brain.

But I say nothing.

And that feral smile flashes again.

"What did you think you were doing, huh? Running from me?" he asks. "Were you trying to make it harder on yourself?"

There is a smart and safe answer. A soft joke that will cut into the intensity of this moment and defuse the bomb I can hear ticking in our background.

And then there's the answer Red comes up with.

Don't... Bernice starts to warn.

But I'm already saying it. Out loud. "Sure, I'm all up for making it harder on myself," I answer, meeting his eyes in the moonlight. "I mean, as long as you don't come too fast again."

A short, deadly beat of silence.

Then a cold chuff, followed by, "You crazy bitch."

He lifts up. Not to release me, though.

He flips me over onto my stomach and yanks down the comfy Christmas pajamas I've come to like so much, along with my underwear. The next thing I feel is the hot brand of his hand across my ass.

"Ow!"

"You think, after making me wait this long, I'm going to put up with you trying to pull brat shit?"

He smacks my butt again before I can answer that question. The pain sears and makes me crawl to get away.

But he grabs me by the hips and drags me back to him. "I was only going to give you three swats: one for making me wait, one for not telling me as soon as you were done bleeding, and one for hiding. But now I'm giving you five because you didn't take your punishment like a good girl."

"That's not fair," I whine. "That's only four reasons. It should be four swats, not five."

"I add on the fifth one because I knew you'd tried to whine about it," he says with a devious laugh.

If he was a cartoon villain, he'd probably be rubbing his hands together right about now. But no...he uses that cruel palm to deliver another spank. This one is so hard. It collapses my knees, and I writhe on the bed, the friction of the soft covers below and the red-hot pain above scrambling my brain.

At least, I think that's why I'm writhing. He massages my butt cheeks, and I moan brokenly when an unexpected bolt of pleasure rocks through me at his touch on my tender skin.

"You're getting there, bad girl." His voice is a mechanic in the dark, figuring out exactly how to fix me.

Then he smacks my butt again.

You'd think he'd go lighter, given that he's already rendered me prone. But this fire palm is the worst of all. He claps it down so hard my hips jerk in the bed. And when they come down again, he shoves two rough fingers into me.

I gasp at the sudden invasion, but it doesn't hurt.

He tells me why without me having to ask. "You liked that spanking. I thought I'd have to get you ready, but this cunt is soaking wet. Feel the way you're clenching around my hand, bad girl? Is your pussy going to hug my dick like that when I'm fucking you for real?"

His crude words make my mind reel. I don't answer. I can't answer. A fever washes over me, and my body pushes back onto his fingers with a mind of its own.

"Yeah, just like that, bad girl," Griff says approvingly as his fingers meet my helpless thrusts. "I'm so fucking excited to take you. I almost wish I didn't have to finish this spanking."

That's the only warning I get before he pulls his hand out of my sex and smacks me a final time, his fingers now wet with my own juices.

The pain...it shrinks me down to one single question: *What is wrong with me?* Right before I implode with an orgasm I didn't see coming.

I claw at the covers and try to flail my legs. But they're still caught in the pajama bottoms he pulled down to mid-thigh earlier. I gasp for air, trying to keep my head above the surface of sanity. I'm lost...lost at sea.

When his heavy weight drops down on top of me, it feels like he's both subduing and securing me at the same time. But really, it's another invasion.

"I told you how this would end," he says, right before shoving his thick erection into my tight space, making it burn. Making it hurt.

Then he begins moving on top of me. Slow, thick strokes that rock my body and keep me pinned at the same time. They also make the hurt better. I keen, welcoming the invasion like a land without water suddenly drenched in rain.

"Why is your cunt so tight?" His voice is coarse sandpaper, scraping my ear. "Even better than I imagined last night when I was beating myself off because I was sick with wanting you."

The thought of him doing that sends a frenzy of wild emotions through me. I arch my pinned back as much as I can to take him even deeper. Something's coming for me. Something big. I'm no longer Bernice. I'm no longer Red. I'm just a woman on the verge of falling apart.

"Look at you....You trying to come again, Red?" he asks with a dark chuckle as his hips slap hard into mine.

Yes, yes, I am. It doesn't matter that I just came a few moments ago. I'm ticking again. Set to detonate.

He presses his mouth to my ear. "You fought me so hard at the roadhouse, but this is where you wanted to be all along, wasn't it, bad girl? Getting fucked. Getting conquered. By me."

With those vicious words, he wraps a hand around my throat and squeezes.

The shudder that goes through me...it's an electromagnetic pulse wave before tick...tick...BOOM.

I scream for mercy, even though I know no pain. It's 100-proof pleasure ripping me apart.

I'm dying. I'm dying as the second orgasm consumes me. And I don't know that I'll survive this blast.

Yes, I'm a bad girl. A very bad girl. And Griff didn't have to worry about getting me a present. This is exactly what I didn't know I wanted. Exactly what I needed.

Merry Christmas to me.

CHAPTER 16

GRIFF

My bad girl comes so hard. And that makes me explode too.

I release so violently it feels like maybe my spine is breaking as I shoot into the condom. But I don't care. I just keep fucking her. I meant what I said. She kept me waiting too long.

Once I start erupting, I can't stop. Not until every ounce of cum is drained from my cock. Not until I'm so deflated I can't pump into her anymore. Even then, only the prospect of me messing up the condom work and creating an oops baby makes me stop.

But I don't want to.

I make myself pull out of her and stumble out of bed. If I'm being honest, I'm not sure if I'm rushing toward the bathroom to clean up and take care of the condom—or just plain ol' running away to keep myself from falling on top of her again.

Gotta admit, no girl has ever rocked my world like that before. Still, I go through my usual ritual of cleaning up the condom. Not just disposing of it, but washing it all the way out so no wastebasket-used-condom-sperm donation business can pop off.

This is the part where the pleasure of fucking new pussy begins to fade. And I wait for the soaring warmth in my chest to be replaced by that dead inside feeling. It never takes more than a minute or two.

But then a minute passes and then another one. And it never comes. What the...?

I stare at myself in the bathroom mirror and jolt at what I see. This morning when I looked in this same piece of glass, all I saw was hangover Griff, messed-up hair, bloodshot eyes, and some deepening forehead lines I was probably going to have to talk to my derm about one of these days.

But now, I barely recognize the guy in the reflection. He's smiling goofily at me in the mirror. Like he's...like he's...

It takes me a few tries before I land on the word. *Happy.* I look happy. Well, how about that...?

Merry Christmas to me indeed, with a yippee ki-yay on top.

Which is why my heart stops when I come back to the bedroom to find her slinking toward the door.

"Where the hell do you think you're going?" I hook an arm around her waist and pull her back into my chest.

Goddamn, she smells good. Like a whole bunch of carbs topped with apple crisp. As spent as I am, my dick kicks to life as soon as it makes contact with her round, soft ass.

"I need to clean up too and sleep for about a thousand years. You wore me out," she answers with a laugh.

"Damn right, I did," I answer. "Can't say I didn't warn you."

She laughs again, that low, wicked sound I still haven't tired of for some reason. "No, I can't say that. But I figured I should stay in the room you gave me. That way, I won't wake you up later on when I leave."

My blood goes from low simmer to ice in an instant. "You were going to leave without telling me?"

She stiffens in my arms. "It wasn't meant to be an insult. I just figured you'd want me gone, now that you've finally got what you brought me here for."

The truth is, I thought that too. It should've been enough. But it's not. I still want her. I still want to fuck her.

And I can't say if I'm pissed because she's planning to leave or because I already know I won't be letting her. Not today. Maybe not even tomorrow morning.

It feels like I'm jumping off a cliff when I say, "Red?"

"Yes?" she asks, her voice careful, like she suspects she might be dealing with some kind of psycho.

Maybe she is. Maybe she is.

But I say it anyway. "Stay with me. One more week. Stay with me until New Year's Eve."

CHAPTER 17
GRIFF

I WAKE UP THE FOLLOWING DAY TO A STRANGE SENSATION. There's a weight pressing against my back all the way down to my ass, heavy and warm, and something's binding me to it.

Two arms...I pop open my eyes. Two arms have me trapped. And that's when I realize I'm being spooned. Red, the roadhouse bartender I invited to stay with me, has turned me into the little spoon inside her cuddle. *The fuck?*

Listen. I rarely do overnights. I don't do cuddles. And I sure as hell don't let girls little-spoon me. But here I am with Red's arms wrapped around my chest. She's even got her legs pressed into the bottom of my thighs—like a goddamn nesting block.

"What the hell?" I ask out loud.

Her breath whispers across my neck, and she presses her tits into my back as she says, "Oh, hey, you're awake." A little laugh escapes her, like she's been waiting a while for me to show signs of life.

And yes, I'm awake now. In more ways than one.

We ended up sleeping most of Christmas Day away—no keto-friendly dinner for us. But I woke her up two times to take her again. After all of last night's activities, I wouldn't have thought it possible to spring a hard-on this fast.

Red must sense the new arrival somehow. She drops her hand down to my sudden erection and says, "Ooh, you're really awake!"

"What are you doing?" I ask, a warning note creeping into my voice.

"Exploooring," she answers, stretching the word out as she works my cock with long, languid strokes. "Can I be on top this time?"

"Hell no," I immediately answer.

"Oh, come on, it's only fair," she says. "You got to dominate me all Christmas. Let me be the one on top today. We could call it my agreeing to stay until New Year's Eve bonus."

She pauses dramatically. Then adds, "Unless you're too chicken."

"I'm not chicken. I just don't let girls—"

She cuts me off with a "Bawk-bawk-bawk!" right before she makes a surprise move and twists on top of me.

She uses the element of surprise and, like, all of her body weight to knock me on my back. Then this girl has the audacity to try to pin *my* wrists above *my* head.

"What the hell are you doing, Red?"

"What can I say? You make me want to do bad girl things," she answers, flashing me that wicked smile of hers. "And just remember, you can always say the safeword if you're not comfortable with any of this."

She actually says that shit to me. Then she says, "Now, just hold still like a good boy, and let me do this"—right before she drops her mouth down on mine.

She kisses me while rubbing herself back and forth on my erection. Her pussy is already slick with desire. It feels so damn good to have her writhing on top of me. I forget for a few moments that she's assumed the dominant position.

She's so wet, and I'm so hard, I could slip it in right now, even from underneath. What would it feel like to take her raw, no condom? Wait, what am I saying?

Alarm bells sound in my head. All the alarm bells. It's bad enough I asked this girl to stay with me until New Year's Eve. I'm not going to let her dominate me—then spend the next eighteen years collecting child support because I couldn't figure out how to take my power back and put on a damn condom.

We end up wrestling for dominance. Really, I pin her with my superior weight and strength. Then I let her go. Then, when she tries to climb back on top, I pin her back underneath me. We do this over and over again until we're both so turned on I pull out a condom. Wrestling, Playing with Your Food—call our game whatever you want. It ends with me pinning her down one final time, with my cock pumping into her sopping-wet cunt and my hand around her neck.

"Wow, you make it real easy to lose," she says with a husky laugh when we collapse back onto the bed.

We lie there for a moment. Her smiling up at the ceiling. Me waiting for that dead feeling to finally hit me.

But it never does.

Not when I take her in the shower a couple of hours later.

And not after I ruin the pancakes she tries to make me for afternoon breakfast.

Watching this woman cook for me makes me ravenous for something else. I set her on top of the kitchen counter, spread her legs, and feast on her instead of carbs. I don't care about the lost pancakes. Let them burn.

And the feeling still never comes. If anything, it's just the opposite. I'm no longer numb inside. I become a monster who lives and breathes fucking Red.

After Christmas, food becomes something I let her make and eat quickly for the sole purpose of keeping us alive. Weed gets smoked, and bourbon gets drunk when she's too tired to go on late at night—we're still on different sleep schedules somehow. So, I only blaze up and visit the Glendaver bottle to distract myself. To let her rest. Also, to give my hands something to do other than her during our now only once-a-day daily movie.

Sometimes we talk too. At one point, I finally run out of weed. So instead of smoking after dinner, we lie on the ground in my dad's office and listen to Death Buddha CDs. Just listen and talk. She tells me about being raised by her grandma and having never left the state of Tennessee, much less gotten on a plane. She has a secret dream to become an event planner, and she even has a paid internship lined up in New York.

I tell her that I'm scheduled to go to Europe with the country star. Then...

"Actually, I don't know what I'm going to do after that. Being on the road all the time is getting kind of old. I've been thinking maybe I could use a challenge," I admit. Only to her.

"The Reapers don't give you work between security gigs?" she asks.

I shift uncomfortably. The lies are starting to fester inside of me, metastasizing and pushing up against the edges of this fantasy world we've made inside my dad's cabin. But I like this. I like hanging out with someone who wants to fuck me—not the country star they saw in a music video on YouTube. And I'm really liking not walking around with a big-old case of dead inside. I don't want anything to disrupt that. But I know in my gut everything will change the instant I tell her who I am. She will start acting differently. And I like exactly where we are.

"I'm more a Reaper in name only these days," I answer carefully. "They don't give me assignments."

She must not know how motorcycle clubs work because instead of throwing me one of those adorable suspicious squints, she just says, "Oh," like that makes complete sense.

Then she asks, "How about your father? You mentioned something about a business he wanted to go into with you and your brother."

"He actually started it already," I answer. "My older brother's moved out to Vegas, and he's almost switched over to running its day-to-day operations full-time. But the position my dad offered me is still open. And it's not half bad. I guess you could say it's kind of in my wheelhouse, and I think it could be...maybe not boring."

"Not boring sounds good," she says, flipping onto her side to look at me. "What's holding you back?"

I shrug. "I guess because I know, in the back of my head, this is Dad's way of controlling me. He wants me to settle down. Get married and start a family—just like my brother, who can do no wrong. But that's not me. I don't want kids. I don't want paperwork. I mean, my parents had that, and look how that turned out."

She makes a considering chuff. "I never thought of it that way. I guess because my parents were in love and dedicated to each other before they died. I've always wanted what they had. Marriage and kids—at least three. I hated growing up an only child."

I think about how lonely I was without Geoff all those years I lived in L.A. and admit, "I hated not having siblings too—that's a big part of why I joined the Reapers. I guess you could say Waylon and Hades are kind of like big brothers to me. But three kids...that's a lot."

She laughs and covers her face. "I know...and it's boring. But I want what I want. First, I need to get all this rebellion out of my system, maybe use this passport I just got, then I'll settle down and have some babies."

Yeah, that's all I am to her...a rebellion. It shouldn't mess with my head. Still, the thought of her finishing up with me and moving on to some guy on the East Coast who wants to do the whole minivan and kids thing. That future isn't what I want—like, at all. But my chest tightens with a weird, jealous ache.

"Hey," she says, cupping my cheek. "We don't have to talk about boring stuff. How about we do it right here on the floor, and you let me be on top?"

The ache gives way to a laugh. And I flip over on top of her to pin her down before she can attack me like she always does when she starts talking about taking the lead.

"You're just going to keep on trying to make that happen, aren't you? Let me explain this to you in Tennessee—ain't never gonna happen."

"That's not Tennessee. That's just any old Southern accent—" she starts to protest before I cut her off with another kiss.

We go on like this, and I get used to whiling away the days with her. Of waking up wrapped in her arms. She insists on calling this position "little spooning" me, no matter how much I punish her. But I prefer to think of it as a preamble for our morning wrestling session.

However, one day I wake up in bed alone. She's not in the bathroom, and I don't smell anything cooking when I come out to the hallway to investigate.

But the door to her bedroom, which has remained pretty much closed since she all but moved in with me, is standing open. I pad down the hallway—then scrunch my forehead when I find her in the guest room. That oversized tote she carries as a purse is sitting in the middle of the bed, and she's throwing things into its big mouth.

"What are you doing?" I ask, stretching out in the doorway.

She looks up and squints. "Is there a reason you always have to look so delicious and naked first thing in the morning?"

"Is there a reason you're not naked this morning?" I ask back, dead serious. "And/or cooking me breakfast?"

"Okay, calm down," she answers, laughing. "I'm going to make us something to eat. But I figured I should get everything ready to go first so I can leave bright and early tomorrow morning."

My heart stops thumping in my chest. "What do you mean?"

She gives me a quizzical look. "Well, I'm not sure when you have to get back to Nashville, but I promised my cousin I'd definitely be there for her New Year's Eve party after skipping out on Christmas. So, I need to head home first thing in the morning to get some real clothes that aren't Christmas pajamas, and you know, check on everything there."

"I mean, what do you mean you need to leave first thing tomorrow," I clarify. "Tomorrow isn't New Year's Eve."

She looks at me like I'm crazy. "How much weed did you smoke before you ran out? It totally is."

"Weed doesn't work that way. It doesn't make you lose time," I bite out.

But I'm not grumpy because of the accusation. I'm grumpy because that's exactly what happened. I lost time. I lost time even though there aren't any drugs in my system. No drugs, except for her. She's the drug. She's the addiction that made me lose track of time.

And now she's preparing to leave.

"Here's your jacket, by the way," she says, holding it up. "And there was something in the pocket. I wasn't sure if you needed it. It looks like some kind of pills or maybe candy."

She holds up a little plastic bag filled with four purple pills with skulls stamped on the front.

I roll my eyes. "My friend Rowdy must have slipped that into my pocket without telling me. It's just Molly."

Her eyes widen. "You mean Molly? Like ecstasy? The party drug? For real?"

"Yeah," I answer. But the way she asked me those questions makes me cock my head. "Have you never done MDMA before?"

She winces. "I've always been kind of curious about party drugs, I guess. I don't know much about Molly, if I'm being honest. But I've heard it makes sex, erm...kind of cool, maybe."

She peeps up at me in that weirdly innocent way of hers. "Is that true?"

I shift from foot to foot. And that strange guilt I've been experiencing every time I think about all the other women I've slept with comes back over me again.

But I answer her truthfully. "I wouldn't know. I do Molly. And I do sex. But I don't do them together."

"Oh." She considers my words like she's adding up a math problem. Then she guesses, "For the same reason you don't let women drink too much around you. I get it."

She turns back to packing. "Well, have fun with that Molly, whenever you decide to take it. All alone. And you know what, I'll make us something to eat first. Then I'll finish packing after lunch. We should probably take it a lot easier today anyway."

She gets it. Good...I think.

But instead of wrestling with her that morning, I wrestle with my inner turmoil.

The dead feeling never came. And there's still a lot of stuff I didn't get to do to her. Handcuffs and rope. Blindfolds and edging.

But I grit my teeth and tamp down the urge to tell her that.

She's right. This has gone on too long. We both need to get back to the real world.

Especially me.

There are probably a million messages from my team waiting on the phone I haven't checked in days, wondering where the hell I've been.

I start to leave, but then she says, "Griff?"

And I immediately turn back around to answer her instead of finding my phone. "Yeah?"

"Okay, I know this is going to sound crazy," she says with a cute little wince. "But since we've been breaking all your other rules this holiday season, do you mind breaking one more? For me?"

I WAKE UP WITH A START. THERE'S A FURNACE AT MY front and cold at my back. What the hell?

I open my eyes to the sight of a bunch of red hair. Cherry-red hair. And beyond that...the lake.

I'm lying underneath a couple of blankets on the cabin's dock with my arms wrapped around Red.

Again. What. The. Hell?

Why would I sleep outside in the dead of winter? How did we even get out here—

Memories of the night before cut off that question.

Taking the Molly after lunch...downing it with a bottle of champagne. Then came all the great ideas we had after that.

We decided we should make our own New Year's Eve party. Who cared if it was December 30th?

There was dancing...lots and lots of dancing. First inside, with The Darkness playing at full blast...then outside wrapped in blankets, both of us singing along with Justin Hawkins under the full moon.

"You sound so good! *Amazing*! What the heck? Why didn't you tell me you could sing so well?"

She made me worry that I'd been found out. Then she made me laugh when she added, "You know, if we were werewolves, we wouldn't be able to sing like this tonight!"

I remember laughing...then telling her the truth.... "You're even more beautiful under the moonlight. You know that?"

I remember kissing her and admitting, "You scare the hell out of me."

Then I drank some more. Straight from the head of the bottles of champagne we brought outside. One for each of us. Then...

Nothing.

I don't remember anything after that. Just waking up here. Naked and partially cold.

I sit up so abruptly she stirs awake beside me.

At first, she just flutters her eyes open. Then she sits up too with an almost comical jerk.

"What the hell?" she gasps out, just like me. For once, she doesn't go with the clean version of a cuss. Her hair is a tangled mess around her shoulders, and she blinks at me, confused in the sunlight. "We fell asleep out here?"

"Yeah, looks like it," I answer. There's a lead balloon in my stomach. "And I'm wondering what else we did."

"What do you mean?" she asks, pushing her snarled locks out of her face.

I spell it out for her. "Did we have sex? Did we use a condom?"

"I don't know..." she whispers.

We both take a moment to look around and peep at the same thing: two empty champagne bottles and two blankets. That's it.

There's no gold foil or any other sign of a rubber around us. And we both know I would've had to have gone back in the house to get one. Something I don't think I would've done hopped up on Molly and champagne.

She gives me a pained but reassuring smile. "You know, I'm so hungover, and I bet you are too. It's possible we just passed out without doing anything else."

I glance at the two empty champagne bottles again—750 ml each, with Molly on top.

It's possible, but...

"Open your legs," I order.

She visibly stiffens. "Why?"

"Open your legs," I command again, my heart pounding. "Remove the blanket and open your legs. Let me see your pussy."

She looks to both sides. "Okay, I know you have, like, an insane sex drive. But I am hungover as all get out. There is no way we're going to have more sex outside—"

She cuts off with a yelp when I rip away the blanket.

"What are you doing?" she yells. "It's too cold to be playing games out here. Give me back the blanket."

I don't answer. Just glare at what I find on her thighs. Her dark skin is stained with my dry semen.

We did have sex. Unprotected sex. While I was wasted.

A new and ugly possibility occurs to me.

"What is wrong with you?" she demands. She snatches the blanket back and wraps it around herself. "It is cold out here, and I am stark naked. Plus, there are houses all around the lake. Anybody could look out the window and see me."

She's speaking. Words are coming out of her mouth. But I'm not listening.

All my fears, all my usual suspicions when it comes to girls, rise like shadows in my side vision.

"Did you do this on purpose?" I ask her.

"No," she answers, her voice irritable. "I did not flash your neighbors on purpose. You're the one who took my blanket."

She's trying to change the subject. Distract me from my real question. That was one of my mom's favorite tricks when my dad asked her about the shady shit she got up to before their divorce.

But I'm not letting Red get away with it.

"Did you do this on purpose?" I ask again. "Did you get me wasted and then have unprotected sex with me?"

She squints, and this time it is not adorable. "What are you talking about? Usually, when conversations like this go down, it's the other way around. I'm the woman here. I should be asking you about this unprotected sex."

Yeah, that's what the media says. But in real life, in *my* real life, girls are always the ones trying to take advantage of men.

"So, was that what your plan was all along?" I demand. "Is that why you stuck around? You figured you'd fuck me then hook me on the line for eighteen years of child support?"

She stares at me. And hurt—real hurt flashes across her eyes.

Then, she cracks her hand across my face. She slaps me once. Twice. Before saying, "Get over yourself."

Then she storms back into the house without another word.

The old, suspicious rage fades as I watch her go. And that's when I know...

I've truly fucked up.

CHAPTER 18
RED

I FIND MY PHONE ON THE PATH LEADING TO THE LAKE right before reaching the cabin's back door. It's lying face down. I pick it up, hoping for the best, but...nope. The face is shattered, and the black screen lets me know it's completely dead.

Of course it is. I'm not a songwriter like Kiki, but this has got to be some kind of metaphor for the disaster I woke up to this morning. My head swims with pain and fatigue as I make my way into the house.

No stopping at Griff's room. That dream's all the way popped. In the cold reality of morning, I make a straight beeline back to the guest room and the tote I should have finished packing yesterday instead of making lunch for that jerkhole—and oh my gosh, *deciding to do Molly* just because I didn't want the good time I thought I was having with him to end.

Well, it's ended now, all right. I pull on my roadhouse shorts and tee since I have no idea where either pair of my Christmas pajamas got off to. And more castigations pile up in my head when

I throw my broken phone into the tote. Even if I manage to get the phone's screen fixed, there's no telling if I'll ever be able to get it to work again considering I left it outside overnight in the cold.

Meanwhile, how am I supposed to find a cracked screen store—or even get home without GPS? Or let Kiki know I'm probably going to be a little late to her party tonight.

"Where are you going?" a voice asks, interrupting my panicked thoughts.

I look up to find Griff doing his naked-standing-in-the-doorway thing again. Just like yesterday. But unlike yesterday, I'm no longer so hopped up on sex endorphins I can't see right through him.

"Home," I answer, keeping my voice hard and clipped.

"Didn't give you permission to leave yet, Red." He holds up one hand, revealing a condom I didn't see before clasped between his index and middle finger.

My chest fills with rage. Is he kidding? He's got to be kidding.

Yesterday, his blend of sexy menace and laid-back humor would have sent a secret thrill through me. Yesterday, Boring Bernice would have handed the keys to our car right back over to my inner bad girl, Red.

But today, I feel nothing but stupid. So, so stupid. Seriously, what was I thinking, spending two whole weeks with a paranoid criminal biker?

"No. I'm not playing any more games with you." I turn away and start throwing the rest of my things into the bag—all the stuff I put on the bed to pack yesterday before he interrupted me. "You accused me of doing something I would never do. Ever. That means the game is over."

Silence. But I don't hear him turn away to leave like he should as I pack up the rest of my things.

And when I haul my bag onto my shoulder and turn toward the door, he's still standing there, naked, save for all those tattoos.

But the sexy menace has disappeared from his expression, replaced by something much graver.

"I'm sorry," he says quietly. "I shouldn't have said that to you outside."

"I would *never* do that," I immediately shoot back. My chest crackles with outrage and hurt. "How could you accuse me of that?"

"I shouldn't have said those things to you. Shouldn't have accused you." He raises both hands in the air with a pleading look. "That's why I'm here apologizing. I fucked up, and I'm sorry. You need to believe that."

His apology tugs at my heart. But...

"No. No," I tell him, shaking my head. "Sorry is not enough. I don't know why you're like this with women. But you don't get to treat me like crap and then have sex with me. At least not without my consent. And you don't have my consent. Not anymore. Now please step aside."

He doesn't step aside. If anything, he becomes even bigger in the doorway.

"So that's it?" he asks. "You're just going to leave?"

"Why do you sound so surprised?" I shoot back. "I was supposed to leave five days ago. Apparently, you were too wasted this whole time to let me. Or maybe that was my plan all along—since it's all *my* fault we had sex without a condom—which could really mess up my plans for the next eighteen years as well, you know. It's not just you regretting last night."

He flinches, as if I slapped him again—like I hurt him. But it's me who feels all cut up.

"Move! Please, you've got to let me pass. All I want to do is leave and pretend like none of this ever happened."

He stares down at me, his entire expression filled with apology and regret. But he doesn't move.

Not even when I drop the bag and shove at him as hard as I can. "Move!"

"Red..." he says, his voice cracked and desperate.

"Please, move!" I beg. "If you don't move, I'm going to cry, even though it was only two weeks. Two weeks I shouldn't have given you. I shouldn't have trusted you. I most definitely shouldn't have trusted myself when it comes to you. And now I can't stop talking. Please, let me by. Just please let me by."

I'm falling apart. I'm falling apart right in front of him, but all he says is, "Red..."

"Just let me by!" I scream.

"No!" he bellows back. Then he grabs me and pulls me into his arms.

"Let me talk," he says into my weave. His voice walks a thin line between plea and command. "You have to let me explain. You're wondering why I treated you like crap. Why I accused you of shady shit. It's because that's who I needed you to be. I needed you to be some trick with a long game. I wanted you to be manipulating me all along because then I could explain it."

"Explain what?" I ask, pushing against his chest.

He eases up his hold, but only so he can look me in the eye when he answers. "Why I feel this way about you!"

I stop fighting. I'm so confused. "What?"

He shakes his head. "You said it yourself. We've only known each other for two weeks. So, if you weren't manipulating me all along, why do I feel like this for you? Why can't I stop with you? Why can't I let you go even though you're begging me to? If you were playing me like I thought, maybe these feelings wouldn't be real. Maybe I wouldn't have to be scared as hell of you...."

Griff shakes his head mournfully. "You're not mindfucking me. I can see that now. But you're trying to leave, and I don't know what to do with all this shit in my chest."

He finally releases me. But only to cup my face.

"Am I insane?" he asks, his voice a hoarse plea. "Tell me I'm stupid, and this is crazy. Hit me. Punch me in the gut. Say the safeword. Do whatever you have to do to get away from me. Just make me stop, Red. Make me stop."

Make him stop? How? All my defenses come crumbling down, and I'm left shaken and confused. Because as angry as I was at him...

"I understand," I whisper, reaching up to clasp his wrists. "I understand exactly how you feel. I don't know why a guy like you is happening to me, of all people. Why I couldn't leave....Why I still don't want to leave. But I understand. I understand exactly how you feel."

Griff's entire face lights up at my words.

"You understand?" he says in the same tone of voice people use on TV to confirm good news. Like hearing they won the lotto.

"I understand," I repeat, feeling like a winner myself.

We stare at each other with tender awe. Then suddenly we're kissing.

I guess the condom was a good idea after all. No more games. No more rules. Griff strips me out of the shorts he wasn't allowed to go beneath when we first met at the roadhouse. Then he hitches me up, and my back hits the wall as he wraps my legs around his waist.

The condom does get put on this time, but other than that, we're primal. He reclaims me with a hard upward shove, and his thick steel fills me up so precisely...as if he were made for me.

"Like you were made for me," he says, echoing my thoughts. He bites at my lip, hard enough to draw pain...smear blood over our kissing and licking mouths...as he ruts me into the wall.

In this position, he reaches a place he hasn't before. He hits it over and over again, and soon I begin to tremble and shake. This is going to be bad. I can already sense it. If the other orgasms made me explode. This one is going to obliterate me. And I don't want to get destroyed alone.

"Griff...Griff..." I moan, holding onto him for dear life. "Come with me, please."

I'm making no sense, but somehow, by some sweet miracle, he understands what I'm asking for.

His hips jackhammer faster, catching up to me until we're exactly where we need to be. He withdraws, and one final thrust blasts us into oblivion. Together.

"Griff…" I cry out, my voice a faraway star shattering in the sky.

"Red…" he rasps, his heavy body shuddering between my legs.

The pleasure is so intense it locks us together, and we scrabble at each other, holding on…trying never to come down.

But eventually, the last of the aftershocks fade, and reality begins to creep into our bubble of bliss.

"We can't stay here," I tell him. "I have to go, and you do too."

He presses his forehead into mine. "I know. I've got my performance, and you've got your cousin's party."

We grieve those truths as one, breathing parting kisses into each other's mouths.

But then he says, "Meet me…meet me later in Nashville. Spend New Year's Eve with me. And I promise you, we'll figure everything out."

CHAPTER 19
BERNICE

"MEET ME...MEET ME LATER IN NASHVILLE. SPEND NEW Year's Eve with me. And I promise you, we'll figure everything out."

Griffin and I are making love in a room bathed in white light. He's inside of me—deep, so deep.

"Meet me in Nashville," he tells me. "Meet me there, and I promise to love you forever."

He makes me that beautiful offer, and I let out a shuddering breath.

Then I ask him, "Boy, are you out of your mind?"

He blinks, and that smooth bad-boy arrogance gives way to confusion. "What?"

I sit up. "What part of 'I've got hopes and dreams' did you not understand when you made me that offer? I have an internship of a lifetime lined up in New York, and you are so obviously the kind of guy who could ruin a girl's entire life. You think I'm just going to let myself fall in love with you? To believe you're falling in love with me? No, I'm not that stupid. And you...you're a monster."

He stares at me for a confused moment. But then that bad-boy arrogance creeps back into his expression.

He pulls out a guitar out of nowhere and begins strumming "Boat on the Sea."

"You sure about that?" he replies. "You sure you're not that stupid?"

"Mommy?" a voice asks somewhere in the distance.

Icicles of foreboding form in my stomach. "Where did you get the guitar?" I ask him.

"Mommy?" the small voice asks again.

And Griffin abruptly stops strumming. "Who's that?" he demands.

"Why did you do this to me? Why did you lie about who you were and ask me to meet you that New Year's Eve?" I demand instead of answering his question. "Was it just for kicks and giggles?"

Griffin stares at me blankly. Then he opens his mouth wide to answer: *"Ladies and gentlemen, we're beginning our descent into Nashville. Please turn off all portable electronic devices and stow them until we have arrived at the gate. Please also make certain your seat back is straight up and your seat belt is fastened."*

I jerk awake to the sound of the descent announcement and O2 saying, "Mommy! Mommy! We're here!"

I pop my eyes open to see my three-year-old daughter staring out the window and pointing down at the city where we're about to land. I don't know how long I was asleep. But even though she hasn't gone anywhere, O2's somehow managed to lose the band that was supposed to secure the end of her bottom left ponytail braid. It's half-unraveled.

"What happened?" I demand, reaching over to re-braid her loose dusky-brown hair.

"Can I wear it down at Thanksgiving?" she asks.

"Sure, I'll do it in the car."

"Then don't do it now," she whines, batting my hands away.

I roll my eyes, but I let her have this one.

I've learned to pick my battles with my sweet but stubborn daughter over the years. Besides, my hands are still trembling a little from that dream.

I always have nightmares when I travel back to Tennessee. But they don't mean anything, I remind myself. It's a location thing. That's all.

"Mommy, what were you dreaming about?" O2 asks.

Probably to distract me from re-doing her hair, but the question feels prescient. Too prescient. And there's no way I can tell her the truth.

I can barely tell myself the truth. In my dreams, I always turn Griffin down when he asks me to go to Nashville, but I said yes that morning in real life. Even though he never promised to love me forever.

And I instantly came to regret it that night....

"Mommy?" O2 says again, and this time her voice sounds wobbly.

I look up to find her dark blue eyes full of fear and her little light-brown face drawn up in pain.

"My ears hurt," she tells me, her voice a little shaky.

"Oh sweetie, that's because of the air pressure change. You need to pop your ears. That happened to me when I moved from Tennessee to New York. It was my first time on a plane, and a nice flight attendant had to explain what was happening to me. Here, try yawning, really wide. Like this…"

I show her, yawning big with a huge stretch of my arms.

She tentatively mirrors me, then nods and yells way too loud, "It's working! It's working!"

Her whole face lights up, like I've introduced her to the wonders of sliced bread. And even though she looks exactly like her father when she smiles at me like that, a wave of love and gratitude washes away all the regrets I expressed in that dream.

No, my life isn't ruined.

Yes, I felt more than a little bit stupid when I looked up from the GPS instructions I'd printed out with the address for the Fairgood Residences building to see Griff. Not the country star he told me he worked for, but Griff himself—looking down at me from a billboard advertising Stone River's big New Year's Eve bash.

It had taken me several blinking seconds to realize what I was looking at—that Griff was also some guy named G-Latham who would be headlining that night's New Year's Eve bash along with a few other country music stars I didn't recognize.

If not for all the horns blaring behind me because I'd stopped dead in the road, I might still be sitting on Church Street with my mouth hanging open.

Instead of collecting the money from Griff—who was apparently really a "country trap" artist named G-Latham—I ended up selling my car to fund my New York dream. So no, that wasn't the most intelligent I've ever felt.

And believe me, I got to feeling even more stupid when I read the pregnancy test I bought on a whim when I couldn't recall the date of my last period. As it turns out, it wasn't because of the buzzy brain fog that came with moving to a huge, loud city and starting a breakneck year-long internship at an elite event planning company.

No, I couldn't remember because I was pregnant! Pregnant by that lying monster!

So, dream interrupted.

The glitzy event planning company suddenly decided that we weren't "a match" after I started visibly showing. And believe me, I felt mighty low pounding the pavement in search of a job that would keep me in New York while nearly eight months pregnant.

Thank goodness for Olivia Glendaver. The bourbon heiress gave me a full-time job at her Women with Disabilities clinic without hesitation. And sure, I was working the same boring job I'd had in Nashville, with a front office one on top. There wasn't enough room in the clinic's budget for a nurse and a receptionist, so I had to do both.

But the job came with maternity leave, prorated access to the university hospital's daycare, and benefits that Olivia made sure kicked in before my baby came. I was so grateful, I named my newborn after my angel of a boss, which is why everyone, including me, calls my daughter O2.

So no, my life didn't turn out quite like I was expecting. But I would never call it ruined.

I do, however, scan the crowd anxiously as we make our way down to the baggage claim.

I know the odds of me running into G-Latham—who's rebranded himself as Griffin Latham these days—are slight. But being back in Nashville always makes me anxious.

"Are Aunt Kyra and Uncle Colin going to send a big black car, like last time?" O2 asks as I follow the signage to the rental car counters.

As anxious as I am, I can't help but laugh. Being only three, O2 can't remember some of the stuff that happened two weeks ago. But that black limo memory from last Thanksgiving stayed with her.

"I told them not to," I answer.

But Kiki, who insists everybody calls her by her given name, Kyra, these days, can have a mind of her own.

Just in case, I bring my phone out to tell her.

> *Hey best cuz! Just landed. Headed downstairs to pick up our RENTAL CAR.*

That warning given, I get in line to pick up the car. I don't drive in New York, so I like to practice whenever I visit Nashville—a city where everybody doesn't drive like they're on freaking cocaine. But it takes forever.

And by the time we climb into the small economy car, I have to let Kiki know:

I'm having major regrets about not letting you spoil us with another limo. But we've got the car, and we're on our way.

Kiki's text comes back almost immediately

KIKI: *Can't wait to see you. You will NEVER believe who RSVPed for the party...*

I laugh. And type, *"Who?"* even though I already know it will probably be some up-and-coming country singer I've never heard of. Now that artists like Kane Brown are sitting at the top of the pop charts, my songwriter cousin is forever trying to make country music that Black folks also like happen.

KIKI: *Colin's cousin, Waylon! And he's best friends with Griffin Latham, so he's coming too.*

My heart stops. Just plain old stops beating in my chest. And another message pops up.

KIKI: *Griffin Latham? You know, G-Latham. He was huge a few years ago. But he's kind of semi-retired now.*

Yes...yes, I know who G-Latham is. Now.

But I don't type Kiki that. I can't...I can't...I can't do anything but sit there and tremble.

"Mommy? Mommy?" O2 calls out to me from her car seat in the back. "Why are you just sitting there? Why aren't you driving?"

CHAPTER 20
GRIFFIN

"LOOK WHO FINALLY MADE IT TO ONE OF OUR PARTIES," Colin Fairgood tells his wife, Kyra, after he and Waylon walk me into their Thanksgiving get-together.

Kyra Fairgood wrote a couple of tracks on my last album. She's one of those bold, arty types who swaps out her hair color at least once a month. She also has a visible scar across her face that she does nothing to hide but never explains.

She's still hot, though. And right now, it's a triple smoke show because she's talking to that reality star babe Colin's brother, Woods, married, and the girl-next-door cutie Waylon's suddenly decided he wanted to go all-in for this year.

I brace myself for some more light ribbing from Kyra. She and Colin have been razzing me about missing their big New Year's Eve party for almost three years straight now. It was just one party, and I still ended up on Colin's imprint over at Big Hill like he wanted. But according to Kyra, me signing with Colin doesn't make up for them never getting to meet the mystery girl I was supposed to bring through as my plus-one.

"I'm going to stay forever curious about the woman who could get G-Latham to actually admit he was dating her."

Them and me both. If they were upset about not getting to meet Red, imagine how pissed I was when she never showed up at my place after promising to meet me there.

It's been years. Not months, but *years*. Yet my stomach still knots up when I remember how, instead of reporting for rehearsal at the soundstage Stone River had rented, I rehearsed my big confession speech in front of the mirror what had to be a thousand times before going down to the lobby to wait for her.

Only for her never to show up, like she promised.

But Kyra looks upset when we stop in front of her. And instead of teasing me, she holds up her phone and tells Colin, "Bernice can't make it now."

"Who's Bernice?" I ask, snagging a glass of champagne from a passing cater waiter. "She sounds boring."

"My cousin, who you know nothing about," Kyra answers.

I was just teasing, but she glares at me like I spit on one of those kids she and Colin keep popping out. "And now that you say that, I'm glad I don't have to introduce her to you."

"Is your cousin as cute as you?" I ask, grinning at her over my champagne glass.

"Nobody's as cute as Kyra," Colin answers.

He used to be cool. But ever since getting married, dude's become a permanent eye roll.

Also, don't think I didn't notice that he didn't answer my question...or say she was already taken like all the other beauties I'm spotting at their boring party.

"But seriously, man, is she hot like your wife?" I press. "Because if she is, I'd like to get that introduction—"

"So, have you two been dating long?" Kyra asks, abruptly turning to face Waylon and his woman.

I don't get any more information from Kyra about her possibly single cousin.

And I'm only at this party because Waylon claimed he needed psycho backup to watch his woman—who apparently may or may not be still trying to run away. He wasn't exactly clear.

But soon, I'm kicking myself for not getting more details.

He and that pretty nurse he pretty much kidnapped have been squeezed up tight like lovebirds all day. I'm the only single guy at this party. And all anybody wants to talk about at dinner is how they all met their spouses.

Fifteen minutes into Kyra's and Colin's meet-cute story, I'm regretting my decision to quit smoking so much weed. I'm also eyeing the kids' table. It looks like Mason Fairgood's adopted teenage son snuck in a Nintendo Switch. I wonder how much cash I'd need to palm him to give me a turn. I would happily drop three figs for some Zelda right now.

"So he tells me to meet him at this cabin in Latham County, of all places...."

Something Kyra's saying suddenly breaks into my thoughts about copping the Nintendo Switch.

"And mind you, this was back before they cleared out the white supremacist motorcycle gang," she adds, popping her eyes wide. "I was like, 'Oh my God. What am I getting myself into?' And I texted my best cousin, 'Listen, if I go missing, it was *Colin Fairgood.*'"

Everyone else falls out laughing. But I stare at her with my heart beating in my ears. "What did you just say?"

Kyra's laugh stutters a little. "No offense. This was before they renamed the place after your father. I hear it's perfectly safe to go there these days."

"No, not that. The other part, about your cousin. Why did you call her your 'best cousin'?"

Kyra looks to both sides. "Because she's one of my best friends," she answers carefully. "And also my cousin."

Suddenly, I'm back at that Latham County cabin I haven't visited in three years, lying on the floor with Red and listening to The Darkness believe in a thing called love.

"What's your cousin's name?"

"It's Bernice," she answers. "Remember, you said she sounded boring earlier?"

Okay. I doubted Red's real name was something as dull as Bernice. But the thing is, I never did find out her actual name. She'd disappeared by the time I went back to the roadhouse to look for her after getting over that ego kick.

And when I asked Nestor if he had any documentation on her, he just said in that heavy Greek accent of his, "This is not a job many girls want on their resume. I do not bother with paperwork, and Red was fine with getting paid in cash, so no checks. But ask my niece about her. She is the one who brought her in for the interview."

And that's how I ended up meeting the girl Hyena called Doc. She turned out to be a thin med student with a pair of A-cups. And she claimed to have no idea where Red had gone. Not that first time or any other time I'd asked after her while visiting the roadhouse.

But just because it was a boring name didn't mean we weren't talking about the same person. I mean, ask Dave Evans, Saul Hudson, and Shawn Carter why they prefer to be called the Edge, Slash, and Jay-Z.

And Kyra's name isn't Kiki, but that cabin story sounds too familiar to just be a coincidence. Plus, the way Kyra's squinting at me...it reminds me of the suspicious way Red used to regard me —like she could see straight through all of my bullshit.

"This Bernice...does she have cherry-red hair. Like, what do you call it? Red weave? All the way down her back?"

Nitra Mello, Wood's reality star girlfriend, snorts. "Are you talking about Kyra's cousin Bernice—the one who stays rocking that Brandy box braid bob like it's the nineties and we're still watching *Moesha* every Tuesday on UPN?"

"What?" I ask.

Nitra just busts into some song I've never heard of, but the other woman must have some idea what she's talking about because they join in.

"Hold on. Hold on!" I leap up from to table to yell over their singing. "Do you have a picture of this Bernice? I need to see what she looks like."

All the Fairgood wives cut off like I've peed in their Thanksgiving dinner, and an awkward silence descends.

Everybody's looking at me like I'm a psycho, including Waylon, who actually is an unrepentant psycho.

"Um...I don't know what's going on here, but my cousin is a hard-working single mom nurse who hates country music," Kyra says carefully. "I really don't think you know her. And I get that you're bored, but this line of questioning isn't cool."

Fuck, a single mother. So not my Red.

I feel like a fool.

Especially when Waylon pulls me aside after dinner to ask, "What the hell was that?"

I rub at my forehead. "Man, I don't know. I upended my whole life for her, and she just disappeared on me without ever telling me why. I guess I'm just grasping at straws."

Waylon dips his head down and gives me a halfway sympathetic look. "Yeah, you are. Red clean disappeared years ago, and it's obvious she don't want to be found. Plus, you've got no idea what she was into. You lied about who you were, and maybe she did too. Woman who looks like that? For all you know, she had a husband stashed away someplace who was real pissed off about her disappearing for two weeks with some rap fucker. But she, for damn sure, isn't some single mom cousin of Kyra's named *Bernice*."

"Country trap," I remind him. But then I have to admit. "You're right. I don't know what I was thinking."

He claps me on the shoulder. "No judgment here. Believe me. I get it. You know I get it better than anybody else in this place. When a woman haunts you like that, it's hard to shake. But I think it's time you got over her."

Right again. And that's not even the craziest thing that happens that weekend.

Less than thirty-six hours later, I get a chance to see firsthand how duplicitous females can be when Hades's woman, Persy, disappears on him without a trace.

To say Hades goes ballistic is an understatement. He literally flips one of the banquet tables at the roadhouse. He promises to find her. Then he threatens to kill anybody who touches her before he does. Then he guzzles a bottle of Buffalo Trace Sazerac Rye like it's a can of Pepsi.

He doesn't stop until he collapses onto the roadhouse floor blackout drunk.

And that's when I see my future if I continue down this path.

Persy's gone, disappeared into the wind, just like Red.

And it doesn't matter how much Hades wants her. That's not going to bring her back.

I look over at Doc, pulling beers behind the bar.

I always ask her if she's heard from Red when I stop in, but this time I don't. I just don't. Instead, I leave without saying a word to her.

I head back to Vegas, and I throw myself into my job as head of A&R for AudioNation. I work to impress my father and manage to tolerate Geoff—barely. And when I need a release, I find some woman to fuck. Then I leave as soon as it's done.

That dead inside feeling is dependable now. Unlike Red. It shows up when it's supposed to. Every time.

CHAPTER 21
BERNICE

KIKI: *Missed you today. Hope O2 is feeling better. Poor thing.*

I RECEIVE MY COUSIN'S MESSAGE ON MY ANCIENT APPLE Watch just as I finish helping O2 wash her face and brush her teeth in the bathroom at the hotel I booked for us last minute.

I feel pretty guilty that I had to lie to Kiki to avoid seeing Griffin and Waylon, but a whole lot more relieved that I got away with it.

Either way, today was too close—way too close. I could have walked into that Thanksgiving party blind. And who knew how that monster would have reacted when he saw O2....

Memories of the New Year's Eve when I found out who Griff truly was rise in the back of my mind. Shadows chilling me to the bone.

"Is that Auntie Kyra? She all better?" O2 asks as we walk out of the bathroom.

The worried expression on her little face twists my insides with even more guilt.

A fresh wave of hate washes over me for G-Latham. I hate lying to her. But since her father's basically the devil incarnate, it's a necessary evil.

But it's not O2's fault I picked the wrong guy to lose my mind with, so I force a smile and tell her, "Yes, Aunt Kyra's feeling a lot better."

"Can we go to her big house tomorrow?"

I cringe. Kiki hadn't said if Waylon would be staying overnight. And besides, I still hadn't come up with a good way to explain to my cousin why I lied to her about O2 being sick.

So... "I'm sorry, but no, sugar pie," I tell my secret daughter as I pull back the covers to tuck her into bed. "But tell you what, tomorrow I'll take you to the zoo. You love that place."

"The zoo's boring!" O2's face goes a little whiny. "I want to go to the Opry again and sing on stage, like last summer with Uncle Colin."

I have to resist the urge to roll my eyes as I tuck her into the hotel bed. Only O2 would consider a tour of the Grand Ole Opry, with a few minutes to belt out whatever she wanted on stage, better than a trip to the zoo.

"I don't think there's going to be tour slots left this last minute," I answer, grabbing our worn-out copy of *Dragons Love Tacos* before I climb in on the other side of the hotel bed. "And I'm pretty sure Uncle Colin pulled some behind-the-scenes strings to get all you kids a turn on stage. I don't have that kind of juice."

I can tell O2's fighting tears now. "I wish you had juice. I wish they didn't have to get sick. This vacation's no fun now. It's boring! Just like you!"

O2's been on an "everything's boring" kick for a while now. And if we were back in New York, she'd be getting a stern talking-to about how I'm not made out of money and it not being my job to entertain her little entitled behind.

But tonight, all I feel is guilty. Instead of chastising her, I pull her into my arms for some motherly comfort. "Oh, sugar pie....I know you're frustrated about it now. But you want your mom to be boring. Me being boring is what keeps us stable, with food on the table and a roof over our heads. Trust me, it's good to be boring."

O2 does not trust me.

I'm treated to a rant about how she wishes we could live here in Nashville in Aunt Kyra's big house and with all her cousins running around. It's so lonely and boring in New York, she tells me. Then, because three year olds have zero ability to read the room, she interrupts me in the middle of *Dragons Love Tacos* to tell me her own made-up story.

It involves her going on a tour of the Opry and running into a famous music star who asks her to come on stage with him when he sees how good she can sing. Then it turns out—big twist—he's her father!

My stomach turns into a vat of acid when she says that. This isn't the first time O2's made up a story about her father. But usually, he's an astronaut or a pirate and once—in a pretty blatant rip-off of her favorite book—a dragon who loved tacos so much, he'd dedicated his life to hunting them all over the world.

But this is the first time she's cast him as a music star. Talk about too close. Before she can finish, I pointedly reopen *Dragons Love Tacos* and insist we read the rest of a story somebody else made up.

I do not feel good about myself as a mother by the time she finally closes her eyes, and I switch off the light to go to sleep myself.

Yes, it's good to be boring. But I'm not sure O2's ever going to be able to accept that like I have. She doesn't know how big the world can be. How cruel some people can be.

But anyway...

We go to the Opryland theme park the next day, then fly back to New York as planned on Sunday. And late that night, I get an unexpected text from Allie.

> ALLIE: *Ding-dong, the witch might finally be dead. G-Latham just walked out of here without asking about you.*

Good, I tell myself, remembering that awful night. Good...

And as it turns out, Allie is right. The monster who introduced himself to me as Griff really does seem to have given up on finding me to finish his game of "mindboink the naïve girl."

I don't get any more "guess who was in here asking about you" texts from Allie.

However, the next time I hear from my old friend, her news is even more alarming than one of her G-Latham texts.

And she doesn't text. She calls—just a few days after my boss, Olivia, asks me to come with her to Kentucky to help set up a Louisville-based version of her Women with Disabilities clinic.

She calls, and before I can even say hi, Allie tells me, "Bernice, I'm in trouble. And I need your help."

CHAPTER 22
GRIFFIN

"C'MON, GRIFF. HELP ME, HELP YOU," JENNI SAYS AS THE car Phantom Zhang's assistant sent for us pulls up to a little backhouse sitting behind the famous Glendaver castle. It's one of those huge, old-world stone and marble mansions that robber barons used to love commissioning for themselves back in the day.

A meager backhouse isn't exactly the kind of green room experience I got used to during my heyday as G-Latham. But hey, I'm getting paid stupid bills to perform at the wedding of Phantom Zhang's brother, so I can make it work—especially if they throw in the five bottles of Glendaver bourbon I asked for on my rider.

That's what Jenni should be concerned with right now. Instead, all she's been talking about since we boarded the company plane in Vegas is some extra photo op she wants me to do.

I haven't performed in over a year, thanks to the pandemic. And I haven't even been back to Nashville in nearly three years—not since that fateful Thanksgiving when I decided to give up on finding Red.

I think Jenni's a little too hyped about being back in the South and actually getting to do her job onsite for this gig instead of from behind a laptop in the Vegas rental house she's been trapped in for way too long with her latest long-term.

"No!" I answer. Again. "And can we quit it with the *Jerry Maguire* refs?"

I swear Jenni doesn't know that dude's totally made up. He's been her patron saint ever since she made the switch from working as my assistant in Nashville to working as my agent/PR/personal branding manager in Vegas.

I climb out of the limo just to get out of another Tom Cruise-inspired speech.

"How about *Succession* then?" she asks, following me out of the car. "Because I'm not the one who's trying to convince Daddy Latham that you have what it takes to run AudioNation. And Geoff's all over the news with his drive-in wedding concert series."

"Please do not call my father that unless you're planning on leaving your girlfriend to become wife number three," I answer. "And that concert series is a stupid bad idea. The last thing people should be doing after a pandemic is throwing marriage on top of their misery."

"They're inspiring people," Jenni insists, jogging to keep up with me as we make our way to the backhouse's door. "And they're getting a lot of AudioNation artists in the press."

"Yeah, and they're also costing AudioNation millions of dollars. We've already lost two summers of touring profits, and now we're paying out the nose for this publicity stunt. I'm telling you, me getting in good with Phantom Zhang is the way to go. No photo ops, just me killing this set I'm about to do, then convincing him to sign on as an official AudioNation liquor sponsor. His VIP3 soju brand is killing with Asian markets all over the world."

Jenni stumbles a bit. "Wait, you actually had a plan for coming here?"

"Yeah, I'm good for more than signing on artists," I answer, my tone salty AF. "And after I land this deal with Zhang, Dad's going to realize that too. Where is everybody, by the way?"

I frown at the closed backhouse door. "You'd think they would have sent someone to meet us. And why aren't the Reapers here for security duty yet?"

Jenni winces. "I might have gotten us here a little earlier than planned."

I narrow my eyes at her. "And why would you do that?"

"Okay, don't be mad," she says.

"Don't make me mad," I shoot back, furrowing my brow. "What the hell's going on?"

She holds out her hands, palm forward, and explains. "So when I was talking with Zhang's assistant about possible photo ops for you, he mentioned a little girl in the backhouse daycare who apparently knows all the words to 'You, Me, and the Music Forever' by heart."

"A lot of kids know that song by heart," I point out grumpily.

I can be cocky, but I'm not exaggerating. I'm honestly kind of wishing I'd never let Kyra Fairgood convince me to voice a growly wolf and put out a track for the animated film she and Roxxy Roxx decided to music supervise for that arthouse animation studio Yinz Entertainment.

Yeah, sure, attending the premiere party with the producer, Victor Zhang, I met Phantom, who let me know his brother was a huge fan. But these days, I can't walk down the street anymore without kids shout-singing some off-key version of the song at me.

"Yes, yes, I know. It's so hard having to put up with adoring fans who don't have D-cups," Jenni answers, dismissing my grouchy tone with a wave. "But the assistant told me this kid is truly talented. She even does the rap! According to him, it's the most impressive, adorable thing you will ever see. And this little girl's, like, your biggest fan."

"Pass," I answer without even a second of consideration.

"*Please*," Jenni begs. "I mean, the daycare's right here, and I told them you'd be stopping by."

I'm already shaking my head. "You shouldn't have done that."

"It's just a few minutes," Jenni answers with a pleading look. "And it's guaranteed to raise your family consumer street cred, which your dad will really like."

I fold my arms, faltering a little bit. I want to just say "pass" again, but Jenni has a point. Geoff's mom, Whitney, told me flat out the other day that my dad wouldn't even be considering me to head up AudioNation if that movie hadn't done what she called, "a perhaps unintentional but much-needed reputation patch-up job."

Jenni pounces on my hesitation. "All I need you to do is visit this daycare for five minutes and watch this girl sing. Five minutes. That's all. Between that and the concert, I can probably stretch it into a couple of weeks of big social media posts."

I expel an annoyed huff of air. But, in the end, I answer, "Fine."

Jenni jumps up and down. And I have to wonder if she has a point about that *Succession* TV series.

When did I go from being an outlaw musician to a character in a show about the scions of a billionaire willing to do whatever it takes to win?

CHAPTER 23
BERNICE

W HEN DID I BECOME A SIDE CHARACTER IN A NIGHTTIME soap about rich-people drama? I'm not sure. But that hot summer evening, instead of dancing with the rest of the guests at the reception I party planned from top to bottom, I go out to the front steps of Glendaver Castle to play my part.

That's why I'm sitting on the steps, reading my Auntie Clara's latest sci-fi novel on my Apple Books app, when Allie arrives to pick her son up from the castle daycare. Olivia's former nanny, my Auntie Minerva, started this daycare for Olivia and all the other parents working at the Kentucky location of her Women with Disabilities Clinic.

"Let me guess," Allie says, stopping in front of me. "You're trying to finally get a quiet moment by yourself for the first time since the pandemic started."

"No," I answer, lowering my phone. But I have to laugh at her guess.

Allie understands the struggle more than most as a single mother herself. And now she has a near similar story to my own. Olivia hired Allie for her already too-popular clinic in Louisville, despite her being visibly pregnant, just because someone she trusted—me—recommended her. The only difference was, she was hired on as a general practitioner doctor instead of a nurse/receptionist.

Throughout the pandemic, we'd become even closer—to the point where O2 insisted on calling Allie's toddler son "Little Brother," no matter how many times we explained they weren't related by blood.

And even though she's the doctor with the least experience at the clinic, she's the best and funniest, according to our online reviews. Olivia adores her and even trusted her enough to be the doctor in charge while she and I were at her former work husband's wedding to her real husband's brother—yeah, I hear it too. I honestly think the East Coast Zhangs might be giving the Southern Fairgoods a run for their dramarama money.

Anyway, Dr. Allison Snow's employment has more than worked out, which makes me feel a little better about the lie of omission I made to get her the job. I told Olivia that Dr. Allison Snow was simply a medical work colleague from my pre-New York days, without mentioning our completely off-the-books jobs at that anonymous roadhouse.

But Allie and I never talked about that under-the-table job anyway, or the fathers of our children.

Hopes and dreams, all day—I could tell you Allie's five-year plan, line by line. But our pasts, well, let's just say that the reason we're such good friends is that we understand what's thoroughly off-limits.

As far as we're concerned, we're exactly what we say we are. A boring office nurse/receptionist and an ultra-capable doctor. The girls we were when we worked at that roadhouse, we've left them far behind.

For us, there's only now, and we try not to think about our pasts ever catching up with us.

"Good guess," I say to Allie in answer to her question about why I was waiting outside the castle. "But really, I'm out here to intercept Dawn, who should be here any second with her husband, Victor."

Allie's eyes widen, "Oh my gosh, are you going to run interference to warn her not to bring up the situation with her brother and the yakuza—"

"Yup," I answer before she's even finished with her guess.

One of the grooms is my old work colleague and Olivia Glendaver's best friend. And she doesn't want anything to ruin his big day —which Dawn Zhang could totally do if she tells the truth when he asks her how her brother, his ex-boyfriend, is doing. So, I've been put in charge of intercepting Dawn as soon as she and her husband arrive—which should be any minute now that their delayed flight out of Rhode Island has finally landed.

See what I mean about nighttime soap drama?

But anyway, my gossip game is A++ after years of being a side character in The Phantom and Olivia Show. So Allie knows *all* the special guest stars in their universe, including the obscure ones she's never met.

"Ooh, I'll wait with you," she says, dropping down to sit on the stone steps beside me. "Maybe his sister will have an update for us too. I can't wait for another episode of that story!"

"See. This right here is why we're best friends," I let Allie know with a wry laugh.

She laughs too, and the Southern accent she tries not to use in her professional day-to-day comes back full force as she declares, "I'm just saying, this single mom Kentucky life is thin on drama. I need an infusion of other people's wherever I can get—"

Roaring engines in the distance cut her off.

And the laughter disappears from our voices. From our minds. From our very souls.

We know that roar. It's the growl of ruin and danger, announcing a motorcycle gang's arrival at the roadhouse. It's the sound of our pasts catching up with us.

Every nerve, every drop of blood, every breath freezes inside my body.

"Don't freak out," Allie says, even as we both rise to our feet. Like prairie dogs who have caught the scent of a predator.

"It could be anybody," she assures me. "It doesn't have to be them—"

But then she stops cold, her pretty face collapsing into horror.

It is them. It's the Ruthless Reapers.

I know that even before I turn to see the ten bikers roaring toward us with their president, Waylon, at the front of the pack.

"Maybe...maybe he won't remember us," Allie says beside me, her voice shaky and hopeful.

"Red, Allie, is that you?" Waylon asks, stopping his bike right in front of us while the rest of the gang drives on toward the parking area around the side of the house.

He knew Allie's real name, but of course, he doesn't know mine.

I didn't give it to any of the bikers at that roadhouse. I wasn't that stupid—at least not until O2's father looked down at me with those piercing blue eyes.

Allie, so capable beyond her years, just stares at Waylon, her face as stunned as I feel.

"What are you doing here?" I ask for both of us.

"Security. Something about a surprise show for the gay brother of some big-shot alcohol guy," Waylon answers. Then he kills the engine. "What are *you* doing here, Red?"

Oh my God! Oh my God!

Panic washes over me in such thick waves it nearly collapses me to my knees. But I shore myself with one last, desperate thought. Isn't Griffin Latham mostly retired and working some bigwig position at AudioNation these days? Maybe the Reapers are working security for some other star—

"Okay, you better come with me," Waylon says with a heavy sigh. "He's been looking for you."

He's been looking for you.

Like it's been five days since I saw him last, not five years.

And that lets me know, without a shadow of a doubt, who's come to perform tonight. There's only one person who the Reapers' prez would refer to as "he"—like he's some kind of deity who needs no introduction.

This is my worst nightmare.

I glance at Allie.

Best friends. We're best friends now for reasons we never talk about.

Without saying a word, we both break toward the castle's front doors.

We run...run through the castle toward the backhouse daycare and our secret children as if we have hellfire at our feet.

CHAPTER 24
GRIFFIN

GOTTA ADMIT, I DON'T HATE JENNI FOR MAKING ME COME out to this backhouse daycare.

I figured Zhang's assistant was exaggerating. But this kid, who everybody calls O2 for reasons nobody bothers to explain to me before she opens her mouth, turns out to be just as stellar as she claimed.

She sings sweet and clear, and without yelling like a lot of kids do —even the professionals with coaches out in L.A. No, her projection game is on lock, and I nearly fall out of my seat when she does the entire rap, matching my animated-wolf-growl note bar for bar.

By the time she's done just killing that song, I'm grinning ear to ear, and my A&R Spidey-tingle is buzzing in the back of my head.

Jenni said all I had to do was clap and tell the kid she did a good job, and the current age of the mask has made it really easy to be a socially distant, insincere dick. But I end up crouching down to tell her, "You've got phenomenal talent, kid."

Now she's the one grinning from ear to ear. "My mom says I should be boring, like her. But I want to be a singer-rapper when I grow up. Just like you!"

"Just like me, huh?" I chuckle, and a long-lost memory of me saying the same thing to one of my rap-star heroes, C-Mello, washes over me.

"Well, guess what, my dad didn't want me to rap either. So you keep doing you, and see how that turns out."

"Okay, I will!" she says.

Jenni appears beside us and clicks a few pictures with her camera phone before saying, "That was wonderful, O2. Now, that's not your real name, correct?"

"No, ma'am, I'm named after Auntie Olivia. So everybody calls me O2."

"Wow, kid's calling you ma'am. We really are back in the South," Jenni jokes.

"Yeah," O2 agrees with a somber nod. "It's not like New York here. You have to talk to adults with respect. That's what my mommy says."

"Well, your mother sounds like a very by-the-books person," Jenni says in that exaggerated, slow tone some adults use with kids. "Could you let me know her name? I'd love to find her and have her sign a release form so that we can showcase your talent on Griffin's social media channels."

O2 claps both hands over her cheeks, like a cute, light-brown Macaulay Culkin. "No shush?"

After a confused moment, I realize that's her kid version of "no shit."

"No shush," I assure her with a laugh. "Just give Jenni your mom's name."

She drops her hands and eagerly answers, "Bernice! Her name is Bernice!"

That name...

I still.

"What did you just say?" I ask the little girl.

At the same time, Jenni says, "Could you spell that for me? And what's your last name?"

Instead of answering either of us, O2 points over my shoulder and says, "Mommy! Mommy! It's G-Latham!"

CHAPTER 25
BERNICE

ALLIE AND I SCREECH TO A HALT AT THE BACKHOUSE daycare's front door.

"Mama!" Allie's son calls out, toddling right on up to her.

But O2...my Olivia...

She doesn't call out my name for a reason that makes my heart nearly give out.

She's deep in conversation with a man who's squatted down to speak with her. He's wearing a cowboy hat paired with a Ruthless Reapers leather vest over a tee. And though his back is turned to me, I recognize all the tattoos running up his neck and down his arms.

I remember allowing my curiosity to roam free one of the weedless days, when we were supposed to be watching a movie on the couch. I crawled over to him like a cat in heat and kissed each inked piece while my hands grazed his hard, lean body—until he put me on my back and buried his mouth in my pussy, aggressively returning all my soft tattoo kisses with a hard, wet one of his own.

The memory floods through me like it happened yesterday, not years ago.

"Mommy! Mommy!" O2 calls out when she sees me over his shoulder. "It's G-Latham!"

I can't answer. I can't speak. I can't even breathe as Griff...G-Latham slowly stands up to his full six feet plus.

"Bernice?" Allie asks, pulling me back into the present.

She's got ahold of her little boy, and she's desperately trying to hide her face and help me at the same time.

But I can't be helped. He's already seen me.

"Run," I whisper out the side of my mouth. "Run while you still can."

O2's face goes from excited to worried when Allie turns and flees without even a word of hello.

"Mommy?" she asks.

I need to say something...reassure my daughter, the love of my life.

But I can only stare at her father.

A few more hopeful maybes spark in my chest. Girls in his world are a dime a dozen. There had to be a million *mes* while he was out on the road. I mean, that was probably why he stopped asking Allie about Red, the bad girl he never got to finish mindgaming.

And I wear my hair in sensible box braids now—not a flashy cherry-red weave. Maybe he won't recognize me. Maybe he won't realize—

"Red," he says, his blue-black eyes narrowing on me, then on my daughter.

Our daughter.

All the hope dies in my chest. Then I spring into action.

"O2, come with me," I say, holding out my hand. "Now. We've got to go. No questions."

Thank goodness she still minds me like she did in the big city of New York.

O2 rushes forward, throwing a "Bye, Mr. G-Latham!" over her shoulder.

"Wait," a slender blonde I didn't notice before calls out. I recognize her as the same woman who dropped off the Roxxy Roxx album—the one I had to sell along with my car to pay for my New York move after everything that went down with Griffin. "We need your mother to sign this release!"

O2 doesn't even pause. Back in New York, when I picked her up at daycare, hesitating to obey an order to take my hand and get to trucking meant standing in a freezing-cold subway station for an extra thirty minutes because we missed our train up to Harlem due to her lollygagging. Lesson still learned.

I grab her hand, and we rush out the daycare's door without even pausing to thank Auntie Minerva.

People are dancing in the distance on the Glendaver Castle's rolling back lawn. Since Allie doesn't live in the castle like me, I bet that's where she went to avoid the Reapers.

But after a moment of calculation, I steer O2 toward the house's side service entrance.

Maybe he won't follow me. He didn't want kids. He said that so many times. Maybe he'll just play along and pretend he never even saw me. Maybe I can live out my boring side character life without ever having to—

"Red!" a voice calls behind me. "Red! Where the hell do you think you're going?"

"Who's Red?" O2 asks.

"Go faster," I answer, breaking into a jog.

But we don't move fast enough. Her little legs can't keep up with me, and she's nearly six years old now—too big to pick up and flat-out run with like my heart's screaming at me to do.

We don't even make it halfway to the servant's entrance before he grabs me by the arm and swings me around to face him.

"Why are you running?" he demands. Then, before I can answer, he glances at O2 and says, "Tell me...tell me she isn't my daughter."

It's not a command, I sense. It's a dare.

He and I both know who O2 is. That she's a secret I've kept from him for over five years.

I open my mouth, but before I can come up with anything to say, O2 screeches, "You're my dad? For real?"

She doesn't give Griffin a chance to answer. She just throws her arms around his waist like only a child with zero trust issues could. "I knew it! I knew it! It's just like in the story I made up.

Mommy said I should stop telling it, but I knew it! You're my dad!"

An unreadable expression comes over Griffin's face, and instead of answering her, he looks to me.

Memories of that New Year's Eve night flash through my head.

You think you're hot shit, don't you? Well, I'm about to show you how fucked up a Reaper can make you.

Why did I go to his apartment that night? Even after hours of mulling over who he really was? I thought I'd get answers, but all I got was nightmares.

So many regrets flood through me as the monster waits for his confirmation. But I have no choice. Denying it now would only cause harm to O2 and make her not trust me if the truth ever gets out. I nod.

Dear God, I nod and finally tell the monster the truth.

"She's yours," I whisper.

Griffin stills, and his eyes...

His eyes light up with rage.

But then, to my surprise, instead of pushing O2 away, he picks her up in his arms.

"Yes, I'm your father," he says, hugging her as tightly as she hugs him. "I'm your dad."

SO I END UP GOING WITH WAYLON AFTER ALL. AFTER Griffin gives a terse explanation to O2 about how he still has "this show to put on," Waylon appears like a henchman in an old vampire movie to keep an eye on us.

O2 is way more excited about watching the short set than me. She asks Waylon questions, like, "Do you have any kids? Are you my dad's best friend? Can you beat Uncle Phantom at arm wrestling?"

The surprises keep on coming. Waylon answers each of her questions with, "Yeah, a little girl, just like you," "I guess so, if you ask him," and "I dunno, probably—matters how much hGH he's pushing to get that ripped."

"What's hGH?" O2 asks.

To my relief, Waylon pretends not to hear her follow-up question.

Maybe he has gotten softer after having a kid of his own. When Griffin runs out for his surprise set, he lifts her up so she can see above the raised stage. And he sings along with her to six of G-Latham's most famous songs. That's how I find out O2 already knows many of the words by heart.

My head's still reeling after the concert when Griffin, Waylon, and I all walk into the castle to escort O2 to her room. And it's a struggle to get her to go down.

"How about if this was all a dream?" she asks when we stop at her door, her voice pitiful and small. "How about if I wake up as soon as I let myself close my eyes?"

She always says things like that when she's had a good time and doesn't want it to end with having to go to sleep. Usually, I give her lots of hugs and reassurances that the good times will swing back around again someday. But tonight, I'm too on edge. Having Griffin there is like standing next to a time bomb with a count-down clock I can't see.

"O2, c'mon," I say, unable to keep the irritation out of my voice. "Let's not do this. It's already an hour past your bedtime.

"But—" she starts to protest.

To my surprise, Griffin crouches down in front of her and says, "I promise you, I'm going to be right here when you wake up. You're going to go to sleep, and your mom and I will talk, then I'll be seeing you for breakfast tomorrow morning. And I'll make this right, I promise you."

O2's whole face lights up, like Griffin eating carbs. "Really?"

"Yeah, really," he answers. "But breakfast in the morning isn't happening unless you go to sleep right now. No more whining about it."

O2 doesn't have to be told twice. She hugs him and says, "Good-night, Dream Dad. I love you. Love you too, Mommy."

Then she dashes into her room like she can't wait to go to sleep.

Leaving me in the hallway with the monster. And his Reaper prez bodyguard.

It feels like my life—my nice, boring life as a side character is slipping through my hands. But maybe I can fix this. Maybe he can be reasoned with. I read all those magazine pieces on him after discovering who he really is. I got to know him inside and out after the fact. Nothing I've learned about him screams, "Yes, I, Griffin Latham, would love to have my wild and luxurious life disrupted by a child."

I mean, at the cabin he pretty much said an unexpected baby was his worst nightmare. That might have been the only thing he didn't lie to me about.

I start off with a compliment to get us off on the right "maybe both of us can be reasonable adults in this situation" foot.

"That was really impressive," I tell him. "She usually makes me clock at least thirty minutes of story time before she'll even agree to close her eyes."

Griffin just smirks, like getting kids to go to bed is on the long list of talents he failed to tell me about when I thought he was nothing more than a criminal biker.

But then his expression softens, and he says, "Hey, Waylon, I know you're dying to get back to that family of yours, so why don't you go on ahead and take my plane back to Iowa."

Waylon glances from him to me. "Seriously?"

Griffin answers with a magnanimous nod. "Yeah, seriously. I have some things I need to take care of here."

Then his eyes swing back to me.

Waylon looks between us again, but then he accepts Griffin's offer with a terse, "Thanks, brother."

"No problem," Griffin answers without taking his eyes off me.

Waylon leaves, and it's just him and me.

"You should go to bed too," he says. His tone is gentle in a way I would never have imagined before this moment.

Now it's my turn to ask, "Seriously? But we have so much to talk about."

"Yeah, we do," he agrees with another nod. "But that was my first show in a while. I'm dead tired, and I bet you are too. I'm going to find a bed someplace in this castle you've been living in and face-plant into it. Then, tomorrow, we'll all get up, and you'll see I meant every word I said to Olivia. That's her real name, right?"

"Right." I let out a breath I didn't know I was holding and even smile a little.

He's being so cool about this. I'm relieved...and confused. I think about New Year's Eve again, trying to reconcile that monster with the man standing before me. It doesn't seem possible.

But then, I think about all the other things I've read about him recently. That he's killing it as the head of A&R for AudioNation. And there was that animated film O2 watched like a thousand times with her play cousins and Little Brother. Maybe that family friendlier version of him wasn't a one-off. Maybe he was trying to change for the better.

"Neither of us are the people we presented ourselves to be at the roadhouse," I say carefully—to both him and myself. "But we're both adults, and O2 is a child, so the main thing is doing what's best for her. Right?"

"Right," he agrees with a solemn nod. "But emotions are running high. We should both get some sleep, clear our heads—so that we can do what we need to do tomorrow morning."

Another wave of relief washes over me. Yes, this is a nightmare, but everything's going to be okay. "Yeah, let's get some sleep. Good night, Griffin."

"Good night...What do you want me to call you? Red or Bernice?"

My cheeks warm. Not just because I'm embarrassed about how I presented myself to him during those wild two weeks, but also because a small part of me—the last bit of the naughty girl I haven't been able to tamp out—wants him to call me Red, the same as he did back then.

But, like I said. We're both adults now.

I clear my throat and answer, "Bernice."

"Okay, Bernice." He gives me one more solemn nod and tips his cowboy hat at me. "Good night. Sleep tight."

"You too," I murmur.

Maybe he's not as big of a monster as I made him out to be ever since that New Year's Eve night. I turn and go to my room and wonder if I got what happened...if I got *him* all wrong.

There are, of course, a thousand messages waiting from Allie when I finally check my phone.

I type her a quick note, just to give her some peace.

> *He took it pretty well. He's staying the night in the castle, and then we're going to talk tomorrow when we get up. I'm pretty sure he didn't see you, so as long as you didn't run into any other Reapers on your way out, you should be fine.*

I lie back on the bed, and that's when I find out that I must have been just as exhausted as Griffin said.

I fall asleep before I receive her return text, and when I wake up the next morning, I find several replies from her waiting on my phone.

> ALLIE: *I didn't run into any other Reapers. TYL!!!But are you sure everything's cool?*

> ALLIE: *I mean, he might be legitimate now. But he's still a Reaper.*

ALLIE: *And those guys don't forgive. They're ruthless. It's literally in their name.*

I walk to O2's room to check on her and type Allie back at the same time: *"Yeah, that's what I thought too. But it's not like he wanted kids anyway. And I'm not asking him for anything. I think he probably wants to be done with this as bad as—"*

I abruptly stop texting when I see that O2's bed is empty. Not just of her, but also Ellie, her favorite stuffed animal.

Oh my God. Oh my God. My blood ices over. Somehow, I know even before I go looking everywhere for her in the castle and the guard at the front gate confirms that he let a car pick up Griffin at two in the morning.

She's gone. He's taken her.

I was right. Griffin Latham isn't as bad as he was five years ago.

He's an even bigger monster now.

CHAPTER 26
GRIFFIN

"SO DAD'S OBVIOUSLY LOST HIS MIND."

My brother storms into my office the Monday morning after our unexpected Zoom call with our father. "I don't know what happened after Dad flew out to Missouri—for reasons I still don't understand—but this is insane. He's clearly not thinking straight, and he needs to be managed. We're both agreed on this, right? I know we've got our stuff, but we'll need to stick together if we want to counter this bullshit barrier he's constructed to taking over his CEO position."

I lean back in my chair and regard Geoff over my steepled hands. Maybe...*maybe* my brother's not trying to be a self-serving dick.

But our corner offices sit in the same building—on the same floor, even—and I can count on my fingers the number of times he's come to visit me here since I started officially working at AudioN-ation five years ago. The fingers of one hand. And I wouldn't have to use my thumb. Or my pinky.

To be fair, we're both territorial bastards. Most of the time, we have to meet in a conference room just to prove neither one of us is ceding any ground.

But today, he bursts right into my office and starts pacing back and forth in front of my desk. Like a lion in a gray suit. With an agenda.

I can't say I'm surprised by this unannounced visit. I'd be shaken by our dad's ultimatum too—maybe even willing to seek out my main competition for an alliance. If I were Geoff.

Lucky for me, I'm not my brother. I have a plan to deal with Dad's unexpected requirement to be appointed to his CEO position—an insane, diabolical plan. And all my chess pieces are almost in place.

Like the Death Buddha song currently floating at the top of the charts, I count my unexpected blessings.

"Let me guess," I counter Geoff dryly. "You've already got a big countermove in mind. You want me to back out of the running and side with you. That way, Dad has no choice but to give you the job."

Geoff abruptly stops pacing, and his face takes on the expression it often gets when he's playing hardball. Neutral and cold. Like he's going to get what he wants, whether you like it or not.

"Let's stop playing around here," he answers. "You and I both know that position belongs to me. I'm the one who took over at Big Hill Records when Dad stepped down to form AudioNation. I'm the one who put in over a decade of hard work to grow the Latham legacy...."

He trails off and glares at me when I lean my head to the side and pantomime a yapping sock puppet with the same hand I use to wipe my ass.

"Let me guess, you want to mock my solution, but you don't have a better idea for getting around this insane provision Dad's trying to give us," he says, his tone set on withering. "Because you're a child who's only pretending to be a grown-up."

"A child who signed Roxxy Roxx, C-Mello, and sasha x kasha to AudioNation touring deals," I remind him. "Colin Fairgood too. Hey, didn't he turn you down when you tried to bring him into the fold?"

"That's why you should stay in your position as president of A&R. You're doing just fine here. And how was I supposed to know he was holding out for a co-deal with his wife? That was just a lucky guess on your part."

Only Geoff would call snagging agreements worth millions in touring revenue "just fine."

"You would have figured it out if you'd bothered to spend any real time with them. You're too much like Dad," I tell him. "That old-school withholding-as-fuck attitude doesn't fly with acts anymore."

Geoff regards me neutrally, refusing to take my bait. "I'm the one who brought Colin Fairgood over to Big Hill in the first place. I'm the reason we were even in a position to negotiate. Let's not forget that."

"And let's not forget, you're also the reason we had to drop serious bank on Stone River to get my early song rights back when I finally came into the fold. If you had just signed me in the first place, you wouldn't have missed the early boat on the country trap explosion. When it comes to future vision, you're just not the guy for CEO."

Geoff smirks, like he's caught me in the act.

"So, this sudden interest in sitting at the head of the table is because you're still pissed off at me for not giving you a record deal?" he asks—like him not believing in me or my talent is some trivial footnote in our history. Something I should just get over.

I put a whole lot of extra needle in my voice. "If you're so worried about Dad's mental health all of a sudden, how about backing me for the CEO seat? Somebody who actually knows how to seal deals with other music acts. And you can stay in your COO lane. You're doing *just fine* heading up operations."

That does it. The cold mask drops.

"You think *you're* more qualified to run AudioNation than *me*?" He starts to explode but then breaks off and narrows his eyes at me. "Wait, why are you just sitting there, cool as a cucumber, after Dad's ultimatum? Why aren't you just as pissed as me?"

Good questions.

Luckily, a tap sounds on my closed office door just a moment after he asks about my non-bothered state.

"Yes?" I call out instead of answering my brother's question.

My mohawked assistant, Kurt, sticks his head in the door, and Geoff eyes him with undisguised disapproval. My guy Kurt's pretty much the exact opposite of Dana, the stalwart assistant he's had since graduating from B-School.

"Your uh...personal law team just arrived?" Kurt tells me. "They're saying you have a meeting with them—but it's not on the schedule. Not sure how I missed it."

Kurt's voice sounds a little shaky. He's probably just as confused as the guest waiting for me downstairs.

"Thanks, Kurt." I shoot Geoff the same smirk he gave me earlier. "Sorry, bro. Gotta go."

"Lawyers? What do you have planned?" Geoff asks, his eyes bouncing from Kurt to me. "Are you going to try to sue Dad?"

Not exactly.

Instead of answering his questions, I put on the suit jacket I traded out for my Reaper leathers when I took this job.

And I can't resist needling him one last time as I walk out the door. "But seriously, let me know if you want to talk more about backing me for CEO. Trust me. Things will go a whole lot better for you if you do."

I drop that last mic on him, but I don't bother to look back over my shoulder to see how he reacts.

My sole focus is going to meet my downstairs guest, who, as it turns out, has very convenient timing.

"YOU SON OF A BITCH! HOW COULD YOU DO THIS? HOW could you? I'm going to kill you!"

Well, here's one person even madder at me than Geoff.

I'm guessing Red didn't like finding Olivia gone the morning after my wedding performance. And I'm getting the feeling she might not have appreciated the Monday meeting invite my team of killer attorneys sent to her email address.

Or maybe she's just pissed off because she's been made to wait in a basement conference room at the AudioNation headquarters ever since showing up exactly at the appointed time for this meeting. I think that was two hours ago. Maybe three?

Anyway, she flies at me as soon as I walk into the room with my law team right behind me.

"You bastard!" she cries out, slapping my face. "Where is she? Where is my daughter?"

Last time I saw Red, she had on a pretty dress and makeup with her braids done up in a classic bun.

Forget makeup. Now she's wearing a jersey pajama set—maybe the same one she went to sleep in when I lulled her into a false sense of security back in Kentucky. She looks frantic and on edge. Her skin is patchy, and her eyes are bloodshot—like she's spent the entire thirty-six hours since I saw her last crying.

Good. Seeing her wrecked like this is worth all the bridges I had to burn with Phantom Zhang and the Fairgoods to put this plan in motion. She never showed up like she said she would that New Year's Eve. I searched for her for years, and she actively hid both herself and our daughter from me.

So, I let her slap at me and scream bloody murder for a few moments.

Then I coldly catch her by the wrists and ask my lawyers, "Should we add physical violence and name-calling to the list?"

The two lawyers have two different last names and aren't related, as far as I can tell. But they look like they might be thirty- and fifty-year-old clones of the same dour-faced man.

"We can add it to the bad character evidence, yes," Friedman, the older lawyer, answers. He nods at the younger clone, Diaz, who pulls out an iPad to make a note.

Some of the righteous fury fades from Red's expression, and she seems to see the lawyers for the first time.

"What is this?" she asks.

"A custody negotiation," I answer. "Now sit down."

Her eyes flash, just like they did back then at the cabin.

And my dick responds like a Pavlovian dog, filling with lead. This power she still has over me...

Self-disgust rolls my stomach, even as I coldly add, "Or you can keep on hitting me and give us even more shit to use against you."

I'm aware Red did everything in her power to not have to take this meeting.

Jenni's been trying her damnedest to rehab my reputation and have me play nice for the media. But I'm still a Reaper by instinct. When I moved to Vegas to take my position at AudioNation, I set up a shadow team of lawyers, criminal connections, and dirty cops, and I never let them go, no matter how scrubbed up my image got.

Red has her own powerful connections, and she's been attempting to get me arrested for taking Olivia across state lines before the official meeting. So, my shadow team has been worked to the brink, keeping this situation out of the news and off official police reports.

It was a nuisance, for sure. But I'm grateful now. Blocking all her countermoves and wearing her down with a multi-hour wait must have worked.

The fight eventually disappears from her eyes, and she sinks into a seat on the other side of the small conference table.

Speaking of which. "You can go," I say to the head of security. "We've got it from here."

He quietly leaves, and Red watches with wary eyes as the lawyers and me take a seat on the other side of the big table. Us against her.

"What's this all about?" she asks.

I let the lawyers answer.

"Mr. Latham has had us draw up a custody agreement regarding the ongoing care of the child he fathered," Friedman answers.

"Wait, you're trying to sue me for custody? That's what this is all about? Why didn't you just ask?" She turns to shake her head at me. "I would have been reasonable. You don't just kidnap a little girl."

I delight in watching her squirm and protest. Like a kid holding a magnifying glass to an ant.

And Friedman just keeps going like she didn't say anything. "You should know, while looking over this contract, that Mr. Latham's terms are final and non-negotiable."

With that said, Diaz slides a thin sheath of paper across the table to her.

She takes the contract with trembling hands. And her expression enflames as she reads over it. "You want main custody? And I'll only be able to see O2 one weekend every other month and on one holiday?"

"That's more time than Mr. Latham has gotten with his daughter for nearly six years," Diaz answers, making another entry into his iPad. "He's eager to make up for lost time."

Red's eyes flare with outrage. "He doesn't want to make up for anything. This is about revenge! He's using my daughter—an innocent little girl—to exact revenge for an ego blow his ridiculous little mind can't handle for some reason."

Again, Friedman acts like he's got an emotions filter installed that doesn't let him hear anything said in the tone of upset. "You have approximately forty minutes to decide whether or not to take the deal Mr. Latham is offering you. Otherwise, you're welcome to bring a suit against him in court. We, of course, will fight it. And who knows how long it will take for you to gain emergency visitation rights, considering how backed up the family courts are after the pandemic?"

And how many people we've paid off to hold up the paperwork, I silently add with an inner smirk. Red might have powerful friends on the other side of the Mississippi, but Las Vegas is my territory. And she doesn't have the resources to fight me here.

Friedman pauses. As if waiting for another outburst.

But I think it's sinking in. How fucked she is in this situation.

Red just sits there, as if her mind has exploded from all the grenades I threw at her, and she doesn't know what to do.

I've got her exactly where I want her.

"Give us the room," I tell the lawyers.

Unlike her, they don't hesitate to follow my orders. They depart without another word. And then, it's just her and me.

"You get it now, don't you?" I say, leaning forward. "This isn't going to go your way, no matter how much you whine and cry."

To her credit, she doesn't prove my point by giving me the satisfaction of her pitiful tears.

"The only thing I'm getting right now is that I was totally right to do what I did," she answers, her voice low and fierce. "You're a monster, willing to use a little girl to prove…what? I have no idea. You're the one who lied to me about who you really were. You're the one who said you didn't want kids. I did nothing wrong—"

I lose it before I can think to hold myself back.

"You did everything wrong!" I roar at her. "You hid from me—hid my flesh and blood from me for years. Not a few months. Fucking years. And now you're acting like I'm the monster for not telling you who I was, *Red*—real name Bernice?"

She jumps out of her seat too. "No, I'm not going to play your game. I'm not going to negotiate with a lying sociopath. And that's what you are. You're toxic—completely toxic. That's why I kept my little girl's existence from you. To keep her safe. From you."

Rage rushes through me, so hot and deadly I have to bunch my fists like Geoff did earlier to keep myself in check.

I hate this bitch.

I hate her for not showing up like she said she would.

I hate her for hiding from me.

I hate her for making me want her more than I've ever wanted anything in my life. For making me believe in us enough to change—then betraying me, like, *psyche!*

She's calling me crazy. Who does she think made me this way?

But she doesn't give me the satisfaction of her tears, and I refuse to give her the satisfaction of letting her see how bad she's wounded me—first with her disappearance and then with her lies.

I flash freeze the fire raging inside of me and let my voice go cold and deadly to inform her, "There are people in this world you can avoid and escape. I'm not one of those people. Sign the contract or don't. Either way, you're not getting Olivia back. Not unless you play by my rules."

I sit back down and steeple my hands like the future CEO I'm about to become. "This isn't the cabin. I'm not going to compromise. I'm not going to bend just because you're upset. As far as I'm concerned, you started deserving whatever I dish out as soon as you decided to keep this secret from me. So, the only questions you should be asking me now is, 'What do you want from me? What do I have to do to get my daughter back?'"

She opens her mouth. Then closes it.

And a cold calm washes over me because I know I've already won.

She doesn't say anything for several moments. But I can tell she understands—*I've made her understand* just how bad she fucked up when she decided to cross me.

From there, it's just a matter of waiting patiently until she hangs her head and asks, "What do you want from me? What do I have to do to get my daughter back?"

CHAPTER 27
BERNICE

> **ALLIE:** *Update please! It's been almost a week since you decided to move to Vegas. How's O2 handling everything? Olivia's saying she hasn't heard from you either. Please, let us know you're both okay!*

I CLOSE MY EYES AFTER READING ALLIE'S MESSAGE AND try to figure out how to answer her.

I mean, what is there to say? No, I'm not okay? I'm still trying to figure out how, after recommitting so thoroughly to being Boring Bernice, I somehow ended up headlining my own nighttime soap? And my mind's still reeling from my final decision to agree in full to Griffin Latham's second offer?

Telling Allie the truth would only upset her. And besides, it wouldn't change anything. I'm in this now.

Griffin told me exactly what he wanted me to do—the terrible things he expected me to agree to. Then he warned me that I still only had forty—no, less than thirty minutes now to decide.

"If I walk out of this room with a no from you on both my official and verbal offers, you'll leave with nothing," he informed me. "Then, I will make you fight me tooth and nail for every minute with her. And believe me when I tell you this, Red. I always win in a fight."

He's a liar, and a monster. But I believed him when he told me that.

He'd proven himself stronger than me and my friend arsenal, and I'd already been apart from my daughter for over twenty-four hours. I couldn't bear to spend one more minute apart from her—not to mention the days to weeks to possibly months it would take to get her remanded back to my custody.

I hover my thumbs over the phone's keyboard. I'm so sick of secrets and lies, but I text:

Everything's fine. Going to meet her grandfather for the first time now. O2's really excited.

After typing out that load of partial lies, I drop the phone back into my clutch without waiting for Allie's reply. I'm too sick to my stomach to read it anyway.

Which puts me in marked contrast with O2. She's happily chatting with Griffin, who's sitting on the other side of the car seat in the limo ferrying us to his father's house in Kingsbridge, a gated luxury community in West Vegas.

I'm still furious that he basically lied to her and told her they were going on a mom-approved trip across state lines. But, thank goodness, she didn't seem the least bit traumatized when I finally reunited with her in the Benton Grand Suite she'd been staying in with that blonde I'd seen in both Kentucky and Tennessee.

O2 was full of stories about all the cool places Jenni had taken her to—like the fountains at the Bellagio, some dolphin exhibit at The Mirage, and what sounded like every gelato stand in every hotel on the Strip.

After our reunion, Griffin left us alone in that Benton hotel suite with a 24/7 guard posted at the door—for our protection, he told O2. But I knew it was really so I wouldn't try to run away with her and go back on our deal.

I told him once that when I made a decision it was done. I always keep my promises. But I guess he didn't believe me—then or now. Trust is still something Griffin Latham doesn't fuck with.

Anyway, that was the last I heard from him for a week until a hotel employee dropped off a bag with the name of some store I never heard of scrawled across the front in elegant cursive.

Inside I found a bunch of accessories, along with an emerald-green satin floral-print maxidress for me and a darling, long, pastel-pink seersucker dress for O2. It was the kind of winsome little girl dress I would have admired in a department store—then passed right up because I knew O2 would have it covered in dirt and food stains before I could even get a good picture for my social media.

"Do I really get to wear that dress?" O2 asked, her eyes saucer-wide.

Apparently. Another team showed up this morning to do our hair and paint our nails, which O2 really got a kick out of—almost as much as she loved being picked up by an actual white limo outside our hotel.

"I feel like a princess!" she cried when Griffin, who decided to revert to his charming "I'm not a total monster" act, got out and opened the door for her himself.

And now she was sitting on her car seat throne between us and asking Griffin, "Will there be cupcakes at Grandpa's party?"

The party you didn't bother to tell either of us about until you had us in the car, I resentfully mutter to myself.

"Dial your expectations down to light finger foods, followed by a real boring three- to four-course dinner," Griffin suggests with a frank look.

"Aw..." O2's shoulders sink. "So no pizza?"

Griffin shakes his head. "Sorry. Dad's first wife planned the party, and you're going to be the only kid."

I scrunch my head, wondering about the brother he mentioned with the pregnant wife when we were at the cabin. Were they not going to be there too?

"Your dad has more than one wife? I have more than one grand-ma?" O2's voice is breathless with the possibility after growing up with zero grandparents.

"Your grandpa's got two *ex*-wives," Griffin answers. "He married my brother Geoff's mom first, then my mom. Geoff's mom is the one throwing the party. They're still really good friends—plus, my dad could never be bothered to find somebody else to do all his party planning after they divorced."

"Your mommy didn't do it when they were married?" O2 asks.

"She really wasn't that kind of mom." Griffin's voice tightens a little. "That's partly why they broke up."

"Is she going to be at the party?"

"Nope," Griffin answers, and his tone makes it clear that he'd like that to be the end of this conversation.

But O2 lives to serve as a walking, talking example of tone-deaf.

"Does she hate him because he broke up with her?" she asks Griffin straight out. "Is that why she's not coming to his birthday party?"

Normally, this would be the point where I'd intercede and give O2 yet another "grown folks business" reminder. But I stay quiet.

Griffin thinks children are just set pieces to use in his scheme. Let's see how he handles actually having to deal with one—especially when it comes to the tough stuff, like his dead mother.

But he just says, "She's not thinking about any of us anymore" to O2, vagueing over her death.

And O2 must finally get it. Instead of asking more inappropriate questions, she rubs his arm and says, "I'm sorry your mom isn't nice, like your brother's mom."

Griffin lets out a wry chuckle. "Me too."

On that awkward note, the car stops in front of a stone villa with an impressive two-story columned portico. The place puts me in mind of a palace. It's ridiculously large, with separately roofed wings flanking each side of the main house. Vegas's answer to Glendaver Castle.

"Wow, Grandpa lives here?" O2 asks, her eyes going wide.

Yes, O2's grandfather lives here. It's work not to gape as we follow Griffin through the house's huge oak double doors.

Mind you, I live in a castle—but only during the pandemic. I've heard about but have never been to the kind of swanky parties the Glendavers were known for throwing before Olivia and Phantom took over the estate.

So I'm wholly unprepared for the sight of a large foyer filled with people who could have been ripped out of a *Premium Living* magazine shoot.

I stare at them. Then freeze when they all stop talking to stare right back at the three of us, standing just inside the door.

"Ring." Griffin suddenly steps in front of me, blocking my view of the party and the party's view of me as he dips his head down to growl in my ear. "Put on the ring."

My stomach cramps with the memory of what else had been in the bag, along with a handwritten note: *Wear this tomorrow.*

I think about telling him I forgot it. But I doubt I can manage that level of subterfuge—not with the eyes of everyone at the party on us.

I pull the emerald-cut engagement ring out of the teeny-tiny clutch and slip the piece of jewelry onto my left ring finger.

A gust of panic threatens to overturn my mind. Did I really agree to this? Did I really agree to marry a monster?

Yes, I did...

I didn't bother to correct Griffin when he assigned that guard to us, but I have to re-tell myself in that moment: The decision is made.

I chant the reminder in my head as Griffin takes me by my non-wedding-ring hand to lead us forward, beyond the double staircases to the raised foyer/living room where the party is taking place.

The deathly silent party.

Everyone's staring at us so hard that I stop right before we reach the staircase to whisper, "Wait. Did you actually tell your family we were coming?"

CHAPTER 28
BERNICE

OH MY GOODNESS, GRIFFIN DID NOT WARN HIS PEOPLE WE were coming.

I can tell in an instant by the way his jaw hardens and his expression becomes defensive.

"Sugar pie, give us a moment," I tell O2 before leading Griffin to stand a few feet away, where neither the little girl nor the rest of the party can hear us.

"I can't believe you," I hiss at him. "Are you trying to traumatize her? This is *not* how you introduce a five-year-old to the extended family she didn't know she had until a few minutes ago in the limo."

"It's a birthday present," Griffin insists. "It's supposed to be a surprise."

Wow, he is really not getting it. This is why I agreed to his insane proposal—so I could remain in O2's life full-time and do whatever it took to protect her.

"You need to *prepare him*—really prepare him," I insist back. "Like, make sure he doesn't have a heart attack or ask questions that will make O2 feel bad. Seriously, what were you thinking just springing us on him like this?"

"I don't know," he answers from between clenched teeth. "What were you thinking not telling me about her for damn near six years, *Red*."

"That you'd make a terrible father, *Griff*," I answer honestly. I'm so angry. I can barely keep my voice at a whisper level. "That she'd be better off without you because, obviously, you do not think about anybody but yourself when you come up with these insanely evil plans of yours."

Griffin's face collapses. Just for a moment—like a stone wall starting, then deciding not to crumble. But in that moment, he actually looks hurt. Like my words cut him.

And, for an equally short moment, I feel bad for hurting his feelings. I mean, how hard did the lesson that O2 was more than an accessory who could fit seamlessly into my planned life in New York hit after she was born? And Griffin's only known about her existence for a few days.

But then I remember how he didn't show me any mercy in that basement conference room. Why should I show him any now? I've got to make him see reason, for O2's sake.

"Just let us go back to the hotel," I suggest. "I bet the car is still there. Tell your dad whatever story you want to make up. Make sure he's cool. *Then* introduce him to O2. Remember, she's innocent in all this."

His jaw ticks. "You can't go back to the suite at the Benton."

My heart sinks. I guess there really isn't any human underneath all that monster.

"But you can go upstairs and wait in Dad's office while I explain everything to him. Then I'll bring him up there to meet you...and Olivia."

Relief unsinks my heart. Sure, I'm still somehow engaged to a truly despicable Ruthless Reaper turned Ruthless Mogul. But at least he's willing to listen to me when it comes to O2's emotional welfare. It feels like a win.

"Thank you," I whisper.

Then I turn to O2—only to have my heart give out when I see that she's no longer standing where we left her.

"Where is she—?" I start to ask.

Then my heart stops again when I spot her addressing a group of adults semi-arced around her, like she's giving a TED Talk.

"Mommy knew my dad was G-Latham, but she didn't tell me, and she didn't tell him. I think she wanted it to be a surprise. Maybe for my birthday at the end of the month. I don't know," she's telling her audience as we approach. "But it's okay. After my dream dad found me, he asked Mommy to marry him. And now they're both going to be my parents. I miss my play aunts and play cousins. But I like it here. And Jenni took me to see the hotel dolphins. Did you see the hotel dolphins?"

Oh. My. God. I don't know whether to grab O2 and run or shake her for doing the exact opposite of staying put, like she should have.

"Are you talking about the dolphins over at The Mirage?" an older woman with a hairspray helmet of blonde hair asks. She's wearing a shimmery white dress that could double for a kaftan but probably costs too much money to just wear around the house. "I adore that exhibit."

"Are you seriously trying to tell us you're Griffin's daughter?" a gorgeous, clean-cut man with dark brown hair asks O2. He looks a lot like Griffin, if Griffin was slightly taller, lean instead of muscular, and loved that classic all-American, clean-cut preppy look as much as he did tattoos.

I step in there to address the two people I'm assuming are Griffin's brother and his mother.

"I'm sorry about this," I say, cupping O2's shoulders. "We're just going to go wait upstairs—"

"You're not the one who should be sorry, darlin'," a voice with a booming Tennessee accent responds.

Oh no...

It's too late to run upstairs. The crowd parts like the Red Sea, and Greg Latham steps forward.

He's a tall man with thick silver locks and the kind of rough-hewn cragginess Southern men who grew up in the backcountry possess, no matter how much you polish them up.

He glares down his large nose at me. "Is what she's saying true? Is this girl my granddaughter? And are you planning on marrying my son?"

Okay, I lived in New York City with all sorts of folks for years, but I was raised in Tennessee. It instantly occurs to me that just because they named Latham County after this man, that doesn't mean he's a paragon of race relations. I recall the face tattoo story. Is that what this is?

Griffin purposefully pissing his dad off by announcing he's about to marry a Black woman—and introducing him to his half-Black granddaughter?

Maybe...

Griffin steps forward and answers for me. "Yes, it's true. It's all true. I brought Olivia to meet you as your birthday present."

Greg juts out his chin. "Did you run a DNA test on this so-called birthday present before planning a wedding this time?"

This time? What the heck? How many people has Griffin been secret-baby engaged to before me?

"Sure did," Griffin answers. "I can have Jenni send you the results, if you need to verify them. And don't worry, my lawyers are working on the prenup paperwork as we speak."

The DNA test is news to me—one more outrageous thing Griffin's done to throw on the pile.

And did I think everybody was looking at us when we were still faraway in the foyer? Now, they might as well have popcorn. They're watching us so close. I cringe, waiting for Greg's reaction, along with everyone else.

The oldest Latham stares at us for a long, hard second.

Then his entire face bursts into a wide smile. "Well, if this ain't the best birthday present I ever got!"

He holds his arms out wide to O2 and says, "Come here, Grand-daughter. Give your old granddad a hug!"

So, I guess I know where O2 got her general enthusiasm for life. Greg Latham happily bonds with me a little over being from Tennessee—especially after I tell him my father was born in Latham County too, before moving away when he was a little boy. Then the Latham patriarch spends his entire birthday party showing her around the house and introducing her to his guests, like she's simply a long-time member of the family they never met.

For the record, I still despise Griffin Latham more than gnats in my sweet tea, but I have to ask, "Is he always like this?"

"No, never," Griffin answers out the side of his mouth. He appears a little stunned. "I guess he really was serious about being ready for grandkids."

Geoff spends most of the party giving us the stink eye from other corners of the room. But we get enthusiastic hugs from everyone else—especially Geoff's mom, Whitney. She's one of those Tennessee belles who grew up so wealthy she never bothered to adopt a Southern accent.

Whitney and Greg seem to have one of those ex-relationships that you're always reading about in celebrity magazines. She congratulates me and happily introduces herself and her totally opposite wife. A short and squat golf pro named Merri.

"Like in Merry Christmas, but with an i," she tells O2.

O2 immediately decides she can work with that. "I *do* have two grandmas!" she cheers.

Apparently, Whitney's already started wedding planning. "I knew you two would want to get married as soon as possible, considering Greg's...ah, enthusiasm to see his sons married. So I've been texting back and forth with our family friend Nora Benton. How does a Benton Ballroom ceremony on the last Sunday in September sound?"

"That's O2's birthday," I immediately answer to explain why that date won't work.

"Yay! That's my birthday!" O2 cheers to immediately invalidate my reason for saying no to a wedding in less than six weeks.

Whitney laughs, beaming down at O2. "Perfect, then. Oh, you remind me so much of how Griffie was when he was a little boy! Just so enthusiastic and full of life."

Seriously? O2 gets it from her father, not her grandfather? Also...*Griffie?*

"Do you sing too, O2?" Whitney asks.

Wrong question.

O2 belts out that dang G-Latham song I haven't been able to get her to stop singing ever since the movie came out On Demand toward the beginning of the pandemic.

But the new grandmas don't seem to mind her impromptu concert. They clap enthusiastically after she's done, and Merri offers to take her to the grass on the back lanai to start working on her golf swing.

"She's delightful," Whitney tells me as we watch them walk away. "And so are you. I'm so happy for you and our Griffie!"

"Thanks," I say, my stomach twisting with even more guilt. We're selling this happy, reunited family stuff. But it's all based on lies.

"Griffie was so messed up after what happened with his mom, poor guy. I thought he'd never trust in love enough to actually get married. But look at you two, back together again! Maybe he'll even invite Elodie to the wedding."

"Elodie?" I ask.

Whitney tilts her head. "His mother? Have you not talked about her?"

"Yes, but I thought his mother had passed," I answer. A confused note creeps into my tone.

Whitney blanches. "He told you that? That she was *dead*?"

I desperately search my memory of the very little he said about her and answer, "He said she went home."

"Oh no, what a misunderstanding!" Whitney's worried expression gives way to a relieved laugh. "Griffie didn't grow up in Tennessee. So you have to understand, when he says go home, he means it literally—it's not a euphemism for death. You see, she went home to France, where she's from, after accepting her music career here would never pan out."

I let out a relieved laugh too. "Oh, so she's still alive? That's good news."

"Well, yes, I suppose...." The humor fades from Whitney's eyes. "She did leave the country during one of Griffie's holiday visitations with Geoff and Greg. And she refused to come back—such a terrible, terrible thing to do to your son. I can't say I was surprised about those rebellious years of his with that motorcycle gang. I'm just glad he's back in the fold and finally healed enough to get married."

I stare at her, stunned.

Wow, yes, that was a terrible thing to do. Having lost both my parents to a tragic accident, I can't imagine losing one just because my mom decided to bounce. As terrible of a position as he's put me into with this forced marriage business, my heart splinters for Griffin.

And I'm not sure what to do when Geoff corners me just as I'm coming out of the bathroom after—Griffin had called it—the four-course meal is done.

"What are you doing here with my brother?" he demands without so much as a hello.

So that talk is super fraught. But eventually, the sun sets, and it's time to go home.

Thank goodness.

Pretending to be perfectly okay with marrying Griffin is exhausting work—not to mention the conversations with Whitney and Geoff. I can't wait to scrub my face and fall into my bed at the hotel.

But the car pulls to another stop in less than three minutes of driving—this time outside a house that looks like a smaller replica of Greg's villa, just without the two side wings.

"I've got one more surprise for you," he says to O2. "An early gift for your birthday that couldn't wait until the end of next month."

O2's eyes go saucer-wide. "Is the gift in the house?"

He laughs. "The gift *is* the house."

"What?" O2 and I shout at the same time—with much different levels of enthusiasm.

I'm hoping I'm misunderstanding again. But I'm not.

Less than an hour after our arrival, I emerge from putting O2 down in a space that looks like a team of fairies got together to make all her fantasy room dreams come true. And I find Griffin waiting for me on a landing that overlooks the same kind of large foyer where Whitney threw Greg's party.

"She is going to be very disappointed when she sees the stuffed dolphin I'm getting her for her birthday," I tell him, too tired to pretend this house isn't seriously impressive.

Griffin just laughs. "I'm glad she likes it. Today went good."

"Yeah, it did," I agree. Maybe too good.

A soft sense of camaraderie flutters through me, and I have to bite my tongue to stop myself from all the questions I have about his ultramodern family. And the still-living mom in France.

We're not friends, I remind myself, after remembering what Geoff told me. He's using me, and I'm protecting O2. That's all.

"What were you talking to my brother about after dinner?" Griffin demands, as if reading my mind.

I decide to answer with the truth: "He wanted to make sure that I knew you were only marrying me because his father made getting married and having a baby a condition of him passing down the CEO seat for AudioNation."

Griffin stills, but his expression stays neutral. No remorse, no apology. What else did I expect?

"How did you respond?" he asks.

"I was surprised, so I didn't say anything," I answer. "I think he took that as an answer, though. He said he was mad that you took it this far. That you shouldn't have dragged O2 and me into your father's business games."

Griffin smirks. "Look at Geoff, pretending he's not a Latham and just as ruthless as the rest of us."

I don't answer. I also don't admit I was kind of relieved when Geoff told me the real reason Griffin insisted we get married. I will never forgive him for dragging O2 into his scheme. But the Greg Latham ultimatum explains why Griffin blackmailed me into this situation instead of making me fight him in court.

He wants to prove himself to his father, just like he wanted to prove himself to the Reapers when he made that sex bet over me. Yet another thing I got to feel stupid about after that New Year's Eve.

I'd gone back to the roadhouse the next day and tried to work a shift. But Allie wasn't there, and the other servers took mean-girl joy in recounting how they'd all conspired to help Griffin get in my shorts. They teased me so badly, I ended up quitting halfway through my shift.

"How much did Geoff offer you not to marry me?" Griffin asks, pulling me from that memory.

I don't bother to ask how he knew Geoff had made an offer. Clearly, the Lathams grew up with the same rule book. I just answer, "A lot."

"And what did you say?" We're not touching, but his gaze presses into my skin.

"That my daughter's happiness has no price."

The smirk becomes a grin. "Good job."

Secrets & Lies. That should be the name of the nighttime drama I've somehow fallen into.

I heave a weary sigh and ask, "Could you show me to my room? I'm exhausted."

"Sure," he answers. "Follow me."

He leads me to a door on the opposite side of the landing, and my heart sinks.

O2 has always been fiercely independent. No running into my room because she's had a nightmare, ever. Maybe that's something else she gets from her father. But I don't like being so far away from her in the house.

"Could you put me in a room closer to O2?"

He regards me with a bland look. "Not unless you want her to hear the sounds you make while you fulfill the second part of our agreement."

My heart drops.

And he opens the door to a large primary bedroom.

Then he says, "Strip."

CHAPTER 29
BERNICE

I'D SOMEHOW LET HIM LULL ME INTO A FALSE SENSE OF comfort.

He made me ask him two questions during that Monday morning meeting: *What do you want from me? What do I have to do to get my daughter back?*

And he answered, *"One: You will marry me. That's the first requirement for me allowing you to act as the mother of my child."*

I was so stunned by the enormity of the first part of the answer to those questions, I'd let it overshadow the rest.

And when he left me alone in that Benton suite with O2, I thought maybe I wouldn't have to honor it until after the wedding.

Tonight, at his father's house, I was wholly focused on pulling off the lie of our happy engagement. It hadn't even occurred to me to think about what he said after dropping that marriage bomb.

"And here's the second requirement: We fuck. Whenever I want you. Doesn't matter if you're bleeding."

Such crude words tacked on to the end of an already insane order to marry him.

No wonder I'd put it out of my head.

But entering the bedroom—the incredibly large bedroom that takes up the entire length of the house and obviously belongs to him—that second part of the agreement is all I can think about.

Behind me, the door closes, and he bites out, "Strip." Again.

My brain explodes with panic. It's been years since I had sex. Not months. *Years.* And the pandemic isn't necessarily to blame.

I'd tried going out with a few guys before the New York dating scene came to an abrupt stop. I'd even gotten far enough along in a couple of relationships where, after some grown-up discussion, we decided to try sleeping together.

Both times it had felt the same. Nice, safe, not Griff. Boring side-character sex. Exactly what I wanted.

Well, exactly what I should have wanted. Both relationships had petered out, with me forgetting to text back or being so busy they just stopped asking me to go out again.

Back then, I told myself, I just had to figure out how to prioritize dating better. But deep inside...deep inside, where I stored those ill-advised two weeks with the biker Rockstar, I secretly wondered if he'd ruined me.

If all sex, for the rest of my life, would feel like a dim shadow of what I experienced at the cabin.

And now...

Here I am.

I let out a shuddering breath and start to push the straps of the gorgeous emerald dress down my shoulders.

"Turn to face me." His voice is a soft command in the dimly lit room. "Let me see you."

Okay, deep breath.

I turn to face him as I strip. It's insane how good he looks in the blue summer suit with an open-collar shirt. The tattoos on his face have mysteriously disappeared. I'm assuming laser removal. But the rest of the tats are still there, and they somehow make for the perfect accessory to his business look.

Okay, question, God? Why would you give so much beauty to such an ruthless man? You would have thought all the booze and drugs would have caught up with him by now, but somehow, he's even more gorgeous than I remember.

He's chiseled mid-30s perfection staring at me.

Not chiseled perfection.

The monster's eyes burn with satisfaction while he watches me do his bidding.

But as I push the dress down, I'm deeply aware that my brick-house body now includes a tummy pooch from having a baby and twenty pounds of weight gain—at least.

Stop this, Bernice, a voice chides inside my head. *Stop worrying about your body. Stop admiring his.*

Don't think about the monster. Don't wonder at his looks. Just do as he says, and get through this.

"I'm not Red, you know," I tell him. "That was a character I put on because I was lost after my grandma died. You keep calling me

Red, but that woman was just something I did for tips. Really, I'm Boring Bernice. That's who you're marrying, who you probably don't really want to have sex with—Boring Bernice."

Silence. Then he says, "Bra and panties too."

Oh God...oh God...

How is this so much harder than getting thrown on a bed and spanked?

I do as he says, but I keep on talking, partly to try to convince him, but mostly to distract myself from the fact that I'm stripping completely naked.

"I get that you think this will balance some scale of justice. But it won't. It will only make things between us worse. It will only make me hate you."

This is technically a plea, but the last sentence comes out a vicious whisper.

"Are you threatening me?" he asks, his voice a soft knife.

"I'm trying to make you see reason," I correct. "I'm not that girl. Not anymore. And the only thing you're going to gain from doing this is a whole bunch of hate from me and a whole bunch of disappointment for yourself when you find out I have nothing in common with that woman you were so eager to mind-game."

"Hmmm..." He makes a considering sound, thrumming my heart with hope. But then he says, "I'll take my chances."

His decision slices through me, and all hope of avoiding this thing I've agreed to drains out of the exit wound.

"Now, do me a favor. Stop talking and get in the bed. Red or Bernice—I'm pretty sure you remember how I feel about having to tell you things twice."

Terrible, terrible words from a terrible, terrible man. Then he starts stripping out of his own clothes, mocking me with that devil beauty covered in so much ink. A shiver of anticipation goes through me—one I quickly quell.

I tell myself the same thing I did in the conference room when I decided to take his second offer.

This isn't the cabin. This is real life. You'll only have to have sex with him once. Then he'll leave you alone.

I hate-read so many articles about him in the weeks following that New Year's Eve, trying to understand, trying to reconcile what had happened.

Serious music magazines liked how he repped for the South with a mixture of dirty trap and a signature country croon, overlaid with the laid-back California sensibility of a Snoop Dogg.

Motorcycle magazines loved him for never forgetting his roots and wearing his Reapers vest or jacket whenever he went on stage —though, like most one-percenters, they were eager to note, he never talked about his MC to outsiders.

But nobody loved him more than men's magazines. I read mouth-breathing piece after piece about his rumored prowess with women, including a cover story written from the viewpoint of an anonymous groupie who managed to turn one night with him into a five-page piece.

One quote stuck with me through the years, as I tried to figure out why he played me like he did:

"G-Latham likes the chase, but he gets bored once he catches you. He's the kind of guy who gives you his full attention in bed, but when

he's done with you, it's like you never met. None of the other girls following the Outlaw Country Festival feel bad for me when he freezes me out at the next stop on the tour after charming me into bed two nights before. 'G-Latham's a pleasure you have to savor,' one of them tells me. 'Everybody knows if he sleeps with you once, he never wants to get with you again. He's just built for shiny and new things.'"

That quote echoes through my head as I stiffly place myself in the bed.

The issue, I'd decided, was that Red had been a perfect storm for the monster. A bet he could win, a challenge he could conquer, someone he could anonymously experiment on—like a scientist without any conscious.

So, all I have to do tonight is not be a challenge. I'll just lie here. Like a starfish. Then he'll get bored of me and move on—

Griffin drops into the bed beside me like a supple leopard. Eyes hooded. Muscles on arrogant display. His cock is a spear between his legs, standing and heavily veined.

He flicks his eyes over me lazily. Like he knows he's going to eat me but wants to play with me first.

Then he says, "You be on top."

I'm not Red, I'm not Red, I'm not. But I blink the same way I would have in the cabin, and I ask, "Are you serious?" in a voice that comes out sounding at least six years younger.

He just smirks and lies back. "Impress me."

The two words slosh over my skin like cold, dirty bathwater. The groupie had mentioned him saying the same thing to her. Like all women were jesters, hired to entertain.

Oh, hey, more mind-games.

I swallow a hard lump of bitterness and go back to my original plan. Don't be interesting. Don't give him any more of your upset to savor, like an appetizer for the full, humiliating meal.

"Condom?" I ask

He raises an eyebrow. "We're getting married, and we already have a kid."

I still. Before the pandemic, a sibling for O2 had been my main reason for dating. I was getting older, and I was ready for another child. I wasn't expecting dramatic levels of love like what Kyra and Olivia had with their husbands. I just wanted to settle down with someone dependable and have another kid—the planned and right way this time.

My stomach jumps at the possibility of getting another child to love with my whole heart out of this marriage of convenience.

But then I remind myself I'm not a silly girl anymore. I'm a woman, a mother, grown enough to know better.

"That's something we should actually talk about like adults," I answer Griffin. "Not while you're playing mind-games with me in bed."

To his credit, he doesn't deny it. He just plucks out a condom and rolls it on with expert quickness.

And then it's showtime.

Not really though. Red would have pulled out all the stops, pushed every button he had, and tried to make him laugh on top.

Boring Bernice just climbs on with a mission: Get this over with.

First order of business, I'm not aroused enough to take his full length without pain. And hell will freeze over before I ask him for the kind of foreplay he gave me at the cabin.

Instead of putting him straight in, like he's probably expecting, I push my sex against the underside of his cock to pin it to his ridiculous abs. I settle on top of the shaft, letting the rigid length part me from the top to the bottom of my fold.

Then I hold on to Griffin's shoulders and press my clit into his erection as I rub myself back and forth on it.

He watches me curiously but doesn't ask what I'm doing. He also doesn't bring his hands up to touch me on my hips or breasts, as most guys would in this position. He just folds his arms behind his head, a Greek god statue, enjoying the show.

I can only imagine how desperate and needy I look, masturbating myself on his erection. And I close my eyes, so I won't have to watch him watch me.

I focus on the sensations, and it doesn't take long after that. He feels amazing between my folds. He's catching my clit, my vaginal opening...he's so long, he even stimulating my back entrance.

Red rises up with a moan. She wants to tease him about how we never explored that space.

And I have to clamp my lips to keep from talking. To keep from becoming her again and getting myself in trouble.

I'm ready, anyway. I shove Red down and take a hold of Griffin's dick.

No, not Griffin's dick—a dick. It's just a dick. The same as a dildo. I keep my eyes closed, lift my hips, and blindly guide it to my entrance.

And I'm ready, but I'm not ready. The feel of it...the familiar stretch and burn as I slide down its length.

It's just a dick, but it fills me so perfectly.

Another moan escapes me. One of sweet anguish. I didn't...I couldn't let myself admit...how much I missed this.

Red wants me to tell him. She's begging to talk. But I can't let her. She'll ruin us.

I re-clamp my lips and undulate my hips until I find a rhythm on the flesh dildo.

Feels so good. Feels so good. I don't let Red talk, but whines and whimpers fall out as I rock my body into the sensations, and the ride becomes wetter and wetter.

I'm almost there....I'm so close when a dark voice asks, "Do you hate me?"

I grind my teeth. Yes, yes, I do. Most of all for talking. For refusing to let me pretend.

I ignore him and keep rocking my hips. Faster and faster. Maybe I can outrun his taunting.

But he finally touches me. Not to caress me or help me along, but to still my hips.

"Open your eyes. Answer me."

The sensations—the sensations I haven't felt in years begin to recede. No!

I'm like a drug addict being led on a string. I open my eyes, not because he tells me to, but because I have to keep going. I have to reach that star in the distance.

He was a lazy leopard when I closed my eyes. But now his dark blue gaze bores into mine, glittering with madness and triumph as he asks again. "Do you hate me? Do you hate me like you said you would?"

He already knows he's won, I realize. He's won the sex.

I stare down at him. Helpless and afraid of what he brings out in me—what he still brings out in me, despite everything that's happened.

And the unvarnished truth drops out of my mouth. "Yes, I hate you more than anyone else on this Earth. And I want you more than anyone else on this Earth. I want you to dominate me and choke me and do all those wrong things you did to me at the cabin. But you don't want me. You just want revenge. And that makes me hate you even more."

His eyes flare, flashing like blue bolts of lightning.

Then suddenly, I'm on my back. And his hand is at my throat, and I don't curse...I'm a good, boring girl. But there's no other way to describe it.

He's beast-fucking me, pinning me down to the bed as he takes me hard with his raging cock.

Yes, yes, this. My thighs spasm, and my nails scratch into his back. And then...And then...he squeezes that hand around my throat.

And the world becomes a silent scream. It's too much, it's too much. I blink out for a second, clawing at the line between unconsciousness and insanity.

But then I'm back. And Griffin's groaning like a wounded animal in my ear. His hips punch forward one more time, then he's shuddering, like he used to, releasing into the condom with violent force.

What was that? The question comes back at full roar as I lie underneath him with aftershocks popping off inside of me like fireworks.

I'm boneless. Unable to think. Or regret.

A happiness I'd forgotten—the happiness of completion—makes me feel like I'm glowing from head to toe.

But then he rolls off me and says, "Get out."

The two words fall out of the dark like acid rain.

"What?" I'm so far removed from the disassociation I wanted to pull over me like a numbing blanket when I got into bed with him. It doesn't even occur to me not to keep the confusion out of my voice.

"You heard me." He sounds like an animal. Something dark and starving that will kill anything that comes across its path. "Get out. I'm done with you."

My heart catches in my throat. And that's when I realize...

My plan...

It worked. He's done with me, throwing me away, just like I guessed he would.

But there's no joy as I climb out of his bed. Just shame—so much I can't form words to speak.

Stones replace the fireworks in my chest, battering at my heart. But I pull on my dress and do exactly as the monster says.

CHAPTER 30
GRIFFIN

I'M NOT A CUDDLER, BUT I WAKE UP WITH TWO ARMS wrapped around me from behind, two thighs nestled underneath mine, and a luscious pair of tits pressed into my back.

Just beyond the window, the lake sparkles under the morning sun.

"What are you doing, Red?" I ask with a warning tone.

"Ssh!" she answers. "Just lie there and let me little-spoon you. This is my favorite position."

"Your favorite position, huh?"

I twist in her arms and roll on top of her, grabbing hold of her wrists.

God, she's beautiful. Looking up at me with that wicked smile. I wipe it off with a kiss and punch forward—for once not worrying about a condom.

She doesn't fight me this morning, just gives in with a sweet whimper as her sopping-wet cunt swallows me whole.

I'm not a believer, like Waylon. But I'm in heaven as soon as I'm back inside her, riding her, subduing her. Making her mine.

"This is where you belong." I drill into her, but I can't get in deep enough.

A bad feeling chews up my chest. She's sand slipping through my hands, and my strokes become fast and desperate, trying to stop it.

"Griff..." she moans underneath me. Her body's even softer than I remember, but her voice is farther away. Fading.

And for some reason her hair is black now, instead of red.

Red...Red...Red...

I slow down with the sense that I shouldn't come. She's here now, but I'll lose her if she comes.

The realization comes too late, though. The coming orgasm ripples off my spine, even after I stop moving.

"Don't leave," I beg as my balls tighten up to shoot. "Red, stay."

"Griff..." she says again. Her voice is so far away, it could be mistaken for the wind blowing leaves into the lake.

"Red, don't le—"

I explode before I can finish begging her to stay.

And then I open my eyes for real.

There's no winter lake outside my windows. No wind blowing leaves.

No Red cuddled up behind me or underneath.

There's just a mess in my boxer briefs.

I wish I could say this is a first-time thing. But wet dreams—what I've been privately referring to as Red dreams—have been a problem ever since I kicked the woman claiming not to be her out of my bedroom a week ago.

I'd had a plan. A plan to punish her. To prove to her and me that she had no power over me. And I was so excited when she told me Red had been a lie. Maybe sex with Bernice, who claimed to be boring, would work the same way as with other girls. I'd fuck her, and that trusty dead inside feeling would steal over me.

But my plan didn't work.

That old-but-never-forgotten hunger reared up inside me as soon as I saw her new body. Curvier and changed by the child she'd carried inside of her. My child.

Putting her on top hadn't worked either. Being inside Red for the first time in years had felt like coming home—the opposite of dead chest. My entire body had lit up, letting me know I was truly alive.

And that made me realize how much I'd missed her. How much I still missed her, even after all this time. Even though she never showed up and kept a baby from me for years because she didn't think I was good.

Something worse than dead chest reared up inside of me as I lay there with her afterward. The realization that I was still 100% obsessed, 100% addicted to this woman.

She lied to me about Bernice. I wasn't bored at all. I just wanted more.

I still want more.

Okay, Griff, stop whining and go to work. I force myself out of bed, like I've done every morning since kicking her out.

And when that Death Buddha song "Count My Blessings" comes on the shower radio, I turn the fucking station.

ANOTHER ONE OF MY PLANS GETS DERAILED THAT Wednesday. So far, Red and Olivia have been absent when I leave for work—on purpose, I'm pretty sure.

We're not even married yet, and Red is playing that estranged-wife card like a pro. She and Olivia eat senior early bird early, so they're always done with dinner by the time I get home from work. And if somebody told me they caught Red watching from the window to make sure I was gone before getting Olivia up for breakfast, I'd be like, "Man, I believe you."

But today as I go downstairs, I catch a scent wafting into the foyer from the kitchen...a delicious and disturbingly familiar smell.

Unable to stop myself, I follow it—only to stop short when I see the scene in the kitchen.

Olivia's wearing a school uniform, for some reason. And she and Red are sitting at the little table in the open-plan kitchen eating fried chicken and pancakes.

With my brother.

They're laughing and talking, like they've known each other forever. But that comes to an abrupt halt when they look up to see me standing there.

"Hi, Dream Dad!" O2 chirps with a happy wave.

"Hi." I barely manage to grit the word out before turning to my brother to ask, "What are you doing here?"

Geoff just smiles, like it's a perfectly normal thing for him to visit me at my home. When it literally hasn't happened even once since I moved to Vegas.

"Mom mentioned that Nora Benton was able to score O2 a last-minute placement at Frederick Academy, and today is her first day of school."

I narrow my eyes. "It's still August. I thought school wasn't supposed to start until September—like, after Labor Day."

Geoff and Red look at me like I'm an idiot. But Olivia shouts, "I know! They start school too early here. Before my birthday. *I hate it.*"

"Sugar pie, stop this. You're going to love it," Red tells her.

She's great with kids. Probably great with all kids. I'll admit I was fucking with her when I gave her a choice about a condom. I knew she'd choose it.

But what if she hadn't? For the first time, I think beyond the wedding that will secure me the CEO position. And another kid... I can't say I find the idea completely distasteful. I mean, we're already in on one.

But then she holds up her pinky finger to Olivia and says, "Bet you Uncle Geoff and me won't be able to get a word in when we pick you up from school."

"Pinky bet!" Olivia agrees. She perks back up.

And I return to glaring at Geoff. "Why are you picking her up from school?"

Geoff smirks. "Mom said you hadn't arranged a car for Bernice yet, for some reason, so I came by to offer her a ride to and from school."

"Thank you again for this," Red tells him. "We really appreciate it. I'm not sure what I would have done without you offering to drive."

So I guess it's on me to point out the obvious. "You could have asked me."

Red has the nerve to look stunned. "Oh, I didn't think you'd be up for that...I mean, usually you're gone when we wake up, so I wasn't sure what time you had to be at work. And we haven't really talked about domestic responsibilities."

"I can take her," I say between clenched teeth. "And I can pick her up."

"Well, then, it looks like I'm not needed," Geoff says with another smirk—like I'm just amusing him to no end. "Good job, finally taking some responsibility, Griffin."

I grind my teeth. These are times I miss being an anonymous Reaper. I'd give anything to put my fist through his mouth without any consequences.

I have to settle for "Bye, Geoff" and watching him hard as he wishes Olivia a good first day of school, then leaves.

Red does not offer me any fried chicken and pancakes after he goes. Just grabs her purse off the counter and says, "I suppose we should get going."

"You don't think I can handle drop-off by myself?" I ask her.

"Oh, I..."

Her inability to answer that question lets me know that's exactly what she thinks.

I might wear a blazer over concert tees to work these days, but I'm still the Reaper who bet five figures I could bang the untouchable server behind the bar.

"C'mon," I tell Olivia.

And that's how I end up taking her to school by myself in my lifted, electric-blue Limited-Edition F-450. I even find a family friendly pop station on the Apple CarPlay.

I'm pretty proud of myself until Olivia asks, "Is Mom going to marry Uncle Geoff now instead of you? Is that why he kissed her?"

CHAPTER 31
GRIFFIN

I CAN COUNT ON ONE HAND THE NUMBER OF TIMES GEOFF has stopped by my office. And my numbers for stopping by his are even lower than that.

Once. And that one time is today.

His assistant, Dana, isn't at her outer desk when I come through, so there's nobody to tell me I can't go in. Not that it would have mattered. I would have barged right past her, no matter what she said, after what Olivia told me in the car.

I find out why Dana's not where she always is as soon as I charge through her boss's corner-office door.

"Dana! Dana! No. Listen to me."

Geoff's doing his king-of-the-jungle, pace-back-and-forth thing in front of his desk and yelling at her on the phone. "You can't quit! I'm not going to let you."

My brother looks frantic. He doesn't even double take when he sees me standing in his office for the first time ever. Just lowers the phone from his ear and says, "Not now, Griff."

Before snarling into the phone at Dana. "You've seen what I do to business rivals. Do you really think I'm going to let you quit without even two weeks' notice? Not that two weeks' notice would matter. You're not quitting on me!"

"Geoff," I say.

"I said, *not now*, Griff!" He yells before I can finish. "Get out!"

Then he turns his back on me to threaten Dana some more. "If you do not want to experience my *known* wrath—not to mention getting sued for breach of that iron-clad contract I made you sign —I suggest you get your ass back at your desk *where you belong*. Otherwise, I promise you I will—"

Geoff gets cut off from finishing that promise when I spin him around.

And punch him straight in his smug face.

MY DAD'S SEMI-RETIRED THESE DAYS, BUT AFTER SECURITY guards are called in to break up our fight, we're escorted into his rarely used corner office to wait for him like...well, like two top-level executives who got in a schoolyard fight in front of everyone in the C-suite.

The Reapers have lawlessness without consequences on lock. But before joining my MC I got hauled into plenty of offices for fighting: principal offices, retail security offices, sheriff offices, dad's office back when he was still in charge of Big Hill. So, I know how this goes.

But Geoff must have never gotten the "don't say shit to your enemy while waiting to get chewed out by an authority figure" memo. After we take our seats in the guest chairs in front of Dad's desk, he only stays quiet for a minute or two before he has to start in on me. "Is this how you plan to solve your problems when you're CEO of AudioNation?"

His right eye's already bruising up, with red marks above and below. I didn't just slam my fist into his face, I got in a few gut and side punches too before security came through. So he winces when he turns in his seat to ask me, "You're just going to punch everybody you have a problem with in the face without giving them a chance to explain?"

"There's nothing to explain," I grit out. "You kissed my wife in front of my daughter."

"She's not your wife yet, and how was I supposed to know your daughter could see the kitchen from the stairs? Besides..."

He mumbles something I don't quite hear.

"What did you say?"

"I only *tried* to kiss her. Mom told me Bernice was considering using a car ride service to get O2 to school. That's a terrible look for a Latham, but she was obviously unwilling to ask you. Adding that to how disappointed she looked at the party when I told her the full truth about your intentions, I sensed an opportunity."

I fist my hands on the arms of the chair, wanting to punch him all over again.

Geoff continues, "I thought she might be open to some extramarital activity—which I, of course, would have immediately reported back to you. It was my last-ditch effort to keep you from getting the CEO position. I figured, if I could blow up your engagement before you made it official next month, I could remove you as an obstacle in my path to CEO. But when I went in for the kiss, she pushed me away. And when I asked why she would remain faithful to a conniving user like you, her answer surprised me..."

Geoff looks off into the distance, like he's fallen deep into thought. *Now* he wants to stop talking?

I let out an irritated huff when I have to ask, "What did she say?"

He glances over at me, like he went somewhere else and didn't realize I was still there.

"She said she made you a promise, and once she makes a decision to do something, she never backs out."

She'd said the same thing to me when she showed up on the porch of my cabin. The memory warms my heart at first. But then I remember waiting in the lobby. For hours beyond our meet-up time because I trusted those words.

She promised me, I kept telling myself over and over again, all the way up until it was time for me to deliver the worst performance of my life because I went in with zero rehearsal.

And it didn't stop there. As soon as I finished taping my segment, instead of waiting until midnight to get one more piece of airtime, I rushed back to my place to ask the doorman if she'd come by.

"No. Sorry, Mr. Latham. But I promise, if she does, I'll send her right on up," the doorman answered with a look that was half-pity and half-confusion. Up until that point, he'd only had to deal with me telling him not to let girls I was done with know I was in the building if they came by.

She hadn't kept her promise. And she wasn't going to, I realized.

In the end, instead of going with Red to Colin Fairgood's New Year's Eve party, like I planned, I called in the Reapers and told them to bring over the only things that could numb the pain: girls, drugs, alcohol, and themselves for a party to end the year. I told Rowdy and Crash that only country music was allowed at the rager that night. Red hated country music.

Then I proceeded to get blitzed out of my mind. It hadn't been a White Christmas, as they call spending the holiday with cocaine. But it was a White New Year, for sure. And when two sober cuties asked if they could come back with me to my bedroom, I was like, "Sure, why not?"

Red wasn't the only one I could break the rules for, I told myself. Yes, she'd made me lose my mind temporarily, but I could get over her. Possibly tonight.

But even while being attended to by two dime pieces, I couldn't forget her. I couldn't come. No...not until I conjured up her image and imagined her watching me from the door.

"She also said I was a worse user than you if I was trying to kiss an almost-married woman just to get a CEO position," Geoff says, cutting into my memory of that New Year's Eve.

He chuffed. "I explained to her that it wasn't just a position. That it was about my due. What I deserved, after all the work I put in— but she just cut me off and said, 'He's your brother. And family comes first, over everything. Try loyalty.' Then she offered to make me her grandmother's fried chicken. And O2 came down, and Bernice acted like I was just visiting and I never tried to kiss her. All she needed was a 'bless your heart' and I would have been right back in Tennessee, where people think food and family solve everything."

"It doesn't," I agree, matching his cynical tone. "I don't know why she tried to use that brother argument on you. You never gave a shit about me. Then or now."

He looks over at me again, scrunching his forehead. "Is that what you think? That I don't give a shit about you? Is that why you signed with Stone River? Why you joined that motorcycle gang? Because you thought they were better brothers than me?"

I shake my head. What else would he expect me to think? "Dad sent me away, and you said *nothing*. You didn't call. You didn't text. And why are you bringing up Stone River when you were the one who said I wasn't good enough for a deal back then, just like you keep on saying I'm not good enough to be the AudioNation CEO?"

"I didn't say you weren't good enough," he sputters. "I said you *weren't ready*. I'd seen this industry eat people alive. And you were already messed up enough—not to mention running with the Reapers. I didn't want you to end up another statistic. Dead at an early age because I didn't pull the brakes. And as for abandoning you..."

He turns his head, as if he can't look me in the eye and say his next thing: "I felt bad when Mom left Dad for Merri, but I got three parents out of that deal. What happened with your mom— that was on a whole different level. And you were so pissed. I didn't know how to talk to you—how to help you. So I didn't do anything. That's the Dad in me, I guess. Business—I'm all over it. Relationships...I shut down."

Geoff lets out a heavy sigh. "But I guess I was wrong. About everything. You killed it as an artist and didn't get too caught up. And that brotherhood you still have going with the Reapers— even after you went legit and cleaned up your act? My branding people wish I could pull that mix of relatability and Q-factor off. But I don't bond with people like that. And you know, after what happened with Mindy."

Geoff goes quiet before admitting, "Work is all I have, man. That's the real reason I was willing to do whatever it took to win this CEO position. Not because I didn't think you were good enough. You're good enough. You've always been good enough."

Geoff rubs at his ribs. "I'll tell you something else. This answer to Dad's ultimatum is a slam dunk—not just because you're going to get the CEO position. That O2 is just like you used to be before Dad and Elodie divorced. And your wife's loyal, even when she doesn't have to be. This family you somehow managed to pull off...they're perfect for you. Right now, I'm not just pissed at you. I'm jealous."

I stare at my brother, looking at him in a new light for the first time in almost twenty years.

Geoff's confession has killed the bitter engine that's always revving in my belly when I'm in the same room as him. But I guess I have too much Dad in me too. I don't know what to say, so I don't say anything.

"Can I give you some advice, though?" Geoff asks, raising an eyebrow at me.

Honestly, it's been so long since we managed a civil conversation that wasn't about business, it feels like I'm rifling through a dusty Appropriate Responses file cabinet to come up with, "Sure."

It's still morning, but he looks all sorts of tired as he says, "She thinks you don't give two shits about her. She won't even ask you for a car to get the daughter you share to school. There's Latham withholding, and there's whatever the hell you're doing with Bernice. You're fucking this up. And my advice is, don't. Don't fuck it up."

There's a pain in my gut now. And it has nothing to do with the measly couple of punches Geoff managed to pull off after I started wailing on him.

"I hear you," I tell him.

Then I let the rare brotherly bonding vibe hang out for about five more seconds before I add, "Never try that shit with my wife again."

Geoff's usual smirk replaces all his sincerity. "She's not your wife ye—"

"Still a Reaper," I remind him. "I will have somebody shoot you point-blank in the face behind Dad's back, and act just as surprised as everybody else at the funeral."

Geoff grits his jaw. "Wow, this new era with you heading up AudioNation is going to be interesting."

We look at each other. Snort. Then burst out laughing for the first time since we were kids. Together.

But then I have to ask, "So wait, Dana quit?"

All amusement disappears from Geoff's eyes.

"She's trying to," he answers, his voice becoming hard as nails.

"What the hell is wrong with you two boys?" our father booms from his doorway before I can ask any follow-up questions.

And I guess Geoff did get that memo about getting in trouble for fighting. We both slump down in our seats, like good little hoodlums, when Dad comes into the office yelling.

CHAPTER 32
BERNICE

ALL OF A SUDDEN, GRIFFIN'S FATHER OF THE YEAR. IT starts with him volunteering to drop O2 off at school and escalates to him picking her up from Frederick Academy and dropping her off at home before heading back into downtown Vegas to finish his workday at AudioNation.

I'm pretty sure Griffin is one of those execs like Phantom who can make his own hours, but he's basically adding a third commute to his day. It's a heck of an extra effort to put in, and I'm doubtful he'll keep this up for more than a couple of days. Like that groupie told *TripleX* magazine, "G-Latham has zero attention span when it comes to anything outside of the Reapers and music."

But that article was from ten years ago, and to my surprise, Griffin keeps going.

By the third day of school, instead of watching something on Disney+ with me, O2's playing on matching Nintendo Switches with Griffin after dinner. O2 starts calling me "mom" instead of "mommy"—maybe to emulate the other kids at school or maybe because Griffin refers to me as "your mom" even when we're in the same room. But he starts calling her by her preferred nickname, O2 instead of Olivia. Like she's a human being—not just a chess piece to get back at me in become the CEO of AudioNation. And that weekend, when I finish my Saturday chores, I have to search all over until I find him and O2 in the rec room/gym in the basement.

I stop short and hover in the doorway when I see that he's teaching her how to play guitar on a gorgeous Gibson acoustic.

It's eerie to watch them like this. Father and daughter in a way I never would have imagined when I was living paycheck to paycheck in New York. He's holding down the chords on the fret while she strums, and he softly sings "Puff the Magic Dragon" to guide them along.

I stare at them from the open door, mesmerized by the scene. Will she pick up the instrument right away, like the secret daughter in *Forever My Girl*? I watched that movie between my fingers like a horror film when Olivia picked it out for our monthly Mom RomCom movie night with Allie back in Kentucky.

The answer to that question turns out to be no. O2 quickly grows frustrated when she tries to move on to the next step of holding the fret by herself and she can't get the first chord progression right.

"I hate this guitar! I'll never learn how to play it!" she wails.

Those dead-serious, big fat tears that kids cry when they can't pick up something like magic after one or two tries start rolling down her face. And, of course, she starts to push the expensive Gibson off her lap. We're still working on her not-breaking-our-things-when-you-get-frustrated skills.

I'm itching to step in at this point, but I hold myself back. This is the not-fun part of parenthood. What happens between all the Kingsbridge Loves Families poster ad campaign moments of school drop-offs, pool parties, and summer concerts on the community lawn.

To Griffin's credit, he doesn't yell at O2 about the guitar—just pulls it out of her lap and sets it aside. "Don't take your frustration out on the instrument, dude. I destroyed at least three guitars on my way to becoming semi-decent—but none of them were Gibsons."

O2 sniffles. "How long did it take you to learn?"

"Well, I started around sixteen—and I was like, twenty-two maybe before I could play and sing at the same time," he admits, scratching at his neck. Truth be told, my picking skills still aren't that great. I do my thing on stage cuz it looks dope, but my number-one guitar talent is finding the right touring and studio musicians to punch up the backing track."

I haven't played guitar in years—not since leaving the roadhouse behind.

But I let my presence be known when I step through the door and add, "You can also try patience and church. Pick a song and learn it. Then play it at church. Then pick another song and learn it and play it at church. That's how I figured out how to play the guitar after Cousin Kiki taught me the basics."

"This is *Sin City*. They don't have churches here," O2 informs me with the superior authority of an almost six-year-old.

"They have churches everywhere," I inform her back, laughing. "Las Vegas does have an ungodly reputation, but Sin City is just a nickname."

Griffin glances at me, then gives O2 a thoughtful look. "I'll admit, that learn and perform method does work if you've got any kind of ego at all—and you're my kid, so I'm assuming you do. Tell you what, I've got a four-month residency scheduled at the Benton, starting in January. We could figure out a song for you to play— something real simple—and you could come on stage and sing it with me."

"Really?" O2 asks.

"I don't kid around about performance guarantees—that's how you get sued. But you have to learn the song top to bottom— vocals too. Something current too. 'Puff the Magic Dragon' isn't a good look for me."

"Oh my goodness, thank you, Dream Dad, thank you!"

O2 throws her arms around his neck. And she spends pretty much the rest of the weekend learning a simple tune by her favorite pop act, sasha X kasha.

And I spend the weekend feeling increasingly alarmed.

This is why I decide to talk to Griffin instead of ignoring him, like I usually do, when he walks into the kitchen that following Monday.

He stops, glances at the empty table. "Where's O2?"

"It's actually Labor Day, so no school," I answer. "Whitney and her wife picked her up about an hour ago to have breakfast at the Kingsbridge Club and get her started on what Merri called her long-overdue formal instruction. If I'd only known she was going to have a golf pro as a sort-of grandma, I would have done my due diligence."

I chuckle, trying to spark some camaraderie.

But Griffin just shifts awkwardly and glances at the coffee pot.

"Do you want some coffee?" I ask, remembering he's gotten in the habit of pouring a cup into an insulated AudioNation travel mug before he takes O2 to school. "I could make you something too. Bacon and eggs. Anything you want."

He glances around, like he's wondering if he's fallen into an alternate universe. Which is fair. This is a 180-degree switch from the almost total silent treatment we've been giving each other since the night he kicked me out of his room.

"Plus, I was hoping you and I could talk," I add softly, laying all my cards on the table. "About O2."

He shifts again and looks toward the door. Like he'd rather eat bees than spend another moment here talking with me.

This is what I wanted. A true marriage of convenience, where the monster ignored me and let me fade back into side character mode. But a wave of rejection washes over me. Does he really think I'm too boring to talk to or even deal with now?

"Uh, sure, I guess." He sounds about as enthusiastic as a cow selling burgers. "Just the coffee, though. I don't do that other thing anymore."

"Bacon and eggs?" I ask as I take his AudioNation mug out of the dishwasher. I don't realize I've still got his coffee preferences memorized until I automatically add cream to his pour without a second thought.

"Breakfast," he corrects, taking a seat at the kitchen table. "Started intermittent fasting toward the beginning of the pandemic."

I wince as I set his travel mug down in front of him and take a seat with my own cup of coffee. "So when you're in the spotlight, you pretty much have to keep on changing up diets?"

"Yes, until you die," he answers gravely. "It's in the 'I Wanna be Famous' contract all us cut-up musicians have to sign with the devil. That dude freaking loves diets. I don't know why."

I nearly fall out at his unexpected joke. I forgot about that dry humor of his. How much he made me laugh during those two weeks at his dad's cabin. How much we cracked each other up.

But then I remember everything that came after that...New Year's Eve.

And those memories chase away the laughter.

So, I set my coffee aside and get straight to the point. "Listen, I need you to understand something about O2's birth."

He sets his coffee aside too. "I'm listening."

I take a deep breath and start giving him the speech I've been practicing in my head all weekend. "We both know the circumstances around her conception. I made an out-of-character decision—quite a few out-of-character decisions. Decisions that could not be undone once my real character took back over. I was living in New York at the time, so I could have chosen a different path. But I chose not to end my pregnancy because of the mistake I made by pretending to be somebody I wasn't."

"You're telling me Red was a mistake?" Griffin's blue eyes darken, along with his expression. "That everything you did when you were pretending to be her was a mistake?"

"No, I'd never call conceiving our daughter a mistake," I answer. "But you have no idea how alone I felt when I made the decision to keep O2. The event planning company I was interning at fired me when they found out I was pregnant. And I felt too ashamed to come home to my people but too much a stranger to let myself be a burden to anybody in New York. That's why I named her after Olivia Glendaver—why I call my baby O2, even when my former boss isn't around. That generous woman gave me everything I needed to survive when all I asked for was a job. And I truly do believe she was sent from heaven above to help me through."

I feel a little weepy with gratitude, remembering everything that came after landing that miracle job. "I was so scared, though. *So scared.* And you need to understand that I count O2 being born healthy as the luckiest day of my life—especially considering all the mistakes that led to her conception. And I know you're not religious, but when I held that beautiful baby in my arms, I promised God then and there that I would love her with everything I've got. That I would *protect* her with everything I've got."

I pause, hoping that Griffin understands what I'm trying to say.

But he immediately goes on the defensive. "Are you kidding me? You're spinning this sad story to me, but you didn't *have* to be alone. I'm a goddamn music star, a Latham, and a Reaper. Whatever you needed, I could have provided. *Anything!* But you never gave me that chance. Why? Because you were trying to protect her from me? That's bullshit."

I'd cast myself in the role of above-it-all mother goddess when I imagined us having this talk. But his reaction sets my brain on fire.

How could he not see things from my point of view after what happened on New Year's Eve? After he basically blackmailed me into marriage—

Okay, Bernice. Stop. Don't go there.

I hold up my hands and reel myself back in from the tidal pool of resentment swirling inside of me. Yelling at Griffin will not help my little girl.

I re-calm my voice and just level with him. "I don't know why you're suddenly so interested in being a dad to O2. But if this is another game you're playing, some challenge you're trying to win to prove something to your brother or me, then you need to stop it right now. O2 is not a shiny guitar you can practice whenever you feel like it. She's clever beyond her years, but she is a child. And she's tough. But that doesn't mean she won't be hurt if you throw her away once you get bored, like you did with me."

"I'm not trying to hurt her," he starts to yell.

But then he too visibly decides to calm down. When he speaks next, his reasonable tone matches mine. "She asked me if you were going to marry Geoff instead of me. Because she saw him try to kiss you when she was on the stairs."

My stomach drops. "She saw that? But—"

"I know," he says before I can explain what really happened. "Geoff and I had words...after I punched him. And he told me you told him to kick rocks. But O2 said something else that got to me. She said she wanted me to be her Dream Dad, and in her dreams I actually spent time with her. She said that was the nicest thing about Geoff's visit. That he ate breakfast with her and asked her questions—like Uncle Phantom does with his kids. I guess that's something she always wanted for herself."

"She told you that?" I fret my hands, and the guilt I've been carrying since O2's birth twists in my stomach. "As a single mom, I wanted to be everything for my daughter. I tried to be everything for her. But I guess there were some holes I just couldn't fill. But I'll talk to her. I'll explain that you're not that kind of dad."

"Or you could let me fill the holes you can't," he says, looking down at his own hands. "I want to do that for her. I want to be a dream dad."

He raises his eyes to meet mine. "I'm not using her—I just want to be a good dad. And the thing is, I don't know how to do that, exactly, but this week she's been helping me figure it out."

His words...they're beautiful. But I'm so confused.

"You want to be a good dad now," I repeat. "What happened to not wanting to be someone's eighteen-year child support check?"

He shrugs and throws me a blasé smile. "You never asked for child support—even when you really needed it. I guess that changed my mind. Good job, Red."

He's joking, but I don't laugh.

I hold his gaze until the humor fades from his eyes. Then, I inform him, "You don't go from monster who's willing to kidnap a little girl for revenge and a CEO position to wanting to be a good dad overnight."

He shifts uncomfortably and lifts in his seat as if he's thinking about running from this conversation. But then he resettles.

"The thing is, I used to be like O2. I used to hug people and stay optimistic, even when bad shit was going down. I loved my family, and yeah, they weren't perfect, but they were mine. And after my mom got full custody and moved us to California, instead of getting bummed about it, I tried to be the one thing not going wrong in the life that wasn't turning out the way she wanted it to.

I guess you could say I was trying to be her Dream Kid. But then she started drinking on another level. Calling me names..."

We're at a kitchen table in a beautiful house, drinking coffee. But he shivers and lets out a pained breath like we're in a dark basement. "Child support check."

He looks sightlessly out the kitchen's window. "That's what my mom called me. To my face. She said that was the only reason she fought for full custody. She was kind of mean when she got drunk. But I kept trying..."

A smile ghosts across his lips, like he's attempting to find this amusing but can't quite pull it off. "I kept trying to be a Dream Kid. I took care of her. Cooked for her. Kept the apartment clean and my grades up. Kicked the guys she brought home out of our apartment when she was done with them. But it wasn't enough. She asked my father for a lump sum alimony and child support payment. He thought he was getting a good deal, but he's the one who ended up screwed. The final check cleared, and she bounced back to France—that's where she's from. She left me with my dad —like I was a dog she needed to re-home. Basically destroyed that kid who used to be like O2. I was pissed. Too pissed off. And instead of stepping up, my dad sent me away to the first of a lot of boarding schools. After that, I vowed that parent-child support check thing would never be me—on either side of the equation."

He finally meets my eyes. "So the child support thing, it wasn't about you—or even the hypothetical kid. It was about me. Finding out about O2 didn't just make me mad. It scared me shitless. Because the truth is, I don't know how to be a Dream Dad. Or even a decent parent. So I'm just doing stuff with her, and letting her lead, and hoping that's enough to not fuck this up."

"Oh Griffin…" It's hard to reconcile the monster I thought he was on New Year's Eve with the man sitting across from me.

He's not a Reaper at this moment. Not a music star. Or even the future CEO of AudioNation. He's just a guy with a really shitty childhood, trying to figure out how to be the best dad he can.

Instead of telling him to back off like I planned, I take a hold of his hands. "A lot of being a good parent is just being there. This is a great turnaround. O2 is so happy right now—so happy it scares me. I'm just glad your intentions are pure, and you're not trying to hurt her."

"I'm not ever trying to hurt her. I promise you that," He squeezes my hands back. "And, I'm sorry for stealing her. I've only been Dream Dad-ing for a week and I'm seeing how fucked up that was. I'm surprised you didn't try to shoot me when I walked into that room."

Weirdly, I find myself chuffing at my worst memory. "They don't let you carry firearms on planes. And when I asked Phantom about having a guy meet me with one in Vegas, he said I should take the meeting as opposed to signing up for guaranteed jail time. He wasn't Team Griffin, but he did have some questions about me deciding to keep O2 from you all this time."

Now it's my turn to shift awkwardly in my seat. "I'm sorry for doing that by the way. I was basing the decision on things that happened six years ago. But that wasn't fair to you or O2. And I can see you're at least trying to change for the better. So, um, sorry."

It's not the best apology ever. It doesn't erase all the years Griffin missed. But a warmth rises between us. One I haven't felt since we were two rebels smoking doobies all day on a couch as opposed to visiting our families for the holidays.

I get up to clear the coffee cups. "Well, I know you've got to get to work. And I've got a thousand more things to plan for the wedding—"

"What did you mean earlier about me throwing you away when I got bored with you?" he asks out of the blue. "Is that really what you think happened?"

I pause and set the undrunk cups of coffee on the counter instead of pouring them out.

"What do you call what happened when we"—I clear my throat—"attended to the second part of the agreement?"

"The opposite," he answers, standing up.

I turn and shake my head at him. "What do you mean the opposite? You basically threw me out of your—"

I stop myself and hold up my hands.

"You know what, I refuse—simply refuse to undo this progress. We both made mistakes in the past. We both lied about who we were. But we can't change the past. So hopefully, we can provide a stable home for O2 by continuing into the future with a marriage based on civility and respect."

It's a beautiful, unplanned speech. And I'm really proud of myself for taking the high road to forgiveness.

But Griffin just screws up his face. "Your vision of marriage sounds boring. Like the most boring marriage on Earth, if I'm being honest."

I stiffen. "What are you trying to say? That you want to go back to playing mind-games and never being able to trust each other?"

"I'm cool with that after school special conversation we just had," Griffin answers. "But I think you might be under the wrong impression about my intentions toward you. Toward this marriage."

He stands up himself. "I don't just want to be a Dream Dad. I want to be a Dream Husband."

My throat dries. "A Dream Husband?" I wonder but can't produce enough saliva to ask what he means by that.

And he comes to loom over me. The tattooed Reaper in a business suit.

Suddenly, I'm having trouble breathing. "Griffin? What are you doing?"

"Trying not to fuck this up," he answers.

Then his mouth crashes down on mine.

CHAPTER 33
BERNICE

WE'RE KISSING...WE'RE KISSING...OUR LIPS CRASHING, tongues tangling, his mouth claiming mine.

But then he pulls back and asks, "You still want two more babies? Does your Dream Husband fuck you raw? Breed you?"

My head spins at his filthy words, but my body....

I thought wanting just sex with him was bad. A bone-deep biological ache pierces my core at his question, makes my sex clench for him. This is yet another secret desire he's managed to excavate.

"Yes," falls out of my mouth, broken and desperate before doubts like "too soon!," "can't trust him..." and "is this real?" can catch up with it.

Something switches off behind his gaze. He looks down, and when he looks back up, he's the wolf from the cabin.

I'm not that girl. How many times since arriving in this house have I reminded him that I'm not Red?

But suddenly I'm running. Daring him to catch me.

There's no confusion on his part this time, though. No chance to hide for me. He's on me in an instant. I only make it to the grand foyer before he catches me and throws me down on the nearest couch.

He yanks at my pajama bottoms, pulling them off with my undies as a unit and tossing them over his shoulder.

His breaths are coming out in growling pants. Like a predator owed a meal. But he takes a moment to stare at the sex he's stripped bare. I look too, and oh God...it's already glistening with need.

That's the last sight of myself I get to have before he falls on top of me. His lips recapture mine. His erection is a living, breathing animal between my legs, searching for my heat.

Then he thrusts upward, taking me in one hard punch. So rough, but I'm slippery with need. I stretch and moan around his invasion.

"You think I kicked you out because I got bored with you?" He pants against my mouth. "Just the opposite, baby. You scared the hell out of me that night...."

He down shifts, pressing my thighs open even wider. Sinking in even deeper.

"Do you know how many women I fucked to try to forget this? How hard I chased even an ounce of the pleasure I feel when I'm inside you like this?" he asks. "Do you have any idea how bad you wrecked me that night?"

He doesn't give me a chance to answer that question. Just lifts up and spears me with his erection, powering into my sex, like it's something he owns. Like it's something he's reclaiming.

*He's taking me raw...*his back muscles ripple under my fingers, as he rides me like a beast god. And I can't stay quiet. I start confessing as well. "I tried to chase it too. I was afraid too...afraid you ruined me for other guys."

He lets out a harsh laugh. "You think I ruined you? Baby, you have no idea how bad I fought for control that night. I thought I had it all figured out when I let you get on top. But then you started scrubbing this wet cunt over my cock, and I couldn't think about revenge. I couldn't think about control. All I could do is try not to spray with my baby, Red, finally getting her turn on top. You said you're not her. And you're right. You're worse. You're worse. All you had to do was tell me what you wanted, and I couldn't not give it to you."

His words from our first morning at the cabin come back to haunt me. *I can get you anything you need. Anything. All you have to do is ask.*

"Griff!" I cry out brokenly. I'm not Red, but I revert back to the name I called him at the cabin. "Please, make me come. Ruin me again. Make me forget New Year's Eve. Please…"

He pauses. His hips almost stuttering to a stop. But then he gathers me in his arms and buries his face in my neck.

He flexes in between my legs, pinning my hips down. Then he takes me hard. Promptly granting my request? Roughly reclaiming me? Completely dominating me? Mercilessly ruining me for any other?

All of the above.

No more explanations. No more dirty talk. The grand foyer fills with the sound of his body smacking wetly into mine, riding me for broke.

All I can do is hold on and whimper against his neck. A subway train is bearing down on me, but I'm rooted to the tracks. He pumps into me faster and faster, his thrusts becoming desperate and sloppy.

"Fuck, take this cock, Red. Forget everything that came before it. Take this baby I'm going to give you. Take it!" He cuts off with a loud grunt and punches up one last time.

And that subway train plows straight into me, exploding me into stars.

This transcendent orgasm. This soul-deep relief. It's like nothing I've ever known. It doesn't matter that it's still morning time, I float in the night like wind and dreams.

But eventually...

Eventually, I have to come down. And when I do, I find myself wrapped around him like a koala. His hips are convulsing into mine as he releases into me. Spurt after spurt, until finally he collapses, heavy between my legs.

I lost control again. So did he. We both did. And I think we might have ruined the couch. There's so much cum...his release has overflowed my sex.

Still, we lie there in the mess we made, breathing together, holding on to each other like tsunami survivors.

But then he rears up, forcing me to release him.

My stomach cramps as he rises to his feet above me. Is this the part where he tells me to get out again? Or maybe he'll just leave, since this is a common space?

He does leave. I'm right about that. But first he scoops me up in his arms. And I guess that twenty pounds really isn't as big a deal as I thought. He carries me with him upstairs, as if I weigh nothing.

No, he doesn't kick me out. He lays me down on his bed like treasure found.

Then he covers me like a blanket and reminds me of one of the major truths he told me at that cabin. He really does have a very short refractory period.

CHAPTER 34
GRIFFIN

STILL NOT A CUDDLER. BUT AFTER TAKING RED LIKE HER hunter, then making love to her like her sheep, I draw her into my arms just to keep from letting her go.

"I think I have a '90s rapper problem," I tell her, settling my head in the crook of her shoulder.

"What?" She sounds both amused a confused.

"You know how those '90s guys all started out angry because most of them were from these backgrounds that were just messed the hell up. Their fans were like, 'Yeah, so-and-so should be pissed. Look at where they came from.' But then those rappers became popular, got rich, bought cars and houses—started living their best lives. But they were still trying to come out with these pissed-off albums, and that's when it was all over for them. Because people were like, 'You *still* mad, bro? Why? Your life looks pretty great. Seriously maybe you need to deal with your shit instead of trying to come at us with the same thing every time.'"

She goes quiet. I know I'm not making much sense. This is why I usually don't do this talking shit.

But then she translates what I'm trying to say perfectly. "You're anger was valid. But now you're wondering if it's past its due date."

This woman...

How the fuck did I let her go? Even for those few six hours I gave her to go home and pack an overnight bag before meeting me back at my place?

Regret fills me up as I try to explain myself to her. "I know I'm fucked up. I hold onto stuff. My mom abandoning me. My dad punting me off to boarding school. My brother not giving me a record deal. If I'm being honest, spite fuels a lot of my drive. Achieving the fame my mom didn't. Rebelling against my dad by joining the Reapers. Scrapping with Geoff over this CEO position. I'm always trying to prove I'm worth not leaving behind, worth believing in—I'm always trying to destroy people who hurt me."

This is the truth finally. A truth I've never told anyone. Not even myself. But I examine the wound. For her.

"I...I wish New Year's Eve had gone differently," I tell her. That's true. Her not showing up triggered the hell out of me. I gave her my trust, and she didn't show up.

But the regret for the things I did after is also true. So, I focus on that. "And I'm sorry. I'm sorry for all of it. For trying to destroy you. "

I tighten my arms around her. "I'm sorry for letting you think that sex the other night didn't blow my mind. I'm sorry...I'm sorry for all of it."

She's quiet. For so long this time, I wonder if she's fallen asleep during my long ramble. But then she says, "Neither of us had a stable set of parents, growing up. And we were both so lost when we met. I was reeling from my grandma's death, and you were trying to hang on to your Reaper Rockstar despite wanting to do something different."

She reaches up and lay her hand over the back of mine. "I think maybe that makes it hard for both of us to trust that anything good that happens is going to last. Thank you for explaining your side of things to me. I um...I wish New Year's Eve had gone differently too. But I think I'm beginning to understand what happened —why both of us did the things we did...."

She sucks in a deep inhale, and breathes out, "I'm sorry for keeping O2 from you. I should have done it the right way from the start. I found out who you really were, and I told myself it was to protect her. But I watched you change and get better from afar. I suspected you weren't the monster I made you out to be, and I still didn't tell you. If I'm being honest, I was afraid. Afraid that you'd put me back under your spell and destroy me."

"So, we were both afraid." I let out my breath, releasing some more of the bitterness I've been carrying since that night. "We scared each other. Then and now."

"Yes," she agrees. "But we can't go on like this..."

I still. Is she going to try to break up with me? Did being vulnerable with her actually lead her to believe that was an option on the table?

"I know we have to get married in order for you to receive the CEO position," she continues, interrupting my fear tornado. "But O2 deserves parents who aren't chaotic. We can't change the past. But we need to figure out how to move forward past all the hurt, without triggering each other and playing mind-games."

Oh, she's not trying to break up. The fear recedes. A little bit. And an idea occurs to me. "It all comes down to that New Year's Eve. That's what destroyed us. So how about we go back to that morning, and we agree to meet up in six years, not six hours. Actually, about two months shy of six years…"

She shifts in my arms. "I don't understand."

"You said it yourself," I answer. "We can't change the past. So why don't we rewrite it?

"Red, let's pretend we're back in that cabin…" I turn her over in my arms and clasps my hands around both of hers. "Meet me in six years. Not at my place in Nashville. But at an altar in Vegas. We'll get married. You'll be my Dream Wife and a Dream Mother to our children, and I'll work like hell to not only be a Dream Dad, but also a Dream Husband. We'll be the parents we never had. And we'll…"

I cup her face. "We'll *trust* each other. We'll trust each other from now on? How does that sound?"

"How does that sound?" she repeats, her voice a little off-kilter.

I can see all the doubts and fears swirling in her eyes. And I wonder if I should back off like a decent, non-fucked up human being. Give her some room and space. Tell her everything—not just the stuff she needed to hear to stop hating me.

But then she says, "Okay."

Her face breaks out into that wicked grin I missed so much, and she tells me like I told her before our first shot at re I'll take my chances."

She'll take her chances. This woman—she's teasing me. She's challenging me.

She's laughing at me as I put her underneath me and punish her for that—but nothing else.

We've wiped the slate clean and agreed, whatever future we have, it's going to be together.

CHAPTER 35
O2

O2 IS PRETTY SURE HER DAD AND MOM DON'T HATE EACH other anymore.

Mom let her stay overnight with her grandmas. And when Grandma Whitney drops her off, her parents are nowhere to be seen, but there's loud heavy metal music blasting.

"What in the world?" Grandma Whitney asks.

They find O2's parents lying on the floor together in the rec room, holding hands and looking up at the ceiling.

"What are you doing?" Grandma Whitney asks them over the music.

"Listening," Mom shouts back. "Want to join us?"

Grandma Whitney says, "No thank you." In that way grown-ups do when you ask them to come outside and play in the mud.

O2 loves playing in the mud after a Kentucky rain, but in this case, she has to agree.

"I don't like this music!" she yells over the singer screaming about love.

"You should!" her dad yells back.

Then her parents fall out laughing for reasons O2 doesn't understand.

And when she leaves them in the room to listen to their weird music, they're still holding hands.

More clues they might not hate each other pile up over the coming days.

The next day, Dad decides he does do breakfast after all.

And when he gets up from the table to drive O2 to school, he kisses her mom. Right on the mouth!

And there's more kissing where that came from. They kiss that morning and then again that night when Dad gets home from work. And sometimes they kiss instead of saying hi when they pass each other in the house.

And when O2 says, "Ew!" they just laugh and give each other more kisses.

That's another clue that maybe they don't hate each other like they used to when O2 and her mom first came to Las Vegas.

Her parents start hugging a lot too. Sometimes, when her mom's cooking, her dad comes into the kitchen just to wrap his arms around her waist and watch her make dinner with his chin on her shoulder. And sometimes when O2 comes downstairs to get a glass of water, they're sitting on the couch in the entertainment room, hugged up together, and just talking instead of watching TV.

Her mom and dad barely spoke to each other before, but now they're always talking, even after dinner when they could be watching TV or playing on their iPads.

"Why do you two have to talk so much?" O2 complains when her mom says she has to finish her conversation with Dad before they can all watch the new Little Pony movie on Netflix.

Dad just laughs. "We've got a lot of catching up to do."

And that's when O2 decides to ask them flat out, "Do you two not hate each other now?"

Her parents exchange soft smiles. Then her mom explains, "We never hated each other. We just had to get out of our own way and remember that."

Then more kisses. O2 makes sure to say "Ew!" a bunch of times. She even falls to the floor and dramatically clutches at her throat, so they know just how disgusted she is by their icky behavior.

But the truth is, she kind of loves her parents not hating each other.

She hopes they stay this way forever.

CHAPTER 36
BERNICE

"SO WHAT DO YOU WANT ME TO DO WITH YOUR HAIR?" THE stylist at the Benton Grand's salon asks for our pre-wedding consultation appointment.

This is the first time anybody's asked me this question in years.

Box braids became my go-to in New York. Practical and long-lasting, with zero upkeep—pretty much the perfect do for a busy mother.

But the past few weeks have brought all sorts of changes to my routine.

Crazy rough sex at night, followed by gentle good-morning loving before I make breakfast for the three of us and Griff takes O2 to school. Weekends filled with family outings and me reading ebooks by the pool while O2 and Griff splash and swam. Lots of dirty words and sweet baby making in between.

I keep waiting for Griff to get bored again.

"Do you ever miss the lifestyle that came with being a big music star?" I asked during one of our morning sleep-ins when he little-spooned me before I could little-spoon him.

"Nah," he answered without a second of hesitation. "Living like that was about dumping shit into holes that couldn't be filled. You and O2 are the opposite of that."

It was a strange way to put it, but I understood.

And I feel glowy now as I look at myself in the mirror. The opposite of boring. Not because I'm trying to pretend I'm someone I'm not, but because I'm finally just being the person I want to be.

"We specialize in extensions, but we have a braider available on an as-needed basis," the stylist tells me. "If you want, we can call her in to give you an updo for the wedding."

Yes, braids would be still the most practical choice for me. But hmm...I turn my head from left to right. "If I wanted to try something new today, do you think you could squeeze me in?"

"Sure," she answers with a glance toward Whitney, who's sitting in a chair right next to Nora Benton herself, the self-dubbed Irish Queen of Vegas.

"What were you thinking?" the stylist asks me.

Griff might still call me Red, but maybe Bernice isn't as boring as I thought after all.

I smile at the stylist in the mirror and tell her exactly what I want.

"Oh, look at you! I love your hair!" Whitney calls out when I come into the nail section of the salon, looking shiny and brand-new.

Apparently, Greg Latham arrived while the stylist was finishing up my do. He and Whitney are doing their ex-besties routine again—sitting in side-by-side spa chairs, with an empty spot on each side.

"Grandpa! Grandpa!" O2 calls out, running to jump into the spa chair beside him. "You're getting your nails done too?"

"Little granddaughter, you do not want to see how bad these hooves would be if I didn't get them buffed and sanded every two weeks. And my favorite ex-wife still insists I maintain well-groomed nails."

"That's right!" Whitney agrees as I drop into the spa seat beside hers. But then she loudly whispers behind her hand, "Plus, Merri refuses to do any of this girly stuff with me."

I just laugh and ask Greg, "How was your trip out to Rhode Island? We missed you at the Sunday pool party."

"Unproductive," Greg grumbles. "But Whitney, tell Bernie about my fundraiser idea while I catch up with my favorite granddaughter."

"I'm you're only granddaughter!" O2 points out with a teasing laugh.

"Yes, she is," Whitney mutters. "Since Geoff refuses to ask out any of the lovely women I keep trying to set him up with."

You know I'm back with Tennessee folk because my A++ Southern Gossip Detector fires all the way back up. Since I can't think of a tactful way to ask Whitney about the pregnant wife

Griff mentioned Geoff having when we first met, I make a mental note to get the full story from my future husband when I see him back at home tonight.

But Whitney doesn't dwell on the subject too long. She switches from dissatisfied mother to socialite-with-an-agenda in the next instant.

"Anyway, Greg was just telling me that I should ask for your help with the Latham Foundation Christmas fundraiser. He reminded me about how Griffie bragged about you being a talented event planner."

I jolt a little. "He told you that?"

"Are you not a talented event planner?"

I shake my head. "No, I am. Sort of. I mean, I hadn't really given it any consideration lately. Really, I'm just trying to get past the wedding. But I was on that path before I got back into nursing when O2 was born. I guess I'm just…"

The manicurists arrive, and I use the small interruption to figure out how I'm feeling right now. I mean, yes, Griff and I have agreed to make it work. And since deciding to let go of the past, we're getting along better than ever. A few days ago, I even came up for an idea to incorporate O2's birthday into the wedding—one I'd need his help to pull off.

He not only agreed, he told me, "That event planning company missed out when they fired you."

Still…"I guess I find it hard to imagine him calling Greg while he was out of town to brag on me."

"Oh, not this week, dear—earlier. Griffie was so excited when he invited us all to meet you, even Geoff. He insisted we were going to love you—told us he'd never felt this way about a girl, and that he couldn't wait to marry you—apparently, you'd completely changed his mind on that particular subject." Whitney pauses to instruct her manicurist, "A light fall beige for both my feet and hands, please."

I think about getting the same thing before remembering my new hair. New hair—might as well get new nails too.

"Matte black, please," I tell my manicurist.

But then I turn right back to Whitney, "I'm so confused. I thought you had no idea we were coming to Greg's party."

"Oh, we did not know to expect you," Whitney assures me. "That was a *complete* surprise, I'll tell you that—just when you think he couldn't top those face tattoos at Thanksgiving."

Whitney lets out one of those Southern-lady laughs—the kind that makes it impossible to tell if she thinks Griff is delightful or a total stinker.

"I'm talking about that New Year's Eve when you were supposed to come to his concert at Stone River records. Of course, Greg and Geoff refused to go *there* to meet you. So they all agreed on Colin Fairgood's New Year's Eve party as neutral ground. But then Griffie texted and said you weren't coming after all."

If this was a conversation about anything else...*anything* else, this would be the part where I'd be saying things like, "What?" and "Shut the door."

But I'm so confused and stunned that I can only stare at her.

"We were all disappointed about not being able to meet you—everybody except Geoff. I swear, that son of mine can't find a nice thing to say in a field of sunflowers somedays. But the rest of us kept asking after you—at least until Christmas three years ago, when Griffie yelled at us that it wasn't going to happen, and he'd given up on finding you, so we should too."

The party is suddenly rewriting itself. Greg Latham asking if Griff had gotten a DNA test before planning the wedding this time. His easier-than-easy acceptance of O2 as his granddaughter. Whitney's delight at our reunion—like it was the perfect ending to a love story she'd been watching on TV....

"Why would he do that?" I ask her. "Tell you to come meet me that night?"

Whitney raises her eyebrows at me. "Can you not see that boy was heads over heels for you from the start? I mean, here he is, still insisting on marrying you as soon as possible, even after Greg took that silly ultimatum off the table and told the boys they'd have to start serving as joint CEO after Griffie's residency at the Benton."

It takes me several moments to process what she's saying. And even then, I feel compelled to verify.

"Wait, are you telling me Griff no longer needs to marry me to become the CEO of AudioNation?"

"No," Whitney answers. She seems confused by my confusion. "Greg became so angry with him after he got in that fight with Geoff, he decided it was more important that the boys learned to work together..."

She trails off when she sees the total blank on my face. And her eyes fill with concern. "Did Griffie really not tell you any of this?"

Now it's my turn to answer "No" as the happy cloud I've been floating around on begins to deflate.

We promised to trust each other going into the future. But he lied to me. He lied to me again.

Whitney and I don't talk much for the rest of the appointment.

And as soon as my nails are done, I grab my phone to call him— only to find a text from him already waiting.

GRIFF: *Hey, can you ask Whit to keep O2 for a bit? I'm at my old place. And I need you to come over here to give you something. Here's the address.*

SINCE GRIFF'S OLD BACHELOR PAD IS IN CITY CENTER, IT'S within walking distance from the Benton on the Strip. That means I have plenty of time to think. Too much time.

Why didn't he tell me about Greg removing the marriage condition? Why would he invite his family to meet me on the same night he showed me what a monster he could be?

I can't wrap my head around it, even after a twenty-minute walk through the busiest part of Las Vegas over bridges, up and down escalators, and shortcutting across as many air-conditioned hotel casino lobbies as I can find on the way to his condo.

The building's doorman smiles when I give him my name.

"Yes, he's expecting you. Go right on up."

I try and fail to smile back. That's the exact same thing his doorman in Nashville said that New Year's Eve.

The doorman tells me that the code for his penthouse is 1219. It's a familiar number that's been emblazoned on my mind since O2's conception.

12-19...December 19th... that was the day we met—the fateful day he asked me to stay...stay for Christmas.

Coincidence? It has to be. Doesn't it? I'm not sure of anything anymore.

My mind is a tightrope, with both the future and the past balancing on it as I punch in the code and go up in the elevator.

This elevator stops at the end of a single hallway leading to a pair of double doors. And I can already hear loud country music blasting on the other side of them.

The urge to run rears up inside of me as memories of that night explode like buried mines in my head.

But I don't run. I need answers. I *deserve* answers...even if that's the same thing I told myself that New Year's Eve.

I ring the doorbell anyway.

And I let out a small sigh of relief when a tall man answers the door—one I recognize. "Hi, Waylon."

Waylon grins. "Hey, Red—thought you were the pizza. C'mon back."

Waylon's here. Actually smiling. He never smiles.

I follow him in a daze. But my legs wobble when I see that the front room is filled with Reapers. Just like that night. My throat constricts with fear.

"How's Olivia doing?" Waylon shouts over the music. "What did Rockstar say you called her? O2?"

"Yeah," I barely manage to answer. It feels like the whole room is closing in on me. "She's good."

I concentrate on not panicking as I scan all the Reapers. So many, and country music is blasting, the same as that night. But it's not New Year's Eve, I tell myself. It's less chaotic. All the lights are turned on overhead, and the place isn't packed with scantily clad girls.

Maybe everything will be okay. Maybe Griff and I can talk this out. I scan the room. All I have to do is find him, so I can ask him about—

My blood freezes when I finally catch sight of Griff.

He's not in the bedroom, like last time. He's sitting on one of the front room couches with a Reaper I recognize—the same Reaper who answered the door that night. They're deep in conversation.

But they both suddenly stop talking and look up at me.

And that's when I realized I've been duped, yet again. Our agreement to go forward in trust...to try to make it work and start a family...

It was all a lie. Part of some sick revenge plan. He has no interest in being my Dream Husband.

I think about how he lulled me into forgiving him and even agreeing to cancel my own New Year's Eve plans at the lake cabin...how he told me we'd talk in the morning just a few hours before kidnapping O2.

How many times had he proven himself a monster? How many times had I ignored the signs and bared my neck to him again?

These last few weeks, all the talking things through, and reconciliation—it was all just a game. The biggest monster game he's played on me so far.

And I fell for it.

CHAPTER 37
GRIFFIN

"ARE YOU SERIOUS?" ROWDY ASKS WHEN I TURN DOWN HIS offer. "Man, Rockstar, what happened to you?"

Can't say I blame Rowdy for asking. The Reapers showed up in town over two hours ago for my surprise bachelor party. And all I've drunk is a beer.

A single beer. No weed. And I waved Rowdy away with a "Nah, I'm good, man" when he dropped down beside me on the couch with a mirror lined up with blow.

I doubt Rowdy would understand or appreciate my holes explanation, so I tell him, "My woman's about to come through, and I don't want to be messed up when she gets here."

Rowdy's around the same age now as I was when I made the switch from celebrity party boy to kick-ass executive. But I guess that 30-something existential crisis stuff passed him right on up.

"So you're serious about this marriage shit?" he asks with a confused look. "It's not just to get out of paying child support?"

Irritation statics over my good-times vibe. What's up with everybody holding stuff I said nearly six years ago against me? Also...

"My kid's not something I need to get out of. She's mine. My responsibility. And I'm happy—happier than I've ever been because I get to step up and be her dad."

I told Waylon a version of the same thing when I called to invite him and the other Reapers to the wedding at the end of the month. And he told me, "Good for you."

But Rowdy doesn't look the least bit happy for me. He frowns, like I'm talking a whole different language. "I just don't see why you decided to start taking bitches seriously all of a sudden. Especially this one."

I still. "What did you say about my woman?"

Rowdy doesn't answer. He's staring at something.

I follow his gaze, and my whole chest lights up when I see the vision standing across from me.

Red...the Red I knew at the cabin is back. But not exactly.

She's taken out her black box braids and replaced them with extensions. Not waves of cherry red down to her butt, like before —but deep-scarlet curls that only fall to her shoulders.

The new style's eye-catching, like Red, but sensible, like Bernice.

It's like she's combined both sides of herself to present to me today.

I was fine with both versions of her. But this one makes my chest rev and throttle up.

I like it so much, I'm already thinking about all the things I want to do with this magnificent combo as I forget all about Rowdy and come to my feet to grin at her.

However, she doesn't smile back. She looks stricken—like someone's just told her I've died.

"Red? What's the ma—"

The question's not all the way out of my mouth before she turns tail and runs.

After a confused moment, I chase after her without thinking.

Outside in the outer hallway, I find her pressing frantically at the elevator down button, like there's a horror movie monster coming after her.

"Red!" I call out again.

I'm the monster she's running from—I realize that when instead of turning to come back after I call her name, she cuts left toward the exit stairs.

Shit. The stairs are only meant for emergencies and lock behind you when you go through them—so that you have to walk all the way down to the garage to get out.

But I let the door close behind me when I see she's made it three floors down.

What the hell is going on?

"Red!" I yell again, bounding down the stairs after her.

I need to stop calling after her. The sound of my voice only seems to make her run faster.

Luckily, I keep my cardio game 100%.

I leap down the stairs and catch up with her about five floors down.

And this time I'm smart enough to wait until I've got ahold of her arm before saying her name again and asking, "Why are you running from me?"

She rears around on me like a cornered animal. And my chest cracks when I see the desperate tears in her eyes—like she's been crying the whole time she's been running. "Red. What the—"

She throws a punch, straight at my throat. And when I block it, she claws at me with her new stiletto nails and kicks her knee up toward my crotch.

I manage to avoid the crotch shot, too. But those stilettoes hurt like a son of a bitch!

I yell out and barely manage to grab onto her by the wrist when she tries to use my pain as an opportunity to take off again.

This time I bear-hug her from behind. Restraining her and her new matte black claws before she can use them on me again.

"No! No!" she yells, her voice frantic and unhinged. "No! I love my daughter. And I'll do anything to keep her, but I can't let you do this to me. I can't! I won't! I'll find a way to escape you. Please, please don't drag me back up there to finish what you started on New Year's Eve. I will hate you. All I will do is hate you for the rest of my life."

The night she threatened to hate me a few weeks ago, I considered that a challenge and rose to the occasion.

But today the only thing rising up inside of me is alarm.

"Red…" I start to say.

"Don't call me that!" she screams, bucking inside my arms. "I'm not her. I'm not some stupid roadhouse girl. And you can't make me do this. I don't care about the second part of the agreement."

"Bernice!" I growl, conceding on the "Red" thing and subduing her at the same time. "I'm not trying to make you do anything! Fuck, forget about the second part of the agreement. You never have to do anything you don't want with me again. I was an asshole for adding it."

She pauses struggling, finally seeming to hear my words. "You're not going to make me go back upstairs?"

"Hell no," I answer. "Not if you don't want to."

"Then why did you invite me over here?" Her voice sounds small and confused. Like she's lost in the woods somewhere and doesn't know how to get out.

I've been keeping things from her, I'll admit that. But this thing, I rush to explain. "The Reapers surprised me. And we're going to take me on a four-day ride out to California for my bachelor party. I wanted to make sure you had a car for getting O2 to school and back—I invited you over here so you could pick out one of the vehicles I keep in the basement garage. That's all."

I hug her tight and assure her, "That's the *only* reason I invited you over here, I swear. You need to believe me on that. This isn't a game, and I'm not trying to hurt you."

She lets out a shaky breath. Then she says, "Okay, I believe you."

I don't realize I'm holding my breath too until it comes out in a relieved whoosh. Still, I hold on to her.

"If I let you go, you promise not to run?"

She doesn't answer right away, but after a few tense seconds, she nods.

I loosen my hold tentatively and brace to grab on to her again if she tries anything with those nails.

But she lets me turn her around in my arms without incident.

She's no longer screaming and swinging at me, but the cowed look on her face is almost worse.

"I'm sorry," she whispers. "I'm sorry I hurt you. Hurt your face."

"I don't give a fuck about my face," I answer. There's a jack-hammer pile driving my heart.

This obviously has something to do with New Year's Eve. And we agreed to call the past the past—to just wipe it clean so that we can move into the future together. But I have to go back on that agreement.

"Talk to me, Red. Explain to me what just happened here. Tell me your side of what happened on New Year's Eve."

CHAPTER 38
BERNICE

I'M SAFE. I'M SAFE, I THINK. BUT MY STOMACH IS STILL roiling from seeing Rowdy—for the first time since that New Year's Eve.

And here's Griff...asking me for explanations. But it's time for me to start demanding answers of my own.

"Why did you lie to me?" I ask him. "Why did you let me keep believing we had to get married for you to become CEO of AudioNation?"

He stills. Then asks, "Is that why you ran away?"

"Answer the question!" I demand, too frustrated to be even remotely calm.

"Red, it's complicated." He rubs his face wearily.

"*No*, you do not get to act like this is too much right now." I jab my finger at the ground. "You're not the one who was just triggered to hell and back."

He blinks at me like I've lost my mind. Maybe I have. Rage courses through me, refusing to be checked.

"What triggered you?" he asks. "Just tell me."

"Why. Did. You. Lie?" I scream back. "*You* just tell *me* why you won't stop lying to me about everything?"

"Because I fucking love you!" he roars without warning.

He spreads his arms, and his voice echoes in the empty stairwell as he tells me, "I've loved you since the moment we kissed in that bar—no matter how much I tried to deny it. And there hasn't been a minute since that moment when I knew how to handle this love I didn't expect to feel without fucking it up."

I falter, my rage giving way to shock. "You love me?"

"Yeah..." He lowers his arms. "That's what I realized that New Year's Eve morning when you walked back in the house, and it felt like my heart was ripping out of my chest. I love you. I love you with my whole soul. And I don't even mess around with God like that."

He loves me? With his whole soul? I shake my head, both wanting and refusing to believe. "But how? Why?"

He's wearing his Reaper vest, but his expression goes weak.

"The reasons keep on changing," he admits. "At first, it was just because you came home with me for me—not because I'm G-Latham. Then it was because it was easy for me to be around you. I just wanted to be around you, even if we weren't having sex...."

He tilts his head with a wry wince. "Not going to lie, that was a first for me. I just...I just couldn't get enough of you. You were this drug in my system. You fucked me up."

His expression pains, then softens. "But you also made me think about the future—a future on the other side of partying and getting laid all the time because I'm famous. By New Year's Eve morning, I just knew...I wanted to be with you forever. My plan was to tell you—tell you who I really was as soon as you got to my place. That's why I agreed to work for my dad at AudioNation after the European leg of my tour. If you wanted to travel the world, I wanted to travel the world. If you wanted kids after that, I wanted kids. I was prepared to give you the world. That ring on your hand was sitting in my dresser drawer for almost six years before I found you again."

I stare down at my huge engagement ring, trying to process what he's saying.

"But you never showed up," Griff continues. Pain flashes across his dark blue gaze. "That's the real reason I was so angry when I found out about O2. If you showed up like you promised, we could have been doing this happy family thing together all these years."

We could have?

I stare at him, my heart melting and freezing at the same time. His words, his claims, and the alternate timeline they set in motion are almost too bittersweet to imagine. But...

"None of this adds up," I tell him. "If you loved me like you said you did, why did you lie to me about the marriage requirement?"

"*Because you never showed up*," he repeats slowly, like I'm someone who doesn't understand English. "I wanted...I needed to be with you. But I knew you didn't feel the same way about me. Otherwise, you wouldn't have ghosted me like you did."

He looks at me, his expression miserable. Like this conversation and the memories it dredges up are physically hurting him. Even after all these years.

"Griff..." I struggle past all the confusion to tell him, "On the way to see you, I saw a billboard with you on it—advertising that New Year's Eve concert. I found out you lied. *That's* why I didn't show up at the appointed time."

I look away. "When I saw that billboard...I literally stopped driving. All these people were blowing their horns at me, but all I could do was sit there and stare at it. And I don't know how much time passed, but I guess it must have been too much because this cop came by—on a motorcycle."

I stop and snort at the irony. But then I sober back up to continue my story. "So, I found this empty bank parking lot, and I sat there. I didn't go to Kyra's. I didn't go home. I just sat there, for hours and hours, trying to figure out why you would do this to me. My good sense was telling me that you were just a liar and that the last two weeks had been some kind of mind-game. But my heart wanted to believe. I told myself that maybe G-Latham was like Red—a mask you put on to protect the real you from real-world pain."

"That's exactly who G-Latham is," Griff said, taking a step closer to me. "And I'm sorry. I'm sorry I lied to you. I was wrong to be bitter all these years about you not showing up. You only knew me two weeks, and I had a hell of a reputation. If that was how you discovered who I really was, I guess I don't blame you for ghosting me."

He balls his fist, like he wishes he could punch the guy he was back then. But he visibly calms himself and says, "Thanks...

thanks for helping me understand why you didn't keep your promise."

He doesn't understand....

"I always keep my promises," I whisper. "No matter what. It took me a long time—a really long time. But I came to your place, like I said I would. I still needed the money you promised me for New York. Plus, I thought I deserved answers from you."

His eyes fill with denial. "No...no, you never came."

"I did." Tears burn in my eyes. "But you didn't answer the door. That guy Rowdy did. And when he showed me to your room, you were already with two girls."

He goes white as a ghost. "My vision of you that night. It was real. Fuck! You were there. You were really there...."

He confirms what I've been beginning to suspect since the start of this conversation—that he didn't know I was there, even though he looked straight at me and kept having relations with the woman bent over in front of him. And, I confirm what he's saying with a nod.

He jerks back and fists his hair, his eyes crazed with regret. "I'm sorry, baby. I'm so fucking sorry. I was an idiot back then and blitzed out of my mind. I thought partying like I used to would fill the hole of you not showing up. But believe me, I figured out by the next morning that hole was unfillable. I was done with that life. That's why I moved to Vegas and started working at AudioN-ation after my European tour anyway."

More explanations. More terrible, bittersweet feelings because they're coming too late.

"I thought...I thought you threw me away. I thought you only invited me to your penthouse because you always give the other Reapers your leftovers. That's what Rowdy said when he grabbed me."

Griff goes deadly still. "Rowdy touched you?"

The memories I've been trying to hold at bay come rushing back like floodwater. Me trying to run out when I saw Griff with those girls. Rowdy suddenly appearing in my path with an affable, "Hey, Red, you can't leave yet. You just got here!"

Like I'd come there to see him, not Griff.

The way he'd shaken a baggie of pills at me...how his friendly face had turned red and petulant when I turned down his invitation to party.

The way he coldly explained the situation to me. "I lost a lot of money on that bet, and Griff always gives me his leftovers."

Like I was his consolation prize. His due.

"Did he try to..." Griff's voice brings me back to the present.

I can't look at him. If I look at him, I'll cry. So I turn my head away to answer, "Yes."

Then I'm back in that hallway with ugly realization after ugly realization sinking in. I thought I was falling in love, but Griff was only mind-gaming me this entire time.

The hallway was empty. It was just me and Rowdy—who was now standing between me and the front door. And Griff wasn't going to help me. In fact, he had only invited me here after he was done with me so that this exact scenario could pop off.

I realized all of that, and then Rowdy reached out and grabbed me.

"I fought him," I whisper to Griff in the present. "I fought him with everything I had, and I still only barely got away...."

I'm trying to hold them back, but the tears leak anyway. "Afterward, I felt so stupid. I hate-read all these once-and-done articles about you. And I blamed you for lying to me. I let myself believe it was all a lie—that you really were the kind of monster who gave girls to your Reaper friends. But now, I can see you had no idea any of this happened. There's nobody to blame but me. I'm the one who put myself in that position—I'm the one who was so desperately trying to be someone other than Boring Bernice."

All the regret, all the memories I've been trying to dam up for years...they come crashing down once the barrier of blaming Griff falls. And then there's no stopping the tears.

"I'm sorry I blamed you. I'm sorry I assumed you were a monster without stopping to give you the benefit of the doubt."

"No! No! Don't you apologize to me," he answers, his voice low and harsh. "You let me have the real you for those two weeks, just like I let you have the real me. You figured out I was lying to you, and you had the courage to come to confront me. None of this is your fault. *None of it.* The only people to blame are that piece of shit, Rowdy, and me for being such a fucked-up bastard that I wasn't there when you needed me most."

Griff pulls me into his chest and crushes me in his arms. "I'm sorry, baby. I'm sorry I didn't protect you. And I can't believe you were able to forgive me enough to try to make this marriage work, even thinking I did what I did. This is my fault for being too chickenshit to ask you straight up why you never showed up on New Year's Eve. I don't blame you for anything...."

His absolution washes over me, salve for wounds I thought I'd carry forever. I've been doubting myself for years. Wondering if anything I felt in the cabin was real. Now I know, it was.

But, I pull back from his embrace. "You lied to me. You asked me to trust you. We've been talking non-stop for weeks. But the whole time you continued to keep things from me. Important things. I didn't truly trust that you weren't the monster I thought you were on New Year's Eve. And you didn't trust me to know we didn't absolutely have to get married in order for you to get that CEO job. How is this going to work? It can't."

"Red...Bernice..." he starts to says.

"No, let me finish." I step back, my heart trembling with all this new information. "You get it now. You understand the bond between parent and child. Will you take O2 away from me if I refuse to marry you?"

He stills. And I hold my breath to see who will show up. The man or the monster.

But in the end, he says, "No. I'll never use her again. She's my daughter too. And I only want the best for her. Even if that means you don't want to be with me now that you know you don't have to."

I let out a small sigh of relief.

"So now I guess it's time for me to finally ask you the question I should have asked on New Year's Eve morning." He takes me by the chin. Tips my face up to look him directly in his blue gaze. "Do you want me forever like I want you? Will you marry me, and make me the happiest man on Earth?"

His gaze is so tender. His expression is more vulnerable than I ever seen it.

Which is what makes what I say next so hard.

"No." I let out a shuddering breath. "No, I won't marry you."

CHAPTER 39
BERNICE

IT'S A QUIET WALK TO THE PARKING GARAGE WHERE GRIFF has two sport cars, two trucks, two luxury SUVs, and three motor-cycles parked all in a row. I take my time looking them over even though I know it's either the Cadillac or Lexus SUV. Did I do the right thing?

No! Red practically wails.

Yes, yes, of course you did, Bernice says at the same time.

Bernice is right. We couldn't even go two weeks without a blow-up. What makes me think we could last a lifetime? I need to sign the custody agreement and return to my boring life.

"I think you should take the Escalade," he tells me, his voice gruff and quiet. "It matches the new hair."

I'd almost forgotten about my new extensions, the ones that were supposed to merge Red and Bernice.

"Of course, it's your choice," he adds, looking away. "You can find something online and I'll have it dropped off to you. Anything. Just tell me what you want."

It doesn't feel like we're talking about cars.

"Griff..." I say. Then I give up. What can I say?

"I know you're scared," he tells me when I can't go on. "I get it. I was scared too. This thing we've got is so intense, I couldn't really talk with you about it. I love you, but I couldn't even say it until you cornered me."

I wait for the "but" and realize that's it. He's just validating my fears—letting me know I'm not the only one.

"I..." I want to tell him the truth. That I love him too. But that would make things more complicated than they already are.

"Have fun on your trip with the Reapers," I say instead. "We'll talk about custody and everything when you get back. Meanwhile...."

I take off the gorgeous engagement ring and hold it out to him.

He averts his eyes to a spot over my shoulder. Like he doesn't see the expensive item I'm trying to return. "That's yours. Hock it if you want."

His voice is flat. I can't tell if he's disappointed or resolved. Either way, I'm left to put the ring in the pocket of my jeans.

We stand there awkwardly. *Am I doing the right thing?*

The question hovers as the silence stretches. But this time no one answers. My heart just vibrates heavy and sad in my aching chest.

And eventually, I'm the one who has to break the silence. "I'll take the Escalade."

I love Griff, and Griff loves me.

But we're not going to make it work. The almost-six-year-old engagement ring feels like a heavy stone in my pocket when I walk in the door of the house about a half an hour later.

I pull my phone out of my cross-body bag as soon as I walk toward the kitchen. I'm hungry as all get-out after eating explanations and tears for dinner instead of food. But I should coordinate O2's drop-off with Carol before I rummage around the fridge for something to eat.

However, I stop in the middle of the kitchen and furrow my brow when I see the wall of texts and missed call notifications on my front screen. They're all from Griff, saying some variation of "call me."

And as I'm trying to make sense of all the messages, a new one pops up.

GRIFF: *FUCK! CALL ME BACK. CALL ME AS SOON AS YOU GET THIS. DON'T GO HOME.*

Don't go home?

I have no idea what this is all about, but I find out in an instant that I trust Griff more than I thought. Heart sprinting, I turn on my heel and head back toward the door leading out to the garage.

"Not so fast, bitch," a voice calls out, stopping me in my tracks.

Rowdy...

Rowdy's standing in the darkened foyer. Just like on that New Year's Eve, he stands between me and the door I need to reach.

But unlike on that New Year's Eve, he has a gun in his hand. One that he raises to point at me as he says, "Hey, Red, you can't leave yet. You just got here!"

CHAPTER 40
BERNICE

"ROWDY...ROWDY DON'T."

My heart clogs with fear as I look at the man...the nightmare that's haunted me for nearly six years.

Waylon was sober as a judge when he opened the door for me earlier, but Rowdy, not so much.

I can tell he's partied too hard over the years since I saw him last. His skinny frame has given way to beer bloat, and his eyes are red-rimmed and bleary.

He looks wasted, and I try to figure out if that's good or bad for my chances of survival as I say, "Rowdy, you don't want to do this."

"Do you know how much money I lost on that bet?" he asks me, like we're picking up a conversation from six minutes ago—not almost six years later. "A lot. And then Rockstar stopped touring and moved to Vegas. And Waylon banned me from deals after I messed up an order—even though it wasn't my fault it came in a little light."

He points the gun emphatically at me. "I'm not rich, like Rockstar. Girls don't just fall over me unless I can supply them with drugs. And now this. How was I supposed to know that of all the bitches that came through Rockstar's bedroom, you'd be the one he kept asking after at the roadhouse? That he'd decide to marry you? This is all your fault!"

No...not my fault.

From the looks of him, Rowdy was the reason that shipment came up light. And how many leftover women had he felt entitled to, even after they said no? I think about all his affable offers of drugs at the roadhouse in a new light...also, how Griff and I blacked out the night we took his purple pills. How much of his friendly dealer behavior had been about getting whatever he wanted from girls who wouldn't have given consent if they were sober?

But he's the one with the gun. And I'm the one with everything to lose. So instead of doubting him out loud, I tell him, "You don't have to do this. Just put the gun down, and we'll get you help. Rehab. Counseling. Whatever it takes."

"What dream world do you live in?" He screws up his face. "That's not how the Reapers work. He's marrying you. I thought maybe it was just a child support thing. But at the pre-ride party, he kept on talking to everybody about you and this kid. I knew if he ever found out about that night, he wouldn't understand. He'd just have Waylon shoot me point-blank in the face—it wouldn't matter that I'm a Reaper. As soon as you ran off and he chased after you—I knew it was all over for me."

Rowdy's words about what Griff said to him in private would have warmed my heart. If he wasn't also pointing a gun at me.

"I can talk to him," I repeat. "I can make him see reason. This doesn't have to end in bloodshed. All you have to do is put down the gun."

Rowdy lowers the gun.

And I let out a sigh of relief.

But then his face turns ugly with bitterness. "Yeah, actually, I think there does have to be bloodshed."

He pulls back the slide and raises the gun.

"Rowdy, no. Do—"

The gunshot sounds before the plea is fully out of my mouth.

I squeeze my eyes shut, and my whole life flashes in front of me.

All the good times.

All the bad.

O2...Griff...The beautiful future I won't get to make with them. My heart shatters when I think of that...and how I never told Griff that I loved him too in the garage.

But then I open my eyes and see that I'm still alive.

As it turns out, Rowdy was wrong....

Griff didn't send Waylon to shoot him point-blank in the face.

Griff shot Rowdy himself, hitting him in the thigh.

Rowdy cries out and drops the gun as he falls to the ground, grabbing at his leg.

And Waylon appears out of nowhere to push me behind him.

Meanwhile, a lone Griff walks over to the fallen biker and calmly kicks the gun out of reach.

Rowdy was all bitter and "poor me" before, but now he holds a hand up to Griff. "Please, man. Please, man, don—"

This time he's the one who doesn't get to finish his plea.

Griff looks Rowdy straight in the eye—and coldly shoots a bullet into his chest. And then another into his stomach.

Then he looks over at me.

"You all right?" he asks me.

I don't realize I am...I am all right until he asks. I mutely nod.

"Good," he says with a grim look. "I'm glad you didn't promise him anything from me. I know you always keep your promises, and I'll love you until the day we die. But there are limits to that love. He touched you. He hurt you. And you are mine. Even before he decided to come into our house with a gun, he was never going to make it out of this state alive."

Allie's texted words suddenly whisper through my mind: *He might be legitimate now. But he's still a Reaper. And those guys don't forgive. They're ruthless. It's literally in their name.*

As it turns out, Allie was right.

"I had to deal with him. That's the only reason I didn't come back to the house with you after you tried to end things with me," Griff informs me while Rowdy suffers at his feet, gurgling blood. "I'm never going to not love you. Or not protect you again."

Griff tells me his violent truth.

And *then* he shoots Rowdy point-blank in the face.

I stare at the man on the other side of the gun. Not a man, actually. Not a monster either. Something in between. A Reaper to the core.

And this Reaper used the word "tried" when referring to our break-up.

The world blurs as my eyes fill up with tears. This is crazy. I need to scream. I need to send him away and tell him we're too toxic to be together.

But all I can do is run to him.

"He was going to kill me," I tell him, sobbing. "And the only thing I could think about was how I wouldn't get a future with you and O2."

He stays in stone-faced killer mode to slide his gun into a holder under his vest. But then...

The violence fades from his eyes and he looks down at me tenderly to ask, "So, I didn't fuck this up? You're still going to marry me and make me the happiest son of a bitch on earth?"

I think about it.

But not for long.

Griff was wrong about a lot of things—just like me. But he was right about the courage it took for me to be Red, and to let a bad-boy biker take me home. And to take a chance on our marriage two weeks ago.

He's asked me to still marry him, and I decide to take my most courageous action yet.

I pull the Ruthless Reaper Rockstar Mogul's ring out of my pocket and put it where it belongs. On my wedding finger, "I love you too, Griff. And I want to spend the rest of my life being not boring with you. So, yes, I'll still marry you."

EPILOGUE
GRIFFIN

NOT A LOT OF PEOPLE CHOOSE TO RECOMMIT TO THEIR engagement over a dead body. But hey, works for us.

And O2 does not say, "Eww!" on the last Sunday of the month as she stands up with us on the altar and watches her groom father kiss her mother, the bride.

She just cheers along with her real cousins, her play cousins, her three grandparents and uncle, and all of her father's biker friends as her parents seal their new-old love with a wedding kiss.

"Best birthday ever!" she declares to anyone that wishes her happy birthday at the reception afterwards.

And that's a whole lot of people. Back when Red still hated me, she told O2 the wedding would be small.

But after we decided we were all in with love on top, a bunch more people got invited.

I figured since O2 was my daughter, not having the spotlight on her special day might be a problem. But she's Red's daughter too.

And apparently, she's also got that main-background character switch inside of her.

Which makes it all that more satisfying when I take the stage in the middle of the reception. "Okay, I know I, of all people, probably have no business asking a surprise guest to come to my wedding...."

I pause because everybody laughs. Especially Phantom Zhang, who told me at the rehearsal dinner he might be interested in a soju deal now that his wife has seen for herself how happy my wife is with me.

Kyra Fairgood still isn't talking to me. But hey, she showed up for the ceremony. And you know what they say about time healing all wounds. Well, I plan to be around for the rest of her best cousin's life, so she'll just have to warm back up to me eventually.

Anyway, enough about them. Back to my speech: "But I'm making an exception because today is also my daughter O2's birthday—the first one I've ever gotten to spend with her. So, in an effort to out-dad all her other parties, I've not only married her beautiful mother—the most wonderful and interesting woman in the world—I've also invited some very special guests to lead us in a round of happy birthday...."

And that's when sasha X kasha—yes, actual Sasha and Kasha—walk in carrying a small birthday cake with six candles.

"Happy Birthday, O2!" they call out to her together. And then they lead the whole room in singing "Happy Birthday" to O2.

Seeing our daughter break down in happy tears when sasha X kasha come into the ballroom isn't worth all the birthdays I missed. But it comes damn near close to making up for them.

Yeah, this is definitely the best birthday present...the best wedding...the very best day of all our lives ever.

"Thank you for getting them to come," Red whispers in my ear.

"Thank you for thinking of it," I whisper back. "We make one hell of a team."

"Right?!" she agrees, nudging me in the ribs. But then she eyes O2 worriedly. "She's really overcome. Should we tell them not to ask her to sing with them? I don't know if she'll be able to get it together."

I can see why she's worried. We're almost done with the song, and O2's still crying and blathering so loudly, you can hear her over all of us singing "Happy Birthday."

Still, I answer my wife, "That's the best part of the present, and she'll be all right. Trust me."

"But..." Red starts to say.

"*Trust me*," I say again before she can finish.

And look how far we've come....she just lays her head on my arm and watches the rest play out.

Sure enough, as soon as we hit the last "to you," O2 pulls it together in an instant to blow out her candles.

And when sasha X kasha asks if she wants to join them on stage to sing that song we've been urging her to practice ever since Red came up with this plan, she takes the mic and jumps right up on stage. Like she was born there.

She doesn't even miss a beat when her mother and I join her and the sister pop duo on stage for the last verse and chorus.

She's a born performer. And we're something I didn't think I'd ever have.

A happy family.

"We made her," I crow to Red afterward, beyond proud of her performance.

"Yes, we did," Red agrees as we watch O2 hug Sasha and Kasha and thank both them and the audience for coming out.

Then she leans over and whispers in my ear, "And guess what else we made, according to the pregnancy test I took last night?"

My chest contracts, then explodes. "We're having a baby?"

She nods happily. And thank fuck for cardio or else I think my heart would have given out right then and there.

But after lots of kisses and telling her how much I fucking love her, I do have to point out, "Wow, Red, you will do just about anything to get out of period sex."

She bursts out laughing, and man, when I say she's the most beautiful, wonderful thing on Earth...

I kick myself again for the last six years. For letting pride take the lead and not just grabbing her up in my arms and declaring I loved from the start six weeks ago when I finally found her again.

I knew this woman would upend my life from the moment I saw her standing on that bar. But I didn't know she'd heal my wounded soul. And give me all the things I didn't know I should be praying for...a soul mate...children...a *real* life.

I was bored before I met her. But after marrying Boring Bernice, I'll never be bored again.

"Can I tell Waylon?" I ask her a little later when sasha X kasha have left the party after signing autographs and taking lot of pictures with Little Olivia *and* Dr. Olivia—who both claimed to be their biggest fans.

"Just him, okay?"

"Just him," I agree—only to hedge, "And, you know, Hades."

"Boy, who else are you going to ask to tell...?" she demands, her voice filled with outrage.

She laughs and looks over to the section of the ballroom where the Reapers are having their own kind of party with bottles of whiskey and cans of beers they definitely didn't get from the open bar. Reapers will be Reapers—which is why my event planning genius wife sequestered them off in the farthest corner the room.

But instead of guessing who else I'll try to include in the news, the smile suddenly drops off her face.

"Where's Hyena?" she asks me. "And the quiet guy, Des-E."

Shit.

She scans the Reapers and her expression becomes increasingly upset. "And that really tall one—Vampire?"

We promised no more lies. So I tell her the only truth I can. "This is Reaper business."

Red takes one look at my grave face and says, "Oh my God...I've got to call Allie."

Then she rushes off to find her phone.

I don't bother to stop her.

She'll soon find out what I already know, and I'll have to figure out how to fix my very last lie of omission. We'll survive this. But as for her friend...

There's no helping her....

Vengeance has her.

Want to find out what happened to Allie?
Make sure to read
VENGEANCE: Snow and the Vengeful Reapers
Get your copy at theodorataylor.com

Thank you so very much for reading GRIFFIN. These two have been with me for a while.

I knew from the moment I met Kyra Fairgood's boring cousin Bernice that I wanted her to have a super exciting romance. And I was stunned when Griffin stepped up for the job. But I grew to love them and their super modern family.

I haven't written a kid since HAN, and O2 was so much fun-if somewhat triggering. Two out of three of my kids are totally willing to tell you more than I want about me. As one of my Ruthless Patreons noted, *"Kids with tell ALL your business."* Lol!

I think we all have a totally different person inside of us—one who only shows up for certain occasions or people. I'm so glad these two found and managed to become vulnerable enough to share their most authentic selves with each other.

If you have someone who you can show all of you, please give them a hug after you finish this book.

So Much Love,
TT

SO many Easter Eggs in this one:

1. Colin and Kyra Fairgood: His for Keeps
2. Waylon and his pretty nurse: WAYLON: Angel and the Ruthless Reaper
3. The Benton Family:
Vegas Baby & Love's Gamble
4. Roxxy Roxx: Her Ruthless Cowboy
5. West Nygard from Death Buddha: Reina and the Heavy Metal Prince (Patreon Exclusive)
6. Dawn and Victor Zhang: VICTOR: Her Ruthless Crush
7. sasha X kasha: Ruthless King
8. Hades and Persy: HADES: Stephanie and the Merciless Reaper

And of course, Phantom and Olivia!

Curious about the original
Olivia and Phantom?
Keep reading for a sneak peak!

PHANTOM

IT WAS TIME TO DEAL WITH THE DOCTOR WHO WOULDN'T stop asking questions about Dawn.

A couple of weeks ago, Phantom's cousin, Victor, had decided to install his ex-girlfriend Dawn into a prison disguised as a house in Rhode Island. Okay, fine. Phantom had a few questions about how this whole kidnap and imprison your ex-girlfriend thing would end. But this was his cousin, plus one of his literal partners in crime, so yeah, sure, he'd agreed to helped him blow up her life.

He'd not only snatched her from her college dorm room, but he'd also hacked into Dawn's school account and sent the email himself that she was quitting the internship she landed at the Women with Disabilities Clinic in Manhattan before it even started.

> *"I changed my mind about taking the internship. Replace me with someone else."*

Blunt and clear. It hadn't been nice, but it had done the job. After a few hours, Olivia had sent a polite but terse email back:

> *Dear Dawn,*
>
> *Thank you for letting us know you wouldn't be joining us for the summer internship.*
>
> *Though your message was brief and received only three days before you were due to start, I'll assume this must have been a hard decision for you to make.*
>
> *Fortunately, we have a long waiting list for this incredibly prestigious internship, and I've already filled your spot.*
>
> *Best of luck with your future endeavors.*

Dr. Olivia Glendaver.

Great. She'd basically said that Dawn was an easily replaceable asshole in the politest possible way. That should have been the end of it.

But a few days later, the doctor appeared to have a change of heart. A new email popped up in Dawn's inbox, which Phantom was still monitoring.

> *Dawn,*
>
> *This is Olivia again. That last email didn't sound like you.*
>
> *Are you okay?*
>
> *Are you safe?*
>
> *I know we never received the chance to work together and get to know each other, but I'm here for you if you need me. And if you're in any kind of trouble, I'd like to help. Just let me know.*
>
> *We need more doctors like you.*
>
> *Your friend,*
>
> *Olivia*

Dammit. He supposed he should have known that a bourbon heiress who worked as a pregnant lady doctor at a clinic for women with disabilities wouldn't be the cold-hearted type. Ah, well...

He deleted the message, figuring that would be the real end of it. But a few days later, a new email popped up in Dawn's inbox.

Olivia again, I haven't heard from you. I'll keep on emailing until you answer one way or another. I'm not going to give up on you.

He'd heaved a huge sigh and typed back as Dawn: *I'm fine.*

They weren't texting, but her reply had popped into Dawn's inbox less than a minute later.

I don't mean to be rude, Dawn, but you don't sound fine. I'm a pretty good judge of character. And the woman I met wouldn't have sent that first email. Or answered my two concerned emails with "I'm fine."

Well, shit.

That was when Phantom decided to pay her a visit. Obviously, some intimidation would be required to get the doctor to back off.

It had been an easy meeting to arrange. The clinic was under-staffed, and though he wasn't a woman with disabilities, it had been easy enough to slip past the over-worked front office clerk and walk down the hallway until he found the door with a *Dr. Olivia Glendaver, MD* plaque beside it.

Even better, she wasn't there when he walked into the simple room, which housed only a desk, two guest chairs, and a book-shelf filled with medical texts. That meant he could use the good ol' "Bad Guy Waiting In Your Office When You Walk In" intimi-dation routine.

Classic.

While Phantom bided his time like the villain he was, he checked out the two framed pictures sitting on top of her desk. One was of an older trim man in a pastel suit flanked by a pair of thin blonds in equally bright dresses and large hats.

Their colorful outfits, along with the horses trotting around in the background, told Phantom that they must be attending the Kentucky Derby. The blonds looked alike with smiles frozen in place by Botox. But they weren't twins.

One had much more triangular and feline features, a sure sign of some face lifting underneath all those fillers. The other just looked like she'd decided that her thirties was the exact right time to start cutting off access to her facial muscles. Mother and daughter, Phantom figured, and one of them had to be Dr. Olivia Glendaver. They both looked like former southern belles, born and bred.

The other photo featured a Ken Doll in a suit, leaning against a bar with a glass of whiskey in one hand. I-banker. Phantom might call Rhode Island home now, but he could still spot an investment banker from a mile away after growing up in Queens. No matter their color or weight, they all somehow managed to look like entitled douches with their shellacked hair and fake smiles.

So that meant the daughter was Dr. Glendaver. Douchebag and Early Botox Girl looked like a perfect match.

Yeah, it shouldn't be too hard to intimidate her, Phantom decided, sitting back in her office chair.

"What are you doing here?"

The question brought his eyes up from the pictures of her loved ones. Dr. Olivia Glendaver's voice was soft petals falling off a flower that could only grow in the lush southern heat. It sounded exactly like he'd figured it would, given her old money Kentucky background.

But the woman...

She stopped his heart.

Tall and ebony and beautiful beyond compare. She was the exact opposite of the blonde in the photo. Yet, he knew who she was in an instant. This, not Early Botox Girl, was Olivia Glendaver.

An ebony goddess statue disguised as a doctor in a white coat.

Adoptee, his brain told him, answering the question before he could ask it out loud. But that only brought up another question.

"Why?" He stood and picked up the photo of the white family. His brain had gone all fuzzy, and later he would think about the risk he'd taken in leaving fingerprints behind after he broke into her office. But at that moment, he had to know, "Why aren't you in any of these photos?"

"Because I took them," she answered with a careful tilt of her head. "Is this...is this about my family? Are you...?"

She didn't finish the question, but she didn't have to. Phantom knew what he looked like. Knew what anybody with half a brain would assume when they found a goon like him waiting in their office.

And usually, that assumption would be one hundred percent on lock. But in this case, he put down the photo and raised both hands to assure her, "No, I'm not here to hurt you. I..."

New problem. Words. He'd never had any trouble coming up with them before, but this woman—she made all his what to say next disappear. The mean-ass things that made a habit of hanging out on his tongue had scattered like cockroaches when she appeared.

And even if they hadn't. He didn't want to say all the usual shit to her. Didn't want to threaten her or do that thing where he pretended he'd ever really lay a hand on a woman in order to inspire them to do what he said.

She already looked scared enough, and he suddenly had no desire to terrify her out of asking too many questions as he normally would.

What the hell was wrong with him?

He stuttered—actually stuttered when he answered, "I'm...I'm a friend of Dawn Kingston's. She...she asked me to come up here to see you."

Phantom had no idea where these words came from. They were the opposite of the truth, even though he prided himself on telling it like it is.

"A friend..." she repeated.

Her voice shook, and she eyed him distrustfully. Plus, her hand was in her expensive Hermes bag, probably poised to call 9-1-1 if he made any sudden moves. But she stayed put even though she was obviously scared.

And that made Phantom admire her all that much more, even as he lied, "Yeah, she told me you were worried about her decision not to go the doctor route and move to Rhode Island with her guy."

He gave the doctor just enough details to sell the story. "And since I was coming into the city, I offered to stop by to let you know she's all right."

Dr. Glendaver considered his words. Then she considered him and asked, "So you and Dawn are together?"

Phantom let out a laugh, sharp and barking because hell no. Even if Dawn didn't belong to his cousin, she was the opposite of his type.

Weird and girly—not to mention the daughter of the man who'd brought their old Red Diamond Triad down.

You'd have to pay him to sleep with Dawn, and even then, there probably wouldn't be an amount big enough.

But this woman—*he'd* pay. He'd pay to be able to...

Stop staring, man. Be cool.

He made himself avert his eyes for a couple of beats. "No, we're not together. She just got married to my cousin."

"Oh, so this is a marriage thing." She looked to the side. "In that case, I suppose I understand, even if I wish she'd made different choices. She was very bright. She would have made a good doctor."

No, she wouldn't have. Dawn was pretty much at the bottom of Phantom's list for people he thought would make a good doctor. But he suspected Olivia Glendaver was one of those women who saw the best in everybody.

Case in point, she brought her hand out of her expensive purse as if the information he'd given her meant he could be trusted.

Which he absolutely could not.

He glanced toward the picture of the i-banker on her desk. He could practically see the silver spoon hanging out of that douchebag's mouth.

And although he knew the answer, he had to ask, "This your boyfriend?"

Is he protecting you? he added silently. *Fucking you right? Like I would if you were mine?*

She had the smarts to start looking afraid again and the even better instinct not to answer his question.

Good. That meant she wasn't an idiot.

"Thank you for letting me know about Dawn, Mr...." she trailed off, obviously waiting for his name.

Phantom wondered what it would be like to hear his name—his real name covered in her flowers and molasses voice. But he wasn't an idiot either.

Instead of answering her question, he simply stood up and left. He walked past the goddess doctor without another word and figured he'd never see her again.

But yeah, *no.*

This story is about how he couldn't have been more wrong about that. So go to theodorataylor.com to read the rest!

SPECIAL THANKS TO MY RUTHLESS PATREONS!

Become a Ruthless Patreon!

RUTHLESS ULTRAS

Jay Alexandria

RUTHLESS MEGAS

MJ Evans
Vernecia McCall
CILYA FRANK
Monique Alexander
Tamara Pustejovsky
Trenita
Colleen

RUTHLESS SUPER DUPERS

Sharon Keyes
Ayanna Bristow

Jessica

April L George

Nickara20

Ashley Green

Anya Alsobrook

Josephine Thompson

Jememia Black

Sandra Wynn

Ayalibis Dowell

Kimberly Crabbe-Adams

Shaneka Nichols

Patricia Cardinal

Madam A

Tanya Dunlap

Vanessa F A

Sonya Barry

Mylene Williams

Julienne

RUTHLESS SUPERS

housthon parks

K. Brown

Sheshe

Fab Cordova

Cynthea Carbon

Ella

Tiesha Whatley

Sandi Hospedales

Hin Lee

Stacey Cohen

Daeterria McLucas

Kay

Darcy Leone
Dreama19
Roynesia Brumfield
OOW
Deanna R
Sonya Som
Nakinah Webb
Dana R
Brenda Fontaine
Biaunca Albury
Lashan Delancy
Jeanine Hawkins
LaShanda
Michele Jenkins
Christine Roth
Andrea
Guerlande Mathieu
Jenetha Williams
Nicole H
Jaha Walgern
Lyndetta Timmons
Latricia Warren
Clustelle Nielle Charles
Regina Jefferson Rudolph
Alice Rutland
Chanda Hill
Tiffany Mays
Erin Joyner
Romance Fan in B.R.
Earline Stephen
Kisha Patton
Petra Malusclava
Brenda

Kenya Baines
Hridhi Islam
Za Smith-Berthe
Anita Allen
Michaelle Avant
denequia washington
Cyn
Taylor
Sonya Napier
Shiva
Dana Sandoval
Marianna Kalonda Okassaka
Tanecia Appling
Sheryl Wilder
Jennifer Dowell
Wanda J Agee
Alexis M.
Stacy Moore
Nicole Jackson
Danielle

RUTHLESS FANS

Kenya Wright
lisa
nanc evans
Beverley Jackson
Chinyere Offor
Ayesha Cruickshank
Sharon McDowall
Nene
Evelyn Green
Yvonn Keen-Zic

Toni

Alex

Manoucheka Chery

Tiffany Burns

Katina

stacey kindles

kymberly burns

M Jones

Anissa M Jones

Courtney McFadden

Nubooti

Alecia Williams

Sabrina Rachel

Katrina Gardner

Free

Andrea

Gen0vefa

Stephanie Glassman

Tiandrea Knight

Kayleen Murray

Shronda Carter

Alisa Keith

Kia Fleming

Jaleda Wyatt

BlkBae

ABABA

RUTHLESS READERS

Naturalbrainiac

LaDonna Jones

Cassandra Chatman

Shawn

Kaswanna K.

Elle

Tonya Collins

Nicole Smart

Lisa Marshall

Lily Deb

Anie Rahman

SD

Toni

Jannette E. Abel

Ylang

Andrea Mclin

Kaneisha Plummer

Kimmey

K Brar

Avion M Lourde

Caroline Jones

Sonya Smith Sustacek

Dinette Dormeus

Beverley Jackson

Sharron B Brown

Deborah Smith

Cherone Malone

Nichelle Echols

kaiesha

Alison

Tiffany Kendrick

Shawnte Reasor

Paula Thompson

Timika Davis

Shemille McClendon

Tykeisha Rice

Barbara Gilbert

Maria Amoroso

AsiaRenee

Cecile

Kelsey

Adaria Miller

April Marro

Armia Hall

Tualla Clemons

Tianne Brown-Soto

Sarkastik Mastermind

Sherri Kenny

Amy Mathews

Ljlw

Stephanie Williams

Antoinette Green

Ramona L Green

Fayth Jones

Letetia Mullenix

latosha johnson

Mary

Marilyn Liburd

Maisha Perez

material.gworl

Gillian Gayle

Billie Henry

Miesha McJunkins

Sonya Williams

Renelle

BF Smith

Toi

Anita Mallari

Kamico Seals

Marielle Sobowale

Nicole Kohlmeier

Shemika Bailey

Ama misa

Karen Palmer

Shayla Curry

Nina Moore

datreon01

Claudia Ferreira

Tara Hogan

Kisha Caldwell

Jacqueline Britt

Sydni

Andrea Gregory

Kiara

Val Zaharia

Lethia M Grimes

Free Peay

Shalaia Walters

S Watson England

Alaides Cruz

Jemma Wu

Kimberly Ellis

Shemille McClendon

Martisa

Denise

Kyrjuan Fleming

Cynthia Marigny

Andrekia Branch

Sheena J

Simone Howard

Julie

Judith

Cynthia Mckissick

B Mercado

Mitzi Allen

Shayna Hayes

Kalis

Lynn Leary

Bry

Shakayla

Debra Crosby

NCH

Dana Clark

Tima D_May

Dimond Preston

Katina Brown

Cathy Rogers

Sonya BD

Natasha

Crystal Frazier

SHANNON MCCLAIN

Ashley Johnson

Neah White

WC Ford

Linda Browne

Monique Biggett-Johnson

Deidre Clayburn

Carol Gindratt

Babette Cooper

Tamila Robins

Rochelle Tunstall

Terri Robinson

Brittney Dowell

Robyn Weekes

FCadS

Ashleigh Dixon

Tiffiany

Kali Murray

Johari Crews

Keosha Bond

Erica Severan

T. Williams

Adrienne Jones

Christian Hibbard

Nakia Wooley

Ava Nichol

Keri Stevens

Anita Burge

Phyllis Harrington

Latasha Towles

Roxanne

Heather Goltz

OAA

LaTarsha Morrison

Kimberly Billups

Cleo Muhammad

Lilith Darville

Melissa Herrera

Become a Ruthless Patreon

ALSO BY THEODORA TAYLOR

RUTHLESS MC

WAYLON: Angel and the Ruthless Reaper Book 1

WAYLON: Angel and the Ruthless Reaper Book 2

GRIFFIN: Red and the Big Bad Reaper

VENGEANCE: Snow and the Vengeful Reapers

HADES: Stephanie and the Merciless Reaper

HADES: Stephanie and the Ruthless Mogul

THE VERY BAD FAIRGOODS

His for Keeps

His Forbidden Bride

His to Own

RUTHLESS TYCOONS

Ruthless Scion

Ruthless Billionaire

Ruthless King

Ruthless Husband

Ruthless Captor

RUTHLESS TYCOONS: Broken and Ruthless

KEANE: Her Ruthless Ex

STONE: Her Ruthless Enforcer

RASHID: Her Ruthless Boss

RUTHLESS TRIAD

VICTOR: Her Ruthless Crush

VICTOR: Her Ruthless Owner

VICTOR: Her Ruthless Husband

HAN: Her Ruthless Mistake

PHANTOM: Her Ruthless Fiancé

RUTHLESS FAIRYTALES

Cynda and the City Doctor

Billie and the Russian Beast

Goldie and the Three Bears

Reina and the Heavy Metal Prince

(newsletter exclusive)

RUTHLESS BOSSES

His Pretend Baby

His Revenge Baby

His Enduring Love

His Everlasting Love

RUTHLESS BUSINESS

Her Ruthless Tycoon

Her Ruthless Cowboy

Her Ruthless Possessor

Her Ruthless Bully

RUTHLESS RUSSIANS

Her Russian Billionaire

Her Russian Surrender

Her Russian Beast

Her Russian Brute

ALPHA KINGS

Her Viking Wolf

Wolf and Punishment

Wolf and Prejudice

Wolf and Soul

Her Viking Wolves

ALPHA FUTURE

Her Dragon Everlasting

NAGO: Her Forever Wolf

KNUD: Her Big Bad Wolf

RAFES: Her Fated Wolf

Her Dragon Captor

Her Dragon King

ALIEN OVERLORDS (as Taylor Vaughn)

His to Claim

His to Steal

His to Keep

THE SCOTTISH WOLVES

Her Scottish Wolf

Her Scottish King

Her Scottish Hero

HOT HARLEQUINS WITH HEART

ABOUT THE AUTHOR

Theodora Taylor writes hot books with heart. When not reading, writing, or reviewing, she enjoys spending time with her amazing family, going on date nights with her wonderful husband, and attending parties thrown by others. She LOVES to hear from readers. So....

Join TT's Patreon
https://www.patreon.com/theodorataylor

Follow TT on TikTok
https://www.tiktok.com/@theodorataylor100

Follow TT on Instagram
https://www.instagram.com/taylor.theodora/

Sign for up for TT's Newsletter
http://theodorataylor.com/sign-up/

Made in the USA
Middletown, DE
10 April 2023

28572462R00186